EIGHT O' MAY

A Novel

WILLIAM T. BROWN

AN IMPRINT FROM ADDUCENT

EIGHT O' MAY

A Novel

WILLIAM T. BROWN

EIGHT O' MAY

William T. Brown

ISBN (paperback) 9781937592974

Published by Escrire
www.AdducentCreative.com
Jacksonville, Florida USA
Published in the United States of America

Cover Artwork by Akea Brionne Brown
Cover Layout Copyright © 2021 by Adducent, Inc.
Cover, Book Design and Production by Adducent.

If the past has been an obstacle and a burden, knowledge of the past is the safest and the surest emancipation.

- Lord Acton

Coincidence is God's way of remaining anonymous.

- Albert Einstein

DEDICATION

For my parents – Juanita and Jesse Brown.

For my daughter Kesha and granddaughter Akea.

For my ancestors and relatives, whose personalities provided inspiration for the story I told.

GRATITUDE

I express my sincere thanks to the members of Writers on the Hill Workshop who provided valuable reviews of my manuscripts: Allie Armitage, Deon Bennett, Gayla Cook, Savanna Jeordan, Majeedah Johnson, Kayla Lattimore, Myrina McCullough, Da'Shawn Mosley, Eric Peterson and Tyrone Umrani.

I owe much gratitude to my granddaughter, Akea, for her art work that enhances the cover of this book.

PREFACE

The US Civil war officially ended with the surrender of General Robert E. Lee at Appomattox, Virginia on 9 April 1865. With the end of the war, came the official liberation of slaves in the Confederate states. But, the date on which emancipation became reality across the country was determined by the time at which Union troops secured the surrender of opposing forces in various locations.

In northeast Mississippi and northwest Alabama, May 8th has long been called "Emancipation Day." This day, popularly known as "Eight O' May" is the date on which tradition says the slaves in those areas learned they were free.

During the Reconstruction era (January 1, 1863 – March 31, 1877), formerly enslaved people experienced significant improvements in their status. But with the end of Reconstruction, these formerly enslaved and their descendants were subjected to significant diminution of their rights. They existed in a tenuous status in which it was understood that they had "no rights which the white man was bound to respect." Regardless of these conditions, in the late 1800s and on into the 1950s, black communities in various towns and villages throughout the region held large "Eight O' May" celebrations that included parades, speeches, picnics, singing, baseball games, and religious ceremonies. The day was a local holiday recognized by local white-owned businesses, who gave black workers the day off.

Many of the communities impacted by the original 1865 emancipation no longer give Eight O' May the attention it once received.

CHAPTER 1

In New Mexico, in the forty-fifth year of my life, on a Tuesday morning, I awoke from a disturbing dream that was the prelude to a series of implausible coincidences that changed my life forever.

After almost three decades of professional dedication to the pursuit of science, I experienced several unusual events causing me to question my belief that all in this world can be explained by basic logic.

While growing up in Mississippi during the 1950's and 60's, I was surrounded by talk of things that were considered superstitious. Much of it was harmless, such as not stepping on a crack in the sidewalk; however, other things were more serious, such as belief in the ability of certain people to cast spells. If I ever questioned the likelihood of stories of strange events, I was warned: 'Don't laugh at what you don't understand.'

I can't remember a prior time in my life when I experienced so many unusual events competing for my attention within less than a week. I know how to calculate the probability of the occurrence of so many unlikely events within a short time, and that number is almost zero. So many things that began with that dream were highly improbable.

***

The first light of that morning fluttered through the branches of the pinon tree outside our bedroom window, and

1

danced across my face, prodding me out of a restless sleep. In my half-awakened state, images from an unfinished dream flashed through my mind. Covering my eyes with my forearm and lying motionless, I tried to coax that dream to return. I'd had the same dream countless times before, something about a flying horse, but I'd never been able to recall more than fragmented images after waking.

The soft snoring of my wife pulled my thoughts back to the reality of the moment, destroying any hopes of getting back into my elusive dream. As we lay there, not touching, I could feel the warmth of her nude body inches from mine. I had the urge to roll over and caress her; but the friction caused by my coming home so late from work the night before meant it would be a futile effort. I knew more fallout was still to come.

I slid out of bed to avoid waking her and did my morning stretches, push-ups and crunches on our bedroom floor. When I paused for a quiet moment and sat on the bench at the foot of our bed, Ada turned softly in her sleep. The sheet slipped from her right shoulder, revealing a distinctive birthmark – a tiny red and black spider. The sight of it brought back memories of the first time we slept together. I had awakened the morning after, spotted the spider and came within a millisecond of smashing it before realizing my error. I later learned the scientific name for that species of spiders: Ceraticelus. In playful moments I would sometimes use a short form - Cera - as a nickname.

I showered and got dressed, then stood in the kitchen slowly enjoying the bold taste of my morning coffee. While mentally prepared for the approaching emotional storm, I looked out the kitchen window and focused on the spectacular scenery to temper my anxiety. From our home in the foothills of the Sandias, I had a great view of the vast land that spread west. The cloudless sky highlighted the land's natural beauty and I hardly noticed the residential sprawl of Albuquerque. In the distance, I could see alternating strips of pink and brown earth, extending all the way to the snow-capped peak of Mount Taylor. The window was open and scents of desert spring soothed me: sweetgrass, sagebrush, pinon and others I could not identify. I heard the distinctive call of a coyote. My mind drifted back to the naked woman sleeping in our bed. I imagined myself walking in, pulling back the sheet, waking her with kisses to her body and initiating a few minutes of unhurried, passionate lovemaking.

My fantasizing was interrupted by the telltale cadence of her impatient footsteps on the marble floor. I was determined to defuse the impending emotional explosion and turned to face her. She stood within a foot of me; her robe hung loosely from her 5'2" frame, and her ample breasts, rising and descending with each breath, looked so inviting. Rays of sunlight streamed through the skylight bathing her in an angelic glow. At that moment, I felt an overwhelming passion for my wife. When I handed her freshly poured coffee, the earth tones of the mug blended so perfectly with the tan complexion of her skin.

"Good morning, baby. Happy birthday!" With a chuckle, I continued, "I was about to bring you coffee and other things in bed, but you were a bit too fast for me."

Ada deftly deflected my attempt to plant a kiss on her lips. "Well, at least you remembered it's my birthday." With a sneer, she added, "Now, Charlie, would you tell me again why presenting a paper about soap bubbles is so important? Isn't travel to this symposium optional?"

I didn't say what I was thinking: *Baby, birthdays just aren't that important to me; they never have been. My project is something I have been working on for a long time. I feel a sense of accomplishment in developing an elegant solution to a problem that a lot of people have been trying to solve for many years. This is what I do; I need to be there.*

Instead, I said, "You may think of it as soap bubbles; however, my talk is titled 'Mixed Phase Equilibrium in Surfactants.' I submitted my abstract almost a year ago. At the time, it just didn't occur to me that this meeting conflicted with your birthday. You know as well as I do, it would have been bad form not to attend after my paper was accepted. I still don't know why you won't come with me to New Orleans."

Placing her hands on her hips, she said, "You know I have to be in Santa Fe on Friday for a deposition. You know the stakes for my career in this environmental case."

"Ada, I still don't know why Fernando can't do the deposition."

"Look, Charlie, it's not up to you to decide. Fernando and I will both be there; this is an important case. Hey, there's nothing to be gained by arguing about it so let's just drop it. I need to get dressed for work, and I'm sure you need to finish packing. Have a great trip."

With that, she turned and left the room as quickly as she had entered. I had intended to give her the squash blossom necklace I bought for her birthday, but now, I was too angry. It was so inconsiderate of her to think I should push my career aside for a birthday celebration when she wasn't prepared to do the same. I thought about it, then put the gift on a shelf in the den, just high enough that she would not easily spot it. I'd tell her later where to find it.

I heard Ada in the shower and went down the hall to my office to get some papers from my desk before leaving. I sat down and noticed the phone's message light blinking. Ada and I had separate lines in our in-home offices. I used mine mostly with my computer modem to access the mainframe computers at the office. Neither of us answered the other's phone.

The first message was a hang-up. The second call was from Harold in New Orleans; we'd been best friends since we met as college freshmen at Dillard. Later, we shared an apartment in Chicago where I was in grad school and he was in dental school. Several weeks earlier, I had left a message telling him I would be in town and that we should hang-out like old times. When I didn't get a response, I didn't know what to think. Harold's message was to the point: "Charlie, I apologize for taking so long to get back with you, things have been crazy. Peggy and I are no longer together. Call me as soon as you get in; we're gonna hang-out. By the way, my man, did you find that picture of the old gang on our last day together? If so, bring it with you."

That message was so unlike Harold; he's usually very talkative, even on recorded messages. We had only seen each other once since graduating Chicago thirteen years prior, but we talked several times a year, sometimes as much as an hour, just catching up on what was new and reminiscing about old times. He casually informed me of the end of his marriage and then moved on to ask about an old photo. He had made passing reference to the picture the last time we talked, but I hadn't thought about it since. I decided I would have time to look for it before leaving for the airport. That's what led me to my life-changing discovery.

I heard Ada as she moved through the house and into the garage. Her Audi started up, and the garage door opened. Then it closed.

In about fifteen minutes I was packed, and decided I had time for breakfast. I scrambled two eggs with chopped green chili and decided it wasn't too early for a beer. I grabbed a cold Dos Equis from the fridge, put on my favorite cassette, turned the volume up, and listened for the familiar opening chords of "Sketches of Spain." As I savored the last few morsels and the last corner of beer, the beautiful blues of *Soleia* from Miles's horn lifted my spirits.

Finally, I headed to the attic to find that photograph. Two rows of boxes, stacked 4-high, were arrayed against the back wall - boxes that probably hadn't been opened in at least five years - were daunting. I had no clue where to begin. A few boxes were marked; a small fraction of those had dates.

After rifling through more than a dozen boxes, I thought I had found what I was looking for – a box marked simply 'photos.' I brushed away a thin layer of dust and peeled off an old strip of brittle tape. I opened the box and I saw that fateful headline. I looked at the masthead: THE JACKSON INFORMER – a Mississippi newspaper, dated May 15, 1951. *What is this? Where did this come from? Millerton – Millerton, Mississippi – my hometown.* A chill radiated through my head. As suddenly as it came, the sensation was gone. In its place, I heard my Casio watch beeping and glanced at it – 10:05 AM. Time to leave for the airport. Nevertheless, I took a few more seconds to skim the article. "...Prince Dawson shot by..."

Aloud, I asked myself, "What's going on? That's Uncle Prince."

The chill returned.

It was time to go and I hadn't found the photo. I kept the paper and hurried through a mental checklist: luggage by the door, music turned off, house alarm set. Finally, I reassured myself that Ada's birthday gift was in a place where she wouldn't stumble upon it, but where I could easily tell her later how to find it.

On the drive to the airport, I reviewed the bit of information I had just read. The 'what' was that my uncle had been shot some 40 years ago by a man whose name I did not recognize; the 'why' I didn't get from my quick reading. The story was important enough to appear as the lead in the state's major black newspaper. But where did the paper come from? At a stop light, I pulled the paper from my briefcase. I skimmed it again and saw that the article continued from the front page to page three. I flipped to the third page, but the article was not there. I realized that the date was not the same; page three read May 15, 1981. Looking back at the front page, the banner above the headline reads: 'The Informer Files A Page Of History From 30 Years Ago This Week.' *Aha, the newspaper has reprinted its front page from 30 years ago. But I should remember getting this paper. Where did it come from?* The horn loudly blaring behind me refocused my attention to the present moment.

Negotiating the light traffic, I reflected on the date. *May 15, 1981 was the date Ada and I reconnected in New Orleans after all those years, the day I learned from her that we had a daughter who was almost six years old. The coincidences are uncanny. What does this have to do with Ada?*

Then I heard the triple blasts of a police siren and saw the flashing red light in my rearview mirror. After moving to the curb, I began searching for my wallet.

"May I please see your license, sir?"

I passed my driver's license to him, asking, "What's the problem officer?"

"Sir, you just went right through that red light. Didn't even slow down."

With the discomfort of a $50 traffic ticket securely tucked in my briefcase, I vowed not to dwell on the newspaper until I was no longer behind the wheel. Turning on my tape deck, I began to sing along with Marvin Gaye – off key; "Mercy, mercy me..."

I parked the Volvo in the long-term lot, took the shuttle to the terminal, and checked in at the Southwest counter. I had a few minutes to concentrate before boarding. Pulling out the newspaper from my briefcase, I re-read the headline:

MILLERTON NEGRO SHOT BY WHITE FARMER

I read the story:

WELDOWNS COUNTY WHITE FARMER AMBUSHES AND SHOOTS NEGRO FARM OWNER IN BROAD DAYLIGHT
No Arrest Or Investigation Results From Brutal Incident
U. S. Department of Justice Has Been Asked To Investigate Case

Millerton, Miss, May 15, 1951 (DSN)- The Negro citizens of this up-and-coming northeast Mississippi town are reportedly deeply concerned and aroused as never before over the brutal killing, on May 9, of a Negro farm owner.

Prince Dawson, a Weldowns County Negro who lives on his own 80 acres farm six miles west of Millerton in the Tomley community, was way-laid and shot today at about 9:00 a.m. by wealthy Weldowns County white farmer, Tom 'Red' Mullins, who also lives near the Tomley community. The shooting was witnessed by, among others, Mike Franklin, another white man, who also lives near the Tomley community.

According to reports, the shooting took place in Miller-ton at about 9:00 a.m. Eyewitnesses said Dawson was driving his wagon and mules into the hitching lot near the Choctaw River Bridge, as Mullins was pulling his Buick out of the lot. A near-collision between the car and the wagon produced no noticeable damage to the car. Although witnesses say he was not at fault, Dawson apologized. Instead, Mullins began shouting "I told you I was going to kill you when (Continued on Page Three).

That was it. I leafed through each page of the newspaper to ensure I had not missed something. This was a commemorative edition and the paper had only reprinted the front page from 30 years ago. *I would have been six years old when this happened. Why didn't I ever hear about this?*

"Southwest Flight 178 for Dallas now boarding at gate six."

CHAPTER 2

TUESDAY, MAY 8, 1990

Just past sunrise, the morning was overcast as I strolled along a path that weaved through a familiar grove of trees. I was about 50 yards behind my parents' home – the place where I grew up. The low angle of the sun lit the greenery with an eerie haze. A light breeze carried the enticing aroma of someone's early breakfast of coffee, country sausage, and biscuits.

"Probably the Mitchell house. Smells really good. I oughta invite myself to breakfast."

This would be a humid day, typical of northeast Mississippi at this time of year. In the distance I heard the sawmill, but I knew that couldn't be because it shut down decades ago.

I continued my walk but became aware of the tickling sensation of coarse Johnson Grass underfoot, and how it carried the dampness of morning dew; I looked down and realized my feet were bare.

"Where are my shoes, and why am I here? I was going somewhere, but at this moment, I have no idea where."

Without warning, I heard a sound behind me and turned. The horse was partially obscured by trees, but I recognized him immediately. Jack, the white Quarter Horse my favorite cousin, Booker, always rode. I remembered Booker saying that his father -- my Uncle Prince -- gave him that horse when it was born. Booker used to ride me on Jack when I was still a toddler. I realized I hadn't seen Booker in decades.

"How long has it been?" I wondered aloud. "If Jack is here it must mean that Booker is nearby. But this can't be Jack; that horse has to be dead by now."

Nevertheless, I approached the horse cautiously, softly calling out to him. Alternating between lightly slapping my palm against my jeans and beckoning "come here," I tried to get the horse's attention without frightening him. "Here Jack, come here boy." As I got within about five yards from him, I realized he was wearing a rein, but no saddle, only a riding blanket. The horse did not move toward me, but from the glint in his eyes he seemed to recognize me - after all these years. Inexplicably, I felt I should mount him. Slowly, I took the reins in hand, and grasping his mane, I easily swung myself into place. I couldn't remember when I had last been on a horse, but it felt natural sitting there. At first, he was motionless, then he casually turned his head and nudged my left foot; I sensed recognition.

Within seconds, Jack began to trot into the woods, along a path that was not familiar to me. The horse needed no guidance. As his pace quickened, the breeze across my face was exhilarating. Then I realized that the horse's feet were no longer touching the ground; Jack and I were rising above the trees – we were airborne. Flying!

This can't be happening. This must be a dream. Now I remember; I've had this dream many times before.

Something brushed my legs, and I saw wings had sprouted from Jack's torso just ahead of the blanket. The wings were flapping rapidly and produced a pulsating sensation, like helicopter blades rotating in slow motion. Within seconds, I realized with horror that those wings were made of thin tissue paper. As our speed increased, the wings began to disintegrate. Jack and I were plummeting toward earth.

"This is okay because this is all a dream. I'm not afraid because I know I'm dreaming."

But as we crashed through tree after tree, the scratches from the leaves and branches felt too real, especially on my face. Suddenly, the horse let out a loud cry. The ground rapidly approached.

"I am ready to wake up!" But I was still falling like a brick. A large branch loomed straight ahead; there was no way to avoid a collision. Instantly, I was ripped from the horse's back and hit the ground hard.

Everything faded and I passed out. When I woke up on the ground, everything hurt. I felt very woozy and everything was a haze. After looking at my watch, which still worked, I estimated I had been knocked out for about fifteen minutes.

"What the hell is going on? Wake up! Charlie Dawson, you are a 43-year-old scientist; your life is based on logic. This cannot be happening; this has to be a dream. Wake up!"

I got up very slowly and checked from my feet to my shoulders. It looked like not anything was broken. A barely audible sound came from somewhere to my left and shook me out of my haze. I saw Jack about twenty yards away, lying very still. I moved closer and I realized that I was now wearing my favorite Italian loafers.

This has to be a dream.

Jack was obviously still alive, but very badly injured. He was crying – very softly. I saw a big branch protruding from his chest. The tree we collided with had become a stake that opened the horse's chest, revealing his heart. It was still beating rapidly. Something compelled me to reach out and touch it. I gently touched that pulsating heart, it suddenly ruptured, spurting blood into my face. I reached up and removed my glasses to wipe them clean, and realized that the blood that hit my body was cold.

***

I looked down at my hands. A woman's hand touched mine and she said "I'm so sorry sir; it's the turbulence. I'll take care of it right away." She held an almost empty plastic beverage cup.

Speaking to the man in the window seat to my right she said: "...and I'll get another drink for you." Before moving away, the flight attendant turned back to me and said, "I'll be right back with a towel."

I could feel my heart beating rapidly. Sweat dampened my face and neck even as the feeling of fear subsided. "My God, that was some dream," I muttered to myself.

My rotund seatmate looked me over with a sneer, then returned to leafing through his Sports Illustrated.

"You certainly did have some dream. I couldn't help but notice and was tempted to wake you. Are you okay?"

The question came from the attractive young woman seated across the aisle from me. The plane shuddered briefly as it encountered more momentary turbulence.

"I'm alright. Thanks for asking. I just need a few minutes to--"

"A drink would help. May I?"

"I appreciate the offer, but no thanks."

"Why not? Let me at least buy you a coke." She chuckled and reached for the attendant call button. "You were asleep like a rock when I boarded. You must have had some night last night."

The flight attendant returned with a large towel and a Bloody Mary for my seatmate. That explained the stain on my shirt.

"Well, I guess I could use a drink. Double Scotch on the rocks. Thank you." I extended my hand across the aisle. "I'm Charlie Dawson; I live in Albuquerque. Are you from Albuquerque too?"

"No. But I know that you are a 43-year-old scientist." She must have seen my surprise and smiled. "I heard you talking in your dream, which must've been a doozy. I just left Santa Fe, heading to Dallas for a couple of days. Then, I'm off to visit with family in Mississippi. As a new divorcée, I'm free as a bird. My name is Sara Madison. It is my pleasure to meet you Mr. Dawson, or is it Dr. Dawson?"

"Please, just call me Charlie. What part of Mississippi? I'm from Mississippi myself."

"I'll be in a little place called Millerton. Do you know it?"

I stifled a laugh and replied, "That's my hometown. This is some coincidence." Another chill came over my body.

Her eyes widened. Then her face relaxed into a smile, as she said, "It really is quite a coincidence; must be an omen. Things happen for a reason. Are you going to Millerton also?

And, by the way, Charlie, are you married?"

That caught me off guard. But I had noted how quickly she had referred to her divorce, so maybe it shouldn't have.

"I'm going to New Orleans for a conference. My wife couldn't join me; she has a business commitment. Unfortunately, I won't have time to get home to visit. But how about you? Did you grow up there?"

She paused for a moment, gazing nowhere in particular. Then, very deliberately leaned across the aisle, reached up and brushed ear-length, dark hair back from her face. I noticed the small, silver studded diamond and turquoise earrings. A small matching necklace clutched her neck. I recognized the work of Melissa Perez, the most expensive jewelry maker in Santa Fe because Ada had bought many pieces during our marriage. With an intense stare, and a feigned smile, she replied, "No, I didn't grow up there. I grew up in hell! A little town up the road from Millerton called Jonesville." She seemed to relax, leaned back and chuckled.

Seconds later, the flight attendant was announcing our impending landing, "Ladies and gentlemen, in preparation for our landing in Dallas, please return all items to the overhead bin, or to the space under the seat in front of you..."

I suffered regularly from congestion in my left ear when descending; I yawned rapidly to clear the congestion. Sara Madison was busy returning items to her small travel bag. In a short time, we were on the ground and taxiing to our gate.

Because our flight was almost half an hour late, I had to rush to make my New Orleans connection. As Sara and I walked down the breezeway to the gate, she stopped, turned to me, and said: "Are you sure you can't come to Millerton? You really should."

She spoke with a curious intensity at odds with her

previously flirty demeanor, "You know I heard almost every word of your dream. I've had similar dreams. We really should talk about it."

I was floored. "People dream about flying all the time. I'd love to talk but I'm going to miss my flight if I don't hurry."

"Here's my card. Do you have one?"

I fished around, found one in my jacket pocket, and gave it to her. "Nice meeting you," I said and started to walk away. She touched my arm, and I saw that her intense stare had returned. Extending my hand, I received her very firm, but sweaty handshake. "Goodbye Sara. I enjoyed our conversation."

Of course, my departure gate was at the other end of the airport. I boarded my flight with only minutes to spare. Once settled in my seat, I looked at her card. It said simply: "Sara Madison, San Francisco," with a phone number. I put the card away, buckled-up, and drifted off to sleep again.

The flight was uneventful.

Shortly before we landed, I remembered the newspaper. I took my briefcase from under the seat, and pulled out the newspaper to reread the article. But I could not concentrate. It occurs to me that I had that dream many times before, but I've never remembered it this clearly. *It must have been this article about the shooting of Uncle Prince that caused me to dream so vividly about this horse. And now, this strange encounter with this unusual white girl going to Millerton. Too many coincidences for one day...*

CHAPTER 3

In New Orleans, the terminal was crowded. After winding my way through the crowds to the baggage carousel, seconds after I got there, my luggage arrived. I took that as a positive sign.

After collecting my bag, I made a beeline for the taxi stand, to beat the crowd. Surprisingly, I got a taxi immediately. My driver was a talker.

"Where you going, mister?"

"To the Fairmont Hotel."

"I know the way, mister. Why you here? You are working? What do you do?"

This guy sure is nosey, but what the hell. "I'm here for a science conference."

Glancing at his cabbie license, I tried to turn the questions on him. "Where are you from, Ahmed?"

"I am from Morocco. I am a scientist also. A chemist. But I can get no work here in chemistry, so I drive this cab. Do you know my country; have you heard of Morocco? Many people here don't know my country."

"Well, yes. I do know Morocco. I think that Marrakesh is a wonderful city; I had a great visit there three years ago."

"You have been to Morocco? Wonderful, I'm glad you had a very good time."

Although I was tired and wanted to rest for a few minutes in my hotel room before connecting with Harold, I was curious about this Moroccan chemist driving a cab in New Orleans.

"How did you get here?"

"I took the bus from New York-"

"No, I mean why did you come to New Orleans?"

"Ha, ha, ha. That was a joke, mister. I understand what you mean. I lived in New York for three years. I did not like it. Too many people, and too cold there. Then a friend told me to come here because he had a sister here, married to an American. I like it better. Not as much money, but I like it better."

I made some gratuitous comment about how I hoped he would do well in New Orleans, and focused my attention on the view beyond the cab. Clouds were gathering; a hint of approaching rain was in the air. Unexpectedly, I saw the bright, shiny object mounted in the middle of Ahmed's dashboard.

"Excuse me," I said, pointing." What is that?"

He reached forward with his right hand and stroked the winged silver horse. "This is my good luck. They call this the Pegasus. Very famous. Do you know about Pegasus?"

"Yes. But why do you have it?"

"In Morocco my father had a fabulous car – the Bentley. The Pegasus stood on the very front of the car. This is all that remains from my father after a great tragedy. I do not want to say more."

"I hope your Pegasus brings you much luck and success."

I closed my eyes and thought about all these coincidences.

"We are here."

I paid the fare, tipped Ahmed generously and grabbed my bag, waving the bellman off. Moving through groups of people in the lobby, I moved toward the check in desk. but was intercepted by my colleague Bob Murphy. From Boston U, – he was my professional rival.

"Well, Dawson." He spoke in his usual blunt and pushy tone. "How are you doing? It's great to see you here. I'm looking forward to your presentation. Read your abstract – interesting paper. But I must tell you, I think it's got some problems. It seems to conflict with my work, but I'll reserve judgment until I hear the talk tomorrow."

Smiling broadly, and extending my hand, I responded, "Bob it's great to see you too. You really don't have to be concerned. My work doesn't conflict with yours, just builds on it. I studied your 1983 Phys Rev paper in detail."

In fact, I had discovered a subtle error in his paper and was as sure of that as anything I had ever done. I'd wait until my presentation to reveal that. "It's been a long day Bob; I want to get checked in. I'll see you tomorrow."

A message from Ada was waiting for me at the front desk: 'Call home right away. It's urgent.'

I got my room key and headed immediately to my room on the 5th floor. Riding on the empty elevator, a Muzaky *Bolero* played softly and reminded me of Jack, the horse in my dream; the image of his mutilation danced uneasily in my head. Abruptly, the elevator door opened. A woman stood waiting to enter. She reminded me of Sara Madison, and the image of the horse evaporated. Did I stare at her? Did she look back at me strangely as we passed each other or did I imagine all that? I looked for room 519.

Inside, I headed straight for the phone. *Did Ada have an accident? I noticed that low tire on her front right wheel last night, but I forgot to tell her about it. What about Maya? She hasn't called from college in more than a week.*

I needed to control my spiraling mind. I tried dialing my calling card number from memory but mis-dialed. After checking my wallet for the card and not finding it, I gave up and charged the call to my hotel room. Ada answered after two rings.

"Hello?!" I heard her nearly scream into the phone.

I tried to sound calm. "Hi baby, what's wrong?"

"Charlie. Everything is fine here, but you need to call Dr. Frank Davis in Millerton right away."

Frank was my best friend in high school, who had established a thriving medical practice back home. Both my parents considered him to be the best doctor in the world. "What is it?"

Ada hadn't stopped talking. "...tomorrow morning. You need to call him right away. He said you have his phone number, but in case you don't, the number is..."

"Ada. Ada, I'm sorry I missed what you said. Please, start over."

"It's your mother, Charlie. Frank says she's very ill." My heart plummeted into my gut, but I focused on her voice. "They want to get her into surgery right away. He wants to talk with you as soon as possible. You need to get down there immediately. I already made reservations for you for a 7:15 flight tomorrow morning. That's the earliest you can fly out of New Orleans. Charlie, do you want me to meet you there?"

"No. No, baby. Uh, let me find out how bad things are. I'll let you know as soon as... as soon as I know something. Thanks for offering. I think I'll rent a car and drive there tonight. It should take me about -"

"Charlie! Hold on, you aren't making any sense. You shouldn't try to drive there tonight; that's a bad idea. That's more than 300 miles. Talk with Dr. Davis; then get some rest. Let me know what's happening after you get there."

I tried to lighten the mood, as much to calm myself as to make peace with my wife. "Yeah baby. I guess you're right. Cera, I'm sorry about this morning. Happy birthday, again.

Your gift is on the shelf in-"

"I know. I found it; it's beautiful. Thank you." She continued with a chuckle, "You always use that same hiding place. At first, I thought it was in the attic. Why were you up there?"

"I was looking for a picture for Harold, but I found something else -- it's a long story. I'll tell you about it later. By the way, when did you last talk with Maya? And, you need to have your left front tire checked. I love you, baby."

"Slow down, Charlie. I know you need to go, but slow down for a minute. I talked with Maya two days ago, but you should call her. I had that tire replaced today; Fernando noticed it. Love you. Now call Dr. Davis."

"Good night, Cera." I suddenly felt so alone. I picked up the receiver again. Frank answered after the first ring.

"This is Dr. Davis."

"Frank, this is..."

"Charlie, I've been waiting for your call."

There was a calmness in his professionalism; but, in the voice of my friend, I heard worry. "Frank, tell me what's happening. How bad is it?"

"She's very sick. I'm on my way back to the hospital now. I just got off the phone with Dr. Larson – he's the best surgeon around. He feels we need to operate immediately. I'm gonna assist. In about ten minutes I'll be at the hospital and scrubbing in. Where are you? How soon can you be here?"

"I'm in New Orleans and can't get a flight out until 7:15 in the morning. Can't you wait until I get there? What is the actual problem?"

"She has an aneurysm near her heart. It could go at any time; that would be fatal. I wish we could wait, but we can't chance it. Your dad just signed the authorization. This is the right thing to do, my friend. I'm handling this as if it's my own mama."

"Frank. Thanks for everything; I know she's in good hands. If I call right now, do you think I can talk with her?"

"I doubt it, Charlie. They should have put her under by now. But I'll be sure to tell her that you're on the way. You would be amazed at the things patients hear when they're under anesthesia. I gotta go. See you tomorrow, my brother."

As soon as I hung up, the phone rang. It was Harold; he was his usual effusive self. "Charlie, my man. You're finally off the phone. Get your butt down here. I've been trying for half an hour to call you. I'm double-parked; we're wasting time. This town is waiting for us. I put out the word that Charlie Dawson is in town."

That was the last thing I needed at that moment. "Harold, I'm sorry, man. I can't. I just got some bad news. My mother is very ill; I can't stay for the conference. I'm leaving early tomorrow morning. I'm sure you understand."

"Oh. I'm so sorry." Harold paused. Then, "My friend, you have tonight. You can't do anything until you get there. The last thing you need is to sit in that hotel room moping. What you need right now is to get out and release some of that tension."

"Okay, maybe you're right. Give me five minutes. I'll see you in the lobby."

"Alright, but if I get a ticket, you're paying." Harold laughed and hung up.

I tried calling the hospital to reach my father. After having him paged in the waiting room, and getting no response after a few minutes, I left a message with the hospital operator telling Pops that I would be arriving the next morning. Because Pops never touched the answering machine I had given him three years ago, there was no point leaving a message at home. On impulse, I called his good buddy Henry Mitchell, who lived two doors away. Mrs. Mitchell answered.

"Miss Susie. This is Charlie Dawson. I'm calling from-"

"Boy, I'm so sorry 'bout your mama. We praying for her. When you coming home?"

"That's why I called. I tried to reach Pops at the hospital, but I didn't get him."

"Yeah, they out there now. Henry went wit' him. I'll tell 'em you coming. When you gonna git here?"

"My plane gets in at 9:00 in the morning. Just let Pops know."

"We'll be there to pick you up. Don't worry."

"I can get a taxi, Miss Susie."

"Boy, ain't been no taxi around here in five or six years. Don't worry; we'll be there."

"Alright, thank you Miss Susie. See you in the morning. Good night."

"Bye, Charlie-boy. Like I said, we praying for her."

It occurred to me that I had not thought of praying, and I made a mental note that it wouldn't be a bad idea, for Mama.

Before heading down to meet Harold, I tried to call Maya at her dorm at Spellman. I got her answering machine.

"Hi, baby. It's your daddy. Sorry I missed you. I haven't talked with you in a while. I'm in New Orleans right now at a conference. I'll call you tomorrow. I love you. Bye."

I splashed some water on my face and headed down to meet Harold. The elevator door opened in the lobby, and I was looking right at him. For a moment I didn't recognize him. At 6ft, Harold had about two inches on me, but all through college, he probably weighed only about ten pounds more than I did. Now he was easily 50 or 60 pounds heavier. He spotted me; the look on his face told me it was him. We embraced like old friends do. I had an urge to cry; the stress of my mother's condition and the joy of reconnecting with a good friend was nearly overwhelming.

"Man, you still ain't grown up. When you gonna grow, Charlie?"

"Well my friend, it looks like you have been doing enough growing for the two of us."

"Yeah, that's right and I'm gonna put some meat on your bones right now. Do you still indulge in the swine?"

"Yeah, I eat a little pork now and then."

"We're going down the road here. This brother has a real nice place- called Big Dizzy's." Suddenly, Harold got very serious. "How bad is it with your mama, Charlie? Tell me about it."

"I really don't want to talk about it right now, maybe later. Right now, I'm counting on you to help me take my mind off it."

He placed his hands on my shoulders. "That's what I'm here for. Let's get going."

Harold's Benz was parked in the circular driveway of the hotel, with the top down. It was nearly blocking traffic, causing other cars to squeeze by.

"Nice ride you got here. What is this, the 450SL? Dentistry must be treating you well."

He threw his hands up in mock-surrender. "Naw, brother. It's a 560SL, top of the line. The practice is good. But I do take time out to do a free clinic a few days each month. My way of giving something back to the community. Get in, let's go."

Harold punched the play button on the tape deck, and I couldn't believe what I was hearing. The familiar, but long-forgotten lyrics flowed out of the speakers, taking me back to the old days: 'The sad young men are growing old, growing old...'

"Damn, I can't believe you managed to locate our old theme song. Man, I remember in that last year, when we realized it was all about to come to an end, this was the tune we always seemed to play at the end of our parties."

Spotting no opening in traffic, he forced his way into the curb lane, quickly sped into the flow of traffic, then down-shifted and accelerated into the center lane, without using his signal.

"I love having the top down, but it looks like it might rain."

"Naw, it ain't gonna rain on our parade. Charlie, I never did like the damn song that much myself – too sad. Some of you fellas seemed to enjoy getting all moody all the time. But you know what, I figured it out." With his rambunctious laugh, he blurted out, "It was those of y'all who wasn't getting none on a regular basis who was into being blue all the time. Me, I didn't have time for being moody; the ladies kept me too busy."

"Yeah, you did get around, always quite smooth with the women. However, I remember Joan from junior year. Man, that girl broke your heart. She got tired of your foolishness, and dropped you so fast you didn't know if you were coming or going. You went out and got drunk; Nelson and I found you sleeping under a bush out on some street near campus, and had to carry you home. You remember?"

He slowed just enough to make a right turn as the first few drops of rain splashed onto the windshield. And our heads. Without saying a word, he slowed to a crawl, pushed a button on the dash to raise the top, and flipped the wipers on.

I said nothing but looked at him as if to say: 'I told you so.'

The transformation was sudden and dramatic. Within seconds, we went from an open-air expansiveness to closed-in intimacy. The wiper, for a moment, seemed to oscillate in rhythm with the closing lines of the song: '...they are growing old.' The silence that followed was uncomfortable. The quiet was interrupted by Wilson Pickett's booming voice reverberating through the car. 'I'm a soul man...'

Harold nodded his approval and responded with, "It's so damn nice of you to remember all that shit that went down way back when. But, I'm a survivor, man. I got over that stuff. And, guess what? Joan and I recently reconnected."

"Aw, man. Is that why you and Peggy split up?" I asked him, in a tone loaded with contempt.

He jabbed his finger in my direction and shot back, "No! You got it wrong. Peggy and I split about nine months back. I didn't have any contact with Joan until about two weeks ago, after I happened to run into her old roommate Betty, who lives right here in New Orleans. She told me Joan lost her husband more than a year ago. We're planning to get together in DC in about three weeks. For a brother who is so careful and thorough when it comes to your work, you sure are quick on the draw when it comes to making judgments about people."

"Man, I'm sorry. I remember how quickly you used to go through the women, except for Joan. But she just stopped you in your tracks." I was sorry I offended my oldest college friend. "So, why did you take so long to tell me about you and Peggy? What happened?"

"There's not much to tell and it's all cliché. Peggy and I just kinda drifted apart. When I think about it, I realize maybe we really didn't have that much in common in the first place. You probably remember a different version of this, but it was really Ada and I who connected first. If you hadn't taken her from me, brother, we would probably still be together today."

"You damn right, I got a different memory of how that went down." I pounded the dashboard for emphasis. "About our second or third week in Chicago, you and I went out to some little jazz club near the Loop. I still remember walking in there and hearing Sonny Stitt performing, still remember what he was playing: 'Cherokee'. When we walked in, he was just hitting that little riff that goes-"

Harold put his palm in my face. "Hey, Charlie. I know how much you're into the music, but can you get back to the point, my man. You are digressing."

"Well, as I was about to say, you with your smooth talking, managed to pull Ada away from a big group of students, and got her to sit off to the side and talk to you. But the next thing I knew, you were telling me you had to leave and asking me to keep her company for you."

"Well, maybe it did happen something like that. But the fact is, if it hadn't been for me, you two never would have hooked up. The only reason I left was because I looked across the club and saw somebody I didn't ever want to see again in life. Just my damn luck; my loss, your gain. You owe me brother."

"You got a short memory. If you think back on it, I was the one who arranged for you to meet Peggy. So, the way I see it, we're even."

"Maybe you could say we're even, but it's all a matter of perspective. As I see it, since you and Ada are still together, you're a few points ahead of me."

"Come on man. This ain't a game; this is life. Nobody is keeping score. I don't know what went down between you and Peggy, but I don't think you can even consider holding me responsible."

A panel truck abruptly cut us off, causing Harold to swerve and slam the brakes. "Asshole!" He quickly followed up. "Not you, Charlie." Then he added, with his wicked laugh: "...but you sure have been putting out lots of shit lately."

"Harold, you've got lots of double talk, and you don't have to tell me if you don't want to. But I sure would like to know happened between you and Peggy."

"For as long as I've known you, Charlie, you latch onto something, and just hang on 'til you've turned it every way but loose. In fact, that's why I didn't like you when we first met. Fortunately for you, I took the time to get to know the good things about you."

"Well, since we're into truth-telling, to this small-town, southern boy, your big-city attitude seemed like arrogance. Turns out, that's one of the qualities I've come to appreciate about you. Seriously, you have proven to be my best and most reliable friend. Now, stop beating around the bush and answer my question."

"Charlie, I promised Peggy that I wouldn't talk about this. But I'm making an exception because this is you. I think you know me better than just about anyone else. When I was single, I was chasing the women big-time. But once I got married those days were over. So, you can understand I was really shocked when Peggy sat me down and told me she was leaving me for another guy. I never saw it coming, but in retrospect, all the signs were there. I just missed every one of them After we got married, she joined the practice of a guy here in New Orleans; she knew him from law school. I found out, much later, that the two of them used to be an item. Now, I feel sorry for her. He had a change of heart, decided to remain with his wife. But too much trust was lost between us to put things back together. We are trying to be friends again, but it's a slow process."

"Man, I'm sorry. I wish you'd told me sooner."

"It's interesting the way people reacted to our divorce. I have friends locally, but nobody who knows me as well as you do. Your first thought was that I was at fault. Imagine how folks who don't know me as well as you do would jump to the same conclusion. On the other hand, I was feeling embarrassed about what happened. It took me a long time to get past that."

Harold pulled to the curb in front of Big Dizzy's. The valet opened his door as soon as the car stopped. "Dr. Mitchell, it's great to see you. It's been a while; thought maybe you didn't like us anymore."

Harold beamed. "Jimmy, you know I can't stay away. Me and my old friend Charlie are gonna throw down on some ribs and check out Alma and her trio. By the way, didn't I tell you to cut out that doctor shit? You know my name is Harold."

In the dimly lit space, the tall, slender vocalist was belting out a familiar song: 'Day by day, you're making my dreams come true...' Those haunting lyrics about dreams pulled my attention back to the events of the day: the nightmare, the newspaper article that triggered the dream, and the strange encounter with Sara Madison.

After we were seated, Harold quickly ordered two bottles of Abita and two slabs of ribs. The waitress brought our beers as I told Harold about my unusual day. I left out the part about how fine Sara was.

"Damn, brother. That is weird, almost like the Twilight Zone. Are you telling me that Ada had that newspaper all these years before you found it?"

"After thinking about it, I think Ada got that newspaper in Jackson shortly before she and I reconnected here in New

Orleans. You remember how she told me we had a daughter who was almost six years old by that time."

Harold nodded. "Yeah, yeah. That was come crazy shit, right there. How's your daughter doing anyway?"

"She's at Spelman, doing very well. I left her a message just before we left the hotel. By the way, I came across that paper because I was searching for that picture you wanted. What did you want it for?"

"The picture can wait; it's no big deal compared to what you're dealing with. That's around the time Ada was traveling all over the south litigating her environmental justice cases. She was here in New Orleans a couple of times."

"Harold, I don't know anything about that. Never heard you or Ada mention it."

"Well, it really wasn't a big deal. Ada, Peggy and I got together once or twice for dinner. You and Ada were totally out of touch at that time, and Peggy didn't think I should mention it to you."

"Why on earth not?"

"Who knows why women keep the secrets they do. I just did what my wife told me." Harold shook his head a little. "And look where it got me. But, back to your strange tale; it's spooky. And now that you're going to Millerton, I know you won't let this go until you find how what's going on. Will you see this Sara Madison?"

I shook my head vigorously. "No, that's still the Deep South. Our worlds hardly intersect. My mission is to be with my mother. She's my only concern."

"I understand exactly where your head is. You go on down there and take care of business. And you have my number if you need anything. Now, let's check out this fine food and drink. You're gonna love this place."

The concern I saw on Harold's face reminded me of how

much I valued his friendship. The trio started to play again; the piano tickled out the first five bars, and that haunting voice returned: '...willow weep for me...'

Between the music and thinking about my mother, I wept. I felt free to be like that with Harold.

CHAPTER 4

WEDNESDAY, 9 MAY 1990

The wings of the narrow-body aircraft flexed as we sped down the runway into a stiff headwind. For a few seconds I wondered if we would make it, but decided since I had no control over the situation, I may as well try to relax. As we gained altitude, I forced my attention to the scenery outside.

Because I was seated in the front row, the flight attendant faced me in her jump seat. She smiled and, in a voice too perky for such an early hour, asked, "Are you okay sir? Don't be nervous, everything is gonna be fine."

I wasn't nervous about flying and resented the assumption from a young woman who had probably flown fewer times than I had. I found myself snapping back at her, "I'm fine!" She responded with a weak smile and turned away without further comment. I decided not to apologize.

My mind was racing from one thought to the next. I was overwhelmed by things totally out of my control. I was worried about my mother but could do nothing other than pray. *God, I know this is my first prayer in a very long time, but I promise to do better.* After so many years of religious ambiguity, I felt I was betraying my creed.

But my thoughts drifted back to the events of the last few hours. I wrote a note to let the program committee know why I could not present my paper, all while imagining Bob Murphy's glee when he learned I would not be there. I decided to resubmit the paper for the Chemical Physics Conference in San Francisco in October. Then, I tried to put it all out of my mind to get a little sleep.

Gradually, a conversation I had before boarding intruded. I realized no one at work knew of my change in my plans. No one would be at the office this early, especially since they were an hour behind. I called our department secretary, Mildred, and left a message on her voicemail. I thought of calling home to talk with Ada but didn't want to wake her. But, I thought I should let Jan know she would probably have to give my project review presentation the following week. I was caught off guard when she answered on the first ring.

"Good morning. This is Jan Collins."

"Jan? Uh, hey. Why are you there this early?"

"Charlie! I was just thinking of you. Nothing's wrong. I wasn't sleeping very well so I came in early to look at the data again. What's up?"

"Well, I was gonna leave you a message letting you know you will have to give my briefing next week. I probably won't be back by then."

"Sure, I can do that. What's going on? You taking some vacation time? Maybe you can read the memo I gave you about the German data."

"Actually, I'm going to see about my mother. She's very sick. It doesn't look good, and I'm not sure how long I'll be gone. I'm skipping the conference."

"Oh, Charlie. I'm so sorry. Is there anything I can do? Anything! Just let me know."

"I appreciate the offer, Jan. Giving that briefing will be a big help. I already left a message on Mildred's voice mail letting her know. After I get there and see how things are going, I will call to let everyone know what my plans are."

"Well, you can call me anytime. You have my home number if you just need someone to talk it out with. And I know how to reach you. I still have your parents' number from when you were there six or seven years ago. Don't worry about the materials I gave you; that can wait."

"Thanks for that, Jan. I have to go catch my flight. But I'll try to find time to read your memo before I return. We should talk about that when I get back. Gotta go."

We had reached cruising altitude and I was awake now. The flight was smooth for a mid-sized plane. I searched for the newspaper article in my cluttered briefcase, and found Jan's memo, which I set aside. I read the article a couple more times but found nothing new – just a lot of unanswered questions. I reluctantly turned my attention to Jan's memo and was pleasantly surprised by its thoroughness. I concluded that maybe she was on to something.

My lack of sleep was catching up with me; I had been running on adrenaline. I found myself dozing, drifting between sleep and wakefulness. Reality merged with dreamlike images. Briefly, I saw the flying horse again – just a few feet from the plane's wing tip. This time, Jack had a calming effect on me. I slid deeper into sleep but was startled by the plane's abrupt bank to left. I peered out the window but saw no obvious reason for the sudden move, and the pilot didn't provide any explanation. When the flight attendant offered drinks, I accepted black coffee and that got me through the rest of the trip. I had no more sightings of the winged horse.

As we began our descent into the Silver Quadrangle Airport, I pressed my forehead against the window, recognizing familiar landforms through the thin clouds. To the south, the thick pine forest was unmistakable. To the west I spotted the Tomley community with its rich black soil, the area in which my father and his family had lived for so long. As our plane banked to line up for a southern approach, the river came into view. From this vantage point, it seemed so much smaller than when I was growing up. Twinges of apprehension bubbled up from deep inside me.

The aircraft entered a mass of billowing clouds that engulfed the plane in whiteness. As we completed our descent, the greenery below contrasted sharply with the beautiful but barren landscape of my adopted New Mexico home.

***

In the single terminal of the small airport, I spotted the Mitchells. Miss Susie waved enthusiastically with a white handkerchief, as she shouted in a shrill voice, "Charlie-boy, Charlie-boy, we over here!"

For a fleeting few seconds, I was embarrassed by her display; but, I quickly remembered where I was, and that her behavior was perfectly normal. Mr. Mitchell stood silently by her side, smiling at me. Remarkably, in the nine or ten years since I had last seen them, there was no noticeable change in the pair. Mr. Mitchell greeted me with a firm handshake, and an even firmer grip on my shoulder. He didn't say a word, just nodded his head as he flashed his broad smile. Miss Susie grabbed both of my hands, obviously holding back tears, before she blurted out a non-stop stream of words.

"Come hug my neck, boy. We gots good news for you. Your mama made it through the surgery; she still got a long way to go but she made it this far wit' the help of Jesus. Your daddy wanted us to wait till you got to the hospital so he could tell you. But I just couldn't wait. Told you we wuz gonna be praying for her; the Lord sure answers prayer. I expect you did a heap of praying yourself."

Unexpectedly, my body stiffened in her embrace. A wave of anxiety swept over me. I realized I was probably having a panic attack.

"Now step back, let me take a good look at you. Charlie-boy, you know I wuz there when you wuz born. Been knowing you all your life. It sure is good to have you back home for a while; but I gotta see if I can fatten you up while you here. Come on, we need to get on out to the hospital."

I felt a sense of relief but had no time to savor it. Mr. Mitchell was grabbing my bags, and she was tugging on my arm.

**

During the trip from the airport, Miss Susie continued to talk with no let-up, informing me of all that had changed since I had last been there; I missed most of what she said. I tried to resist the thoughts about whether I should have stayed to present my paper and left later in the day, and felt ashamed.

"...bet you don't remember what used to be over there. Can you believe that place used to be the old icehouse? Now look at what they done done to it..."

As we got closer to the hospital, my anxiety increased. My body was shaking, and a cold sweat formed on my brow. Mama's surgery had gone better than expected. Gradually, I realized that we were not going to the hospital to celebrate her recovery; instead, I was participating in a dress rehearsal for my mother's death. While it might not come that day, it was inevitable.

Walking into that hospital room, and seeing my mother lying there was a sobering experience: the oxygen tube in her nose, two IV tubes in one arm, the heart monitor beeping at her bedside, the hiss of the intubation system. The horrible hospital smell I remembered from childhood overwhelmed the room, a smell I always associated with death.

The entire effect was overwhelming.

Pops, was sitting by the bedside and seemed to be napping, but he rose suddenly from the chair after he realized I was there. At first, he looked somber, but he chuckled: "I told Susie to let me tell you what the doctor had to say, but I know she told you already. Woman can't keep a thing to herself. Charlie, your mama shore is gonna be glad to see you."

"I can't wait until she wakes up. I'm not going anywhere."

"Doctor says it's okay to wake her for a little bit but she probably won't remember much anyway 'cause the medicine still ain't wore off." He shook her gently. "Martha, Martha, look who's here. Wake up."

Her eyes opened slowly, and she appeared to be trying to bring me into focus. "Well, well, well, Charlie-boy. Looks like I have to get sick to get my baby boy to come home. I'm so glad to see you."

As I leaned over to kiss her, she smiled softly, then faded back into sleep, and a world of who knows what dreams.

"She's been like that since she got out of surgery. Her mind is clear as a bell when she wakes up, but she don't stay awake very long. Doctor says she should be coming out of that in a day or two. He said to tell you to try to be here when he comes back around 4 o'clock. Me and you may as well get outta here for now. Let's go home for a little while; I can use some rest, and I bet you can too. The car is outside; I'll let you drive. Susie and Henry said they don't mind staying for a while."

Miss Susie said, "That's right, we don't mind at all." Mr. Mitchell just nodded his head in agreement.

As we left the hospital, Pops seemed to be happier than I had seen him in a long while. He gave me a play-by-play of all that had occurred over the last few days, and he seemed to release layer upon layer of tension. By the time he got to his pre-surgery conversation with the doctors, I interrupted.

"Pops, just before I left Albuquerque, the strangest thing happened. I found an old newspaper article about Uncle Prince's murder." I paused, but Pops had no reaction. "I remember being at his funeral when I was about six," I prompted; still nothing. "But until now I didn't realize he had been shot. How did I grow up without hearing anybody talk about this?"

Pops remained silent for what felt like minutes, so I turned to look at him. I had never seen my father so obviously uncomfortable. He stared blankly ahead, seemingly focused on the emblem on the hood of the car. Then a deep sigh, pursed lips, tension in his neck -- everything about him told me, before he opened his mouth, that my father was about to lie to me. But I didn't know why.

"Newspaper? What newspaper are you talking about? I don't know nothing about that."

"Well let's forget about the newspaper for a minute. I sure would like to understand why I never heard anybody talk about Uncle Prince being murdered."

"Where are you getting all this stuff from boy? You been here in town for just about an hour, and already you asking questions about stuff from way back, years ago. Stuff you don't know nothing about. That was a long time ago, and my memory ain't what it used to be. You need to be thinking about your mama; she's still real sick."

"I know she's sick, but we're having a different conversation right now. Pops, this is your older brother I'm talking about. Why can't you talk about it?"

I had just turned onto Spring Avenue, entering my old neighborhood. Everything looked different; the houses were more dilapidated, the streets narrower than I remembered, no kids playing in the streets...

"All right. Pull over right here. Hold on just a minute."

Before I came to a complete stop, he was opening the door. "Pops, where are you going?"

"I'll be right back. I'm going in Slick's Place here. He's got the best catfish in town. I'm gonna get us a couple of lunch plates."

The loud thud of the car door as it slammed against the dangling seat belt told me the conversation was over.

CHAPTER 5

We were finally home. I walked slowly up the steps of 741, onto the front porch. The loose top step squeaked, interrupting my concentration – my mind-numbing focus on nothing. Just ahead of me, Pops was saying something to Chit about getting somebody to do some painting. Chit was a constant fixture in this neighborhood. When Pops had walked out of Slick's Place with him in tow, Chit was along for the ride - and the catfish. I knew why Pops had brought him along. During the short ride to 741, the two of them had engaged in non-stop conversation about miscellaneous nonsense, blocking my efforts to get answers from Pops.

741 was the name my brother and I had affectionately bestowed upon our house. In the 1950s, during the Cold War, Mike had decided we needed a code for communicating when the Russians rolled-in to take over our town and our neighborhood. Because of my fascination with numbers, I had come up with a grand scheme I had long since forgotten. It involved something like taking Mike's age (eleven at the time), multiplying it by my age (seven), adding in the number of toy guns we owned, and after a few other manipulations, finally arriving at the number 741. In similar fashion, homes of various other friends in the neighborhood had received secret number designations. Directly across the street, the brick rambler was once known as 862, and a few doors down the only two-story frame within blocks was known to us as 131.

As those childhood memories started to come back to

me, I realized no one had contacted my brother Mike. He had just left for Germany the previous week. As a newly promoted Air Force squadron commander, he was busy with a three-week training exercise. I realized Pops probably would have no idea how to contact him. I needed to leave a message with his home unit in South Carolina - they would know how to reach him.

The absence of my mother was noticeable as I walked into the house. I had been there many times when she wasn't home, but this was different. The signs were intangible, but real: no smells of greens and cornbread cooking, no gospel tunes playing on WHVN, no hum from that rotary fan she always had on in the kitchen. She had only been in the hospital a couple of days. I went into the back room Mike and I had shared. Although I had been back home a few times since leaving for college, I was always struck by the sharp contrast of returning as an adult to the room I had grown up in. Threads of childhood were still weaved tightly through that room. High school pendants still hung from the walls. The furniture was unchanged, right down to the spreads on the twin beds. I left because I was not ready to face childhood memories.

I called the clerk at Mike's home unit. The airman efficiently took the message and promised to pass it on immediately. I noticed, as expected, the tape had not been changed in the answering machine that Pops never used. I found a new one where I had left a box of twenty under the table and replaced it.

As I walked into the kitchen, Pops was saying: "This fish smells so good, may as well eat it now."

Pops and Chit sat there enjoying the steaming catfish; it was drenched in hot sauce and resting on sliced white bread. They guzzled Colt-45 Malt Liquor and engaged in meaningless banter. My impatience grew by the minute. Chit or no Chit, I was going to have this conversation. It occurred to me I had never addressed my father man-to-man, only son-to father.

"Joseph Dawson, we need to talk – now!"

From the look on his face, I knew I had gone over the top. But Pops was caught totally off guard, and only managed to muster a weak response. "Uh, uh – about what?"

I realized I had gotten in a good body punch and wanted to keep him on the defensive. "You know what it's about. I want to know what happened when Uncle Prince was shot."

I had him on the ropes; he was dropping his guard. "Okay but..." He glanced at Chit, signaling him to leave.

I was caught flat-footed when Chit spoke up. The name Chit was the reason no one took him seriously. The man who was once known around town as Hot Daddy had come by that name in a most undignified way. Everybody in town above the age of 25 knew the story. One Saturday morning after staying out all night, he stumbled home still drunk, and tried to use the wrong key. His common-law wife, Olla Mae, was in the kitchen cooking, and didn't hear him banging on the front door because the radio was turned way up playing the morning blues program, and she was singing along even louder. Thinking she had deliberately locked him out, he went around back, threw his full weight against the door, and broke it down. Startled, Olla Mae grabbed the first thing in sight – a pot full of hot chitlins–, whirled around and flung it in his face.

The permanent scar on his right cheek had a grotesque shape the pale grayish color of chitlins. 'Chitlin Face' eventually became 'Chitlin', and finally only 'Chit'. That incident had changed his whole life. He had gone from being a sharp dressing, brash loudmouth to his current state as a perpetual joke.

"Charlie", he said. He didn't say 'Charlie-boy,' he said 'Charlie.' He said it more resolutely than I ever heard him speak. "Charlie." His eyes locked onto mine, and he didn't blink. "That is your daddy you talking to. You need to re-member that." His finger jabbed the air in front of him, punctuating each word. He continued. "I don't care what you might have on your mind, you got to remember your mama is out there in the hospital, a very sick woman. Your daddy has a lotta stuff on his mind that's a lot more import-ant than stuff you trying to dig up from 25, 30 years ago."

I relented and did not press the point. But Chit was on a roll. "Yeah, Charlie. Like I was saying, this man right here is your daddy. You ain't got no way of knowing all the things he done did for you. Sure as my name is George Armstrong Williams, I...."

That was news to me. The fish was tempting, but as Chit continued to rant on and on, I needed to be away from that house for a while. "I gotta go somewhere, be back in about an hour. You two enjoy the fish."

***

I drove aimlessly, with no destination in mind. After a few blocks, I realized I was in front of my old high school – now a middle school. In Millerton, as in countless towns across the south, as schools integrated, the buildings of the 'col-ored' schools were judged inadequate, and downgraded to junior high, middle school, or even elementary school sta-tus. I parked for a few minutes, but when memories of my awkward teen years started, I pulled away.

I turned the corner to see a familiar house, slowing the car to look closer. Aunt Tillie sat on the front porch, sipping iced tea, fanning herself with a cardboard fan, the type at churches and funeral homes. She was focused on her bible. I could have passed without her seeing me, but if I stopped, it could be a two-hour visit. I stopped anyway.

I walked the five yards or so from the car to her front steps, and she didn't move. Not until I reached the second step, did she look up.

"Saw you when you turned the corner. You better had stopped to see me. Come on up here Charlie-boy and give your auntie a big hug." She placed her fan and bible on her lap. I embraced her and she started to weep softly. "Boy, it sure is good to see you. Look just like your daddy used to look when he was a young man. But all of us getting old now. Stand back and let me take a good look at you. Yes sir-ree, look just like Joe when he was your age."

"Aunt Tillie, you're looking fine yourself. It's great to see you. You know I wasn't gonna come by here and not stop. But I can't stay long."

"Have a seat, boy. You can take a little time for your old auntie. But before you sit, go in there and get yourself some sweet tea, and bring me a little bit more. You know where everything is. And when you come back, tell me about your mama."

She and Mama didn't get along very well, but as sisters-in-law, they tolerated each other. I walked into her small, tidy front room and was struck by how much cooler it was inside. A fan in the open window was pulling a gentle breeze into the room. I smelled collards cooking. Before heading to the kitchen, I walked over to the photographs on her wall; I remembered a few. The most prominent one was a picture of her and her children: Ruby, Linda and Tommie, but no father in the picture. There were three more recent pictures of Ruby and Linda with their husbands and children. Next to those was the solitary picture of Tommie in his uniform, taken just before he departed for 'Nam, the adventure he so looked forward to, and the one he never returned from. I lingered to look at him as I remembered him -- the cousin who had arrived into the world only seventeen hours before me.

I turned to another large picture. All of us kids were in that picture, taken when I was only five. There was me, my brother Mike, Cousin Tommie, a baby (probably Cousin Linda), and several other cousins whose names I could not quite place with the faces. And of course, there was Booker – about seventeen or eighteen at the time and looking like a man of almost 30. Next to that was a picture of the five of them, the four brothers and one sister. Pops was on the left, Uncle Sam was next, Aunt Tillie in the middle, Uncle Abe next, and finally Uncle Prince. Sam, the oldest, had died almost twelve years ago in Dallas. Abe was in Detroit and rarely came back for visits. Pops and Tillie were the two who never left home. Had it not been for his murder, Uncle Prince probably would have also been around, still farming.

"You alright in there Charlie-boy? I know you can't be having no trouble finding the ice box, much time as y'all used to spend in there."

"Just looking at the pictures. Be right out."

Being in the kitchen brought back memories of the many times Cousin Tommie and I raided her 'icebox,' one of us standing watch while the other grabbed some ribs, fried chicken, a couple of pieces of pie or whatever was handy. When Aunt Tillie used to cook and keep house for the Martin family, some of the wealthiest folks in town, she always brought home much better food than anything I ate on a regular basis. Seeing the collards simmering on the stove brought back even more vivid memories of her cooking and the flood of memories was starting to get to me. I returned to the porch with our drinks.

"This is real good tea, something special. You ought to bottle this stuff and sell it. You could be a rich woman."

Her body shook when she laughed. "Boy, you just messing wit' your old auntie; ain't nothing special about this tea. But I sure wouldn't mind being rich. I promise you if there was any money to be made off this, the white folks I used to work for would have me making it by the barrel full and they'd be selling it. Now, tell me about your mama. I got word last night she made it through her surgery okay. Sorry I ain't been out there to see her, but this old Arthur-ride-us just don't ease up on me. Just won't let a body have no rest."

"I just got in this morning. We went straight to the hospital; she woke up when I came in, seemed to recognize me. She may have made it through the surgery, but she's still got a long way to go. I haven't talked with the doctor yet. We're gonna do that this afternoon; that's why I can't stay long..."

"Sure glad she came through her surgery. Everybody was praying for her. Lots of folk go under the knife like that and never come back home. You know Lula Smith, lived up there near Second Baptist-"

"Aunt Tillie. Maybe you can help me with something. Mama is gonna have to be in the hospital for at least another week, but when she gets home, she's gonna need some help. I'll stay in town for a while, but I want to find somebody who can come in to help out for a few weeks."

A car passed and whoever it was waved at us. We both returned the wave.

"I think I know just the right somebody. Mary Miller do that kind of work all the time. I don't think she's working anywhere right now. She lives just about three or four blocks from y'all. I'll call her."

"That would be great. Let me know what she says. I want to get with her real soon."

"Charlie-boy, you know I'll do what I can. Before you go, remind me about your family. Feel like I don't really know them. Your wife and daughter ain't spent much time down here. You still got just the one daughter?"

"Yeah, just the one daughter. Maya is in college in Atlanta. Ada keeps busy with her law practice. How are Linda and Ruby? I saw the new pictures of them with their families."

"Everybody doing just fine. Ruby 'bout to have another baby; I think Linda getting a little jealous. They come over here about every other month or so; Birmingham ain't too far. I might go over there around the 4th to visit for a while."

"That's great; glad to know they are doing well. I would love to see them; it's been a long time. I hate to rush off, but I gotta go. By the way, I was looking at some of your pictures and I saw Uncle Prince. Tell me about his murder."

She tried not to reveal her surprise, but the blank stare said it all. After what seemed like minutes, she replied, "Did you ask your daddy? What did he have to say about it? You know I'm getting old; my memory ain't what it used to be."

"I asked Pops, but I didn't get much out of him. Thought you might be able to tell me something about it."

She took a sip from her glass and shook her head. "Well, like I said, my memory ain't what it used to be. Where you getting' your information from?"

"I read about it in the newspaper I found..."

"Newspaper! Wasn't nothing about that in no paper," she blurted out.

"It was a Jackson paper. I guess you're starting to remember something about it."

"Um, uh, what I mean is, I don't remember nothin' about anything being in the paper. What you asking all these questions for? Prince died a long time ago. Let it be. You couldn't have knowed him very well anyhow. You had to been a baby when he was kilt, uh, I mean when he died."

"I was six years old. I remember the funeral; it was the first funeral I went to. I was so scared to see Uncle Prince in that casket. Then, when they put him into the ground and started piling the dirt on, I didn't cry. But I still remember I got really cold and started shaking, and it seemed to take forever to stop."

"Yeah, Charlie-boy. I remember that funeral like it was yesterday. It was hard on me. I still miss my brother... he was such a good man." I saw her tears, but they didn't flow. She was trying hard to hold them back.

"Aunt Tillie, I remember how hard you took it. You know what else I remember? Booker was not there. They were burying his daddy and Booker was not there. In fact, I never saw him again. Why? And why are you and Pops afraid to talk about it? Something that happened so long ago."

"Well, like I said, you need to talk to your daddy. But right now, you need to get on over to the hospital to see about your mama. Let me have my walking stick over yonder next to you. I'm gonna get on in here and finish my cooking. Later, I'll call Mary Miller about helping y'all out. I'll let you know what she said."

With her cane in hand, she got up carefully, and started for the door. I had been dismissed.

CHAPTER 6

Aunt Tillie's claim that 'Wasn't nothing 'bout that in no paper,' piqued my interest. I sat in the car in front of her house and it occurred to me this should have been a simple matter to resolve. I just wanted to know how Uncle Prince's story ended. Instead, my family wouldn't even acknowledge he was murdered.

I saw Aunt Tillie peep out her doorway, checking to see if I was still there. Since I had almost two hours before Pops and I were to meet Dr. Larson, Mama's surgeon, I decided to visit the local newspaper – The Millerton Appeal. In that small town, it wouldn't take more than about seven minutes.

I took a closer look at Northfield, my old neighborhood. Spring Avenue ran east-west, and was Northfield's main artery. When I was a child, it was the economic and social heart of black Millerton. All kinds of business – juke joints, cafes, barber shops, beauty parlors, pool halls, small grocery stores, service stations, and even a hotel – were interspersed among homes of teachers, preachers, bellhops, dentists, domestics, laborers and what-have-you, along that once-thriving avenue. My brother and I were forbidden to go near the seedier places along 'the Avenue'. Somehow, I occasionally managed to sneak into the pool halls to learn the game and listen to the exaggerated tales of neighborhood hustlers. I learned to love the blues by hanging around outside of juke joints, where we could hear licks of the Blues greats – B.B., Bobby and countless others on the Chitlin Circuit. But as I drove along the Avenue now, the deterioration was glaring.

Properties once kept up by proud owners were either abandoned or neglected by the current occupants. 'The Avenue' had more potholes than asphalt. It seemed so much shorter than I remembered.

Traditionally, 8th Street had defined the boundary between the black and white neighborhoods. When I was growing up, there were no black people living west of 8th and no whites to the east of that line. There were still no white folks to the east, but a few black folks lived west of 8th. As I approached the intersection of 8th and Spring, my light was green. Just before I reached the corner, a battered blue pickup roared into the intersection and made a screeching two-wheel turn that almost took off my left fender. I slammed on the brakes as events seemed to unfold in slow motion, and I got a good look at the driver: ruddy complexion, dirty blond ponytail, a sweatshirt with the sleeves ripped off and bulging biceps larger than my thighs and covered in tattoos. A confederate flag hung in the rear window. After my car skidded to a stop, I immediately named him Bubba.

"Hey Bubba! What the hell is your problem, you stupid asshole?! Don't you know what a red light means?!"

He slowed enough to lean out of his window and shout, as he flipped me the finger, "Up your black ass, boy!"

My heartbeat quickened with anxiety. Bubba triggered unpleasant memories.

***

In the fall of 1962, a momentous event occurred in Mississippi, bringing both turbulence and the promise of great change. During that September, the Mississippi Highway Patrol and the state's National Guard were dispatched to Ole Miss to assist the governor in keeping James Meredith out of the state's flagship university. Encouraged by radio DJs throughout the area, every good ole boy within 150 miles of the campus showed up with his rifle, pistol or shotgun to do a little 'coon hunting.' After two days and nights of white folks rioting, Meredith, with the aid of more than 500 U. S. Marshals and approximately 3,000 federal troops, was finally able to register as the 'first Negro student' at the University of Mississippi. Scores of people were injured, and two were killed. Eventually, the highway patrol returned to its normal, mundane tasks of operating speed traps and giving tests for driver's licenses. About ten days later, after things had apparently quieted down, I went to take the test to become a driver for the first time – a big deal for a sixteen-year-old boy. In spite of all the civil rights turmoil, my thoughts had been centered on becoming a driver.

After school on the appointed day, my father drove me to the Motor Vehicle Department at the county fairgrounds. He waited in the car while I went in to do my paperwork and take my road test. I knew I was ready; I had all the rules of the road down cold. I had become a confident driver and could even parallel park, although there was not a single parking place in town requiring that skill. As I approached the front door, a black man who appeared to be about 30, rushed out. The rage in his eyes startled me. He blurted out, "You may as well forget it; man say he ain't issuing no licenses for colored today."

It made no sense to me so I silently nodded but

continued to the door. As I entered, there stood a beefy highway patrolman blocking my way. His beet-red complexion clashed with his gray uniform. His belly strained so much against his shirt that it seemed likely that two or three buttons could come flying off at any moment. His right hand rested heavily on his service revolver, and his left hand firmly clutched a Billy-club that swung threateningly in a short arc at his waist. He spat out the words, "What the hell are you doing here, boy? Didn't that other boy tell you to turn 'round and go home? Y'all ain't getting no license from me today."

Nervously, I managed a weak reply. "Heh, heh, uh, uh, I comes to get my driver's license, sir."

He raised his club and the pace quickened as he rapped it against the palm of his other hand. "This ain't no joke, boy! You better get outta here 'fore I crack your head op'n. If you wont a license, take your black ass up to Oxford and let that nigger Meredith give it to ya."

He was dead serious; I was scared to death. The veins in his neck swelled, his face got even redder and beads of sweat formed on his brow. I turned to walk away, but my legs barely cooperated, threatening to crumple under me. With all my strength, I walked towards the door. Behind me I heard the dull, rhythmic thud-thud-thud of the club against his palm. He barked out, "Gon' boy, git outta here! And if you run into any more nigras out there, you tell 'em to turn 'round and g'on home."

Despite my fear, I managed to make it back to the car without wetting my pants. After frantically telling Pops what just happened, I expected him to do something. What, I wasn't sure. Instead, what I got was, "Quick, get in the car. Hurry up, let's go."

As I slid into the passenger seat beside him, I took my disappointment and frustration out on him. "Pops, ain't you gonna do something?"

He gripped the steering wheel tightly with both hands and bit his lip. Turning to face me he asked slowly, "Just what do you expect me to do, Charlie-boy?"

"Well, couldn't you go back and talk to him, or maybe call the police?"

By then, Pops was accelerating rapidly through the bumpy, gravel-covered parking lot. The car fishtailed to the right, but Pops didn't slow down; I gripped the door handle tightly and braced against the dash. I saw fear in his face.

In halting speech, he said, "That man will use that stick on me faster than he will on you." After pausing, he continued, "And, in case you forgot — he is the po-leece. You know what these white folks 'round here can be like; don't start pretending that you ain't lived here all your life. Now, we'll just come back in a week or so, after things settle down."

He was right; things did settle down, and I got my license after a couple of weeks. Pops and I never talked about it again. But, for a long time I was sad and angry about his failure even to try to help me.

When I told my friends about it later, leaving out the part about how scared I was, we all decided that the cop's name was Bubba, and that all 'colored folks' around him called him Cap'n Bubba. After all those years, Cap'n Bubba's image had not faded from my memory. The asshole who just ran the red light was his exact replica, only younger. I chuckled to softly to myself. Some things still haven't changed around here.

It occurred to me that I was about the same age as Pops during the Capt'n Bubba incident. I told myself that I would have acted more forcefully, but deep inside I understood times were different and there was no comparison. It was time to get over it.

***

Near Downtown Millerton, the character of the neighborhoods changed dramatically. The roadway, free of ruts and potholes, had been recently paved. There were sidewalks with neatly trimmed grass abutting the curbs. The houses were nicer, especially the large antebellum ones. Mike and I had helped Pops do various carpentry jobs during countless sweltering summers. I saw the old Simmons' place where we had torn out the walls of two rooms to make a large sunroom. I spotted the Milner house, where I fell from the roof in '61. Driving by, I could almost see myself hanging from the rainspout as Pops and Mike rushed over with the ladder. It seemed that every iota of fear I experienced back then was oozing slowly out of my deep, deep memory.

I turned on the radio to block out that thought. Barbara Streisand sang: 'What's too painful to remember, we often choose to forget.' I turned the dial until I found a talk radio station.

In the downtown area, I circled the block several times before finding a place to park. Some streets had been reconfigured since I'd left; surprisingly, I had to parallel park.

In all my years of growing up in Millerton, I never had

a reason to go into the offices of The Appeal. During the countless times I had walked past the building, I paid little attention to it. The building was one of the most ornate in town, probably second only to the courthouse. The two-story brick structure, on the southwest corner of Main and Jeff Davis, was bordered by well-cared-for rows of magnolia trees. Two tall, white columns framed the entrance to the building. The large mahogany door, constructed with more glass than wood, was embellished with ornate brass handles. Hand-painted on the glass in large black lettering was 'Millerton Appeal, Established 1852,' and below that: 'Millard A. Lampson, Publisher.' In smaller, bright red letters was the phrase: 'All the news you need to know!'

Through the door, I could see a 20-something, red-haired, young white woman seated behind a reception counter. She was focused on a document in front of her and didn't see me when I entered. I approached the counter and she looked up at the sound of my footsteps on the stone floor. Her expression transitioned from surprise to fear; finally settling into a quizzical look that seemed to ask: 'Why are you here?' I asked myself what she saw when she looked at me. After all, I was wearing a blue shirt with buttoned-down collar, no tie, almost-new beige slacks, a lightweight sports jacket and brown loafers. There was no issue with my attire, and the reason for her reaction was obvious.

In a voice that seemed somehow strained, she asked simply, "Can I hep yew?"

I tried to set the right tone. "Very well, thank you. How are you today?"

Her own tone changed to frustration, "Fine. Can I hep yew?"

With a hint of humor, I said, "Well, I sure hope so." No reaction. I continued, "I would like to look at some newspapers from May 1951."

"What date, do you know the date?"

"Several dates. Actually, all of them: May 1st through the 31st." That threw her off balance. She started to walk away from the counter, hesitated, started to punch intercom buttons, changed her mind again, and dialed someone. With her back to me and in almost a whisper, she said, "There's a black guy out here who says he wonts to look at ALL the papers from May 1951."

Replacing the phone, she told me someone would be right out. She didn't offer me a seat, but I sat anyway. In preparation for whoever was about to arrive, I took out my business card. Within minutes, a 30-some young man arrived. His attire said a mid-level manager: khaki slacks, white shirt with sleeves rolled up and a red-striped tie loosened at the collar.

He had no accent. "Um, can I help you?"

I got up. Standing, I was about two inches taller than he, and I straightened my back to emphasize the difference. I pulled out my business card with one hand while extending my other to shake his. He hesitated for a moment, then took the card and offered a limp handshake. Rotating my elbow upward slightly, I thrust my hand forward to ensure a firm grip, and responded, "Good afternoon, I'm Charlie Dawson."

Slightly tightening his grip, he raised my card to eye level, the way a police officer examines a driver's license. His eyes darted back and forth between my face and the card: *Charlie Dawson, PhD / Senior Member, Research Staff / Manzano Research Institute.* By then the receptionist had come to stand by his side, stretching her neck to read the card. He finally relaxed his grip on my hand. "Well, Dr. Dawson, Christie says you want to see our entire collection of newspapers from May 1951."

"Actually, I only need to look at a few days around the 8th of May." I smiled at her and continued: "I was only kidding, Christie, about the entire month." Turning back towards the man, I asked "And, you are...?"

"I'm really sorry. My name is Kevin Nelson, the Operations Manager. Why don't you have a seat while I go talk with the editor about this."

Sensing that he was stalling, I tried a different tack: I lied. "Sure. But usually, when I do this it's not a big deal. The receptionist is able to take me straight to the archives." I glanced in Christie's direction; she instinctively took a step backward.

He stroked his chin for a second or two, looked at the ceiling and said, "Well, okay. I guess I can let you in. Christie, get the third-floor key for me."

As we climbed the stairs, he made small talk. "So, I guess it's awfully hot in New Mexico."

"Actually, it's very pleasant; the weather here is much hotter and more humid than the high desert."

"Did you come here just to do this research? What's this about?"

"This is my hometown; just doing a little family research."

That seemed to have grabbed his interest. "So, did you graduate from Millerton High?"

I slowed my pace, and turned to face him. "No. I was born too early to be allowed to attend."

The small talk stopped.

On the third floor, Kevin opened the door to a spacious loft. From outside, the building had seemed like two stories, but the attic was almost a full floor. As the door opened, the musky smell of the room oozed out, surrounding us. In the beam of light shining through small windows in the corner of the room, I could almost see fingers of dust creeping toward us. I sneezed twice and Kevin seemed to be trying hard to stifle one.

I had expected mostly microfiche; instead many of the papers were on shelves in large binders. Kevin explained that everything after 1975 was on microfiche, but they were working backward to get the remainder of their collection transferred. Furthermore, nothing existed before 1941 because of a fire in November of that year.

Uncle Prince was murdered on the 9th of May; I thought the article would have appeared on the 9th, at the earliest. I selected the binder with papers from April through June. I sat at a large, dusty oak table, and opened the binder, Kevin stood there, curious about my research. Most of the papers were turning brown and starting to crumble. Gingerly, I turned to the front page of the May 9th edition. My palms became sweaty; my heartbeat quickened. I felt I was on the verge of something. The sensation was like when I was close to completing a long or difficult experiment or a tedious set of calculations. I scanned the page for the story, but it wasn't there. Carefully, I flipped through the remaining pages – nothing. Turning to May 10th, the result was the same. I went back to the 9th of May; still nothing. My mood had gone from elation to disappointment. I leaned back in the chair, rubbed my palm over my eyes and slowly shook my head.

Kevin cleared his throat, "Are you having trouble finding what you are looking for?"

I was tempted not to answer, but I looked up and saw his earnestness. I gave him a terse summary of why I was there. He looked around, then said, almost in a whisper: "I was afraid of that. I'm not from around here; I grew up in Atlanta. But in the five years I've been here I've come to realize that back then, and on into the late 60's this paper didn't print most of what was going on in the black community, especially if they thought it would incite people." He hesitated, looked around again, and added: "Give me your uncle's name and a local number; I'll see what I can do. No promises."

CHAPTER 7

I left the newspaper office. My thoughts returned to my mother's situation, and a wave of despair came over me. The thrill of my hunt had held my attention, but I realized I was likely to hear very bad news. My failure to find anything in those old papers added to my despair.

I went to the place that had always made me feel I was somewhere else: the Choctaw. The view is breathtaking down River Road as the afternoon sun starts to set. The two-lane road dips abruptly and takes a sharp bend to the right, but from the hilltop, it felt like I was on the verge of plunging into the river. The muddy Choctaw, still swollen with spring runoff, flowed to the south with a ferocity that caused my heart to skip a beat. As a kid, I used to be frightened of that stretch of road. Countless times I'd huddled in the back of the car with my eyes covered, expecting disaster at any moment. As I got older, the drive became a cheap thrill – a short, but free roller coaster ride. In my teens, that vista became an escape for me. When I needed to escape Millerton, that view allowed me to be somewhere else. Where? I was never sure, but I always knew I was some other place – some place wonderful.

I turned the Impala along the riverbank road, relishing a few moments of serenity. I headed north and the memories returned.

***

It was a warm Sunday in late May; summer was approaching fast. There were thirteen of us standing in a cluster on a high section of the riverbank, waiting for the word to start down the path to the river. One of the church matrons organized us in six pairs; Kenneth stood alone in front of the group. He was the oldest, probably fourteen or fifteen; most of us were twelve or thirteen. Everyone seemed animated and enthusiastic about what was about to happen. Everyone but me, because I didn't want to be there. It was my mother's idea, not mine, that I be baptized.

As we walked the dusty path toward the river, the mass of on-lookers became a blur. I heard the singing, but couldn't understand the words. Five of my fellow candidates went in before me, but I hardly noticed what was happening. When my turn came, someone moved in on each side, took my hands and led me toward Reverend Phillips. He looked like God to me. He placed one hand behind my back, the other on my forehead and began: "I baptize, you in the name..." As my head entered the water, a sense of calm descended over me. The river had become my friend.

***

My memories faded. I parked the car on the embankment and moved close to the water's edge. I longed to be in the river, floating away. Again, I felt a total sense of calm. But the sound of a couple of speed boats zigzagging up and down the river pulled me back into the moment. From the town above, I heard the clock at the bank striking 3:00, and at the same time the bells at First Methodist began chiming.

Pops and I had a 4:00 PM appointment with Mama's doctor to discuss her prognosis. I walked back to the car, then cruised just below the speed limit along River Road for a few minutes more. The Impala climbed from the river up into the Highlands, and I headed home. After a few blocks, I heard three quick bursts from a siren and saw the flashing blue and red lights in my rearview mirror. Glancing at my speedometer, I confirmed I was below the speed limit. I moved right to let the car pass, but it pulled in behind me. I was seething. I had been driving almost 30 years without a traffic ticket, and now I was about to get my second ticket in as many days. In the mirror, I watched the cop get out as I reached for my driver's license, then realized I had forgotten my wallet. I opened the glove compartment for the vehicle registration and found a mass of papers. I had started sifting through them when I heard the cop speak gruffly.

"Please step out of the car."

"What's the problem officer?"

"Please step out of the car!"

He opened the door and stepped toward the rear of the car. I got out slowly, trying to decide on the least confrontational way to explain my predicament.

"Don't you know that you have to check in wit' the police when you git in town, boy?" He removed his sunglasses.

For the first time I looked closely at the officer and realized he was black. "I'll be damned. Al! What the hell are you doing here? I didn't even realize you'd moved back! I thought you were still in Detroit."

Al Jackson grabbed me in a firm embrace. "Charlie, it's good to see you, man. About six months ago, I decided I'd had enough of being a big-city cop. Me and Shirley packed up and moved back home. I was just asking a couple of the guys about you last week. Nobody around here seems to hear from you; I had planned to stop by one of these days and ask your folks about you. How are they doing?"

"Well, Al, that's why I'm here. Mama needed emergency surgery. It went well, but she's still got some rough times ahead of her."

"I'm really sorry to hear that. If you need anything from me or Shirley, just let me know. I'm in the phone book." The radio in Al's cruiser had been crackling in the background, but something grabbed his attention. "Hold on a minute; I think that's for me."

Al moved to his car, then reached in to speak into the mike. He trotted back to me. "I gotta go, but let's get together. Tomorrow night a group of folks from high school are coming over, about 7:30. 6211 Hope Road. Come on by Charlie, you might be in for a surprise." He sprinted the few feet to his car, hopped in and took off, burning rubber as he flipped on his lights and siren. I headed home carefully.

I approached the house and saw Pops sitting on the front porch fidgeting. He seemed impatient. When he saw me, he got up and walked to the car. "Where you been, Charlie-boy? Don't you know we gotta go talk to the doctor?"

"Pops, we have almost an hour to drive ten minutes. I'm going in here to freshen up. Give me about five minutes."

"Okay, but hurry up!"

I noticed the blinking red light on the answering machine. I went back outside to ask Pops why he hadn't answered the phone.

"Yeah, I was here. But after Chit left, I took a little nap. I turned the phone ringer down low; turn it back up when you go in there. Hurry up; we gotta go soon."

I played the messages on the machine. The first was from Mike letting me know he'd be arriving from Germany by way of Andrews Air Force Base about 11:00 AM the next day.

The second message was from Ada. She sounded worried. "Charlie, you said you'd call and let me know about your mother's condition. Call me as soon as you get this message."

The next message was from Harold, calling from New Orleans to check on the situation.

The final message was from Jan. She started out official. "This is Jan Davis, Charlie's coworker from Albuquerque." After a pause, she continued apologetically. "Charlie, I pray that all is well with your mother. I am sorry to call at what I know must be a very difficult time, but I need to talk with you as soon as possible. Something has come up at work that you need to be aware of. Call me as soon as you can."

Jan's message was disturbing. I went to change my shirt, and I heard Pop enter the house and head for the bathroom.

"Hurry up, Charlie-boy."

After a few minutes, I walked out to go to the car. There was a familiar pickup truck parked in front of the house. It was Buddy's truck. I looked around and saw him sitting alone on the porch. I'd been in such a hurry to appease Pops, I'd walked right past him. Buddy was a distant cousin who sold the vegetables from his farm door-to-door from the back of his truck.

We greeted each other with a brief, obligatory embrace and Buddy gave me a wide smile that revealed a missing front tooth. "Charlie-boy, you looking good, finally starting to look like a man." He was muscular, and well over six feet, but could always be counted on with a ready joke, or a funny story.

"It's great to see you too Buddy; it's been a long time."

"I just stopped by here to find out how your mama is

doing." His face looked more serious than I could ever remember. "I called out to the hospital, but they told me she couldn't have no visitors yet."

"Pops and I are going to meet with the doctor now. I'll let you know when you can see her." I shook my head, smiling. "I don't recall exactly when I last saw you but it looks like you're doing well. Must be all that hard work keeping you fit."

Buddy nodded his head, still smiling. "Yeah, it sure is a lot of hard work, but I enjoy it. Wouldn't want to do anything else. I found that city life..." He trailed off and just shook his head, smiling that wide smile. "Guess y'all doing all right down there in Mexico; guess you and your wife like it down there. I only seen her one time, but your wife sure looks like a nice girl." He paused again. "You ought to bring her down here wit' you more often."

"Well, it would be nice if she had been able to come. But Mama's surgery was last-minute."

Buddy nodded. "Your daddy told me you and him is about to go out there to see her. Y'all tell her we all praying for her."

We just stood there, nervous and uncomfortable. "Well Buddy, we need to get going out to the hospital. I also better see what Pops is up to." Suddenly the obvious occurred to me. "By the way, Buddy. Did you know my Uncle Prince very well?"

He didn't appear surprised by the question but seemed to ponder how to answer. He scratched his face, rolled his eyes upward, took a deep breath, and nodded slowly. "Yeah, I knowed him, knowed him well."

I realized at that moment, I had no idea how Buddy was related to us. "What do you know about his murder?"

Again, he revealed no surprise, but his eyes misted up

a bit before he answered. "Well, now I'm not exactly sure what-"

Pops stepped out of the door and Buddy turned to face him. "Charlie here was just asking me 'bout your brother."

Pops interrupted angrily, as angry as I had seen him since I had started asking questions. "Charlie-boy! What's wrong wit' you? Why don't you just get all of this outa your head. Come on; we gotta go meet the doctor and see about your mama. Gimme the key, I'm driving." Pops snatched the car keys from my hand and stormed to the car. Buddy shook his head, smiled and said, "Charlie-boy, you need to go see bout your Mama. Maybe we can talk later."

CHAPTER 8

"When we get out there to the hospital, Charlie-boy, don't you be bothering your mama with all that foolishness you been trying to dig up about Prince." His tone reminded me so much of the way he used to chastise Mike and me when we were kids. "You just let it be. You understand?" Pops gripped the wheel tightly and stared straight ahead. He never took his eyes from the road.

"Look, Pops. I know Mama is very sick. She's-"

Pops slammed on the brakes and I watched as his head was thrown forward to within an inch of the steering wheel. He had almost run a red light. He pulled over to the curb and parked.

"That's why you need to be wearing your seat belt, Pops. Are you okay?" I waited for an answer. "Do you want me to drive?"

He shook his head without looking in my direction. "I ain't wearing no seatbelt, so don't start bothering me about that. I been driving longer than you been alive, boy. I can drive out to the hospital without your help."

"Okay Pops. But, tell me something about-"

For the first time since we had gotten in the car, he turned toward me. "Why can't you just stop this? You keep on worrying me with this thing-"

I raised my hand and shook my head. "No, I'm not asking about that. I was just gonna ask you about Buddy. Who is he? How is he related to us? In all these years that I've known him, I don't really know our connection."

Pops seemed relieved and loosened his grip on the wheel. He let out an audible sigh. "Well, he's just a cousin, I guess what you would call a distant relative."

"But who's his family? Does he have a wife? Kids?"

"His wife died about seven, eight years ago. Her name was Lula. You oughta remember her. I'm pretty sure we told you about it when she died." Pops pulled back on to the road. "They had two girls. They grown now, one of 'em is in Detroit; I can't remember exactly where the other one lives. Ain't seen 'em in a long time, but they was some real pretty girls."

As we approached the next traffic light, Pops eased his foot onto the brake and came to a smooth stop. Suddenly a horn was honking. Although the road had only two lanes - one in each direction - a car pulled alongside us.

"Brother Dawson, how's your wife doing? We heard that she was in the hospital." The Franklin sisters were leaning forward, stretching their necks, and waving frantically. "Is that one of your boys in there with you? We knew it wouldn't take long for them boys to git down here to see about they mama. We praying for her."

Before Pops could reply, they were pulling away through the green light.

"Them women sure is some busy bodies. Can't slow down long enough to listen to nothing. But they got to be the hardest working women in Northfield Baptist Church."

I nodded as Pops drove. From as far back as I could remember, Miss Anna and Miss Carrie had been fixtures in that church and were involved in every possible thing that happened there. Some of my fondest memories were the church picnics they organized during summer. I could almost see, taste and smell all of the food in their wonderful picnic baskets: ice-cold lemonade, fried chicken, potato salad, deviled eggs, chocolate cake...

I asked again about Buddy.

"Charlie, I don't know what else to tell you. Wish I could help you out, but that's about all I know."

There was a smile on his face, but from the tone of his voice, it was clear I could expect no candor from Pops. Neither of us said anything more. We turned a corner and the Silver Quadrangle Regional Medical Center loomed in front of us. The building seemed so different from earlier in the day. Situated on a knoll at the edge of a small pine forest, the entrance of the six-story hospital had been brightly illuminated by the sun earlier that morning. Now, with the sun descending and clouds moving in, the building's gray drabness was a stark reminder of Mama's situation.

Pops parked and sat there, staring blankly. A shadow seemed to have descended over his face.

"Are you okay Pops? Are you ready?"

"Just sitting here thinking. You go on in; I'll be there in a minute."

I didn't argue. Walking toward the hospital, I prepared myself for bad news. At the entrance, I looked back to see Pops emerging from the car. At the lobby's information desk, I asked for Dr. Davis, got an update, and I waited for Pops to catch up.

"Frank Davis and Dr. Larson are gonna meet us in a family room on the third floor. They have been examining Mama and should be just about finished. We had better get on up there."

Pops nodded and waited for me to lead the way. I was apprehensive, but eager to know what the doctors had to say.

Frank was waiting for us. When we walked in, he moved toward me, looked me squarely in the eye, then embraced me without a word. Tears welled in my eyes. He stood back to look at me. His face betrayed no emotion, just an unspoken acknowledgement of what I was feeling.

Turning to Pops, he shook his hand. "Mr. Dawson, it's good to see you again. When we spoke after last night's surgery, I know it was upsetting to hear how sick your wife was, But she's very tough; she's hanging in there."

Pops nodded again. Worry lines seemed to have been chiseled into his face.

There was another person in the room I hadn't noticed. He got up from a chair in the corner and walked over. Gesturing to me, Frank said, "This is my good friend Charlie Dawson. We've been friends since first grade. Charlie, this is Dr. Larson; he's Mrs. Dawson's heart surgeon."

I shook Dr. Larson's hand; I looked into his steel gray eyes and was pleased with what I saw: concern. Looking more closely, it became clear that he was much younger than he had first seemed. His thick gray hair provided an aura of maturity, but youth was written all over his face.

Pops must have noticed the same thing because he blurted out, "You look like you just a boy. How old is you?"

Dr. Larson chuckled softly, and suggested that we all have a seat. He did most of the talking, carefully explaining the details of Mama's aneurysm and what he had done to repair it. His demeanor was a careful balance of the appropriate level of detail, sprinkled with compassion. From time to time, Frank chimed in to amplify something. Pops nodded silently in reaction to most of what he heard. When Larson reached the part about prognosis, he silently passed the baton to Frank.

Frank spoke directly to me. "Charlie, I'm gonna be straight up with you. Your mama is very sick. Her situation is not hopeless, but it's a very delicate situation right now.

We're doing everything we can. The next 24 to 48 hours will be critical. She's in ICU." Frank turned to Pops and smiled. "Now, the two of you should go on up there to see her. She's not awake, but I think she'll know you're there."

I had so much to say to Frank, but I felt my emotions rising so I said nothing. We embraced again, and Frank simply said, "Go do what you need to do. We'll have time to talk later."

Pops put his hand on my shoulder. "Okay Charlie, let's go upstairs to see about your mama."

"You go on up Pops. I'll be there in a few minutes. I'm gonna make a couple of quick phone calls first."

Pops scowled but he said nothing.

"I'll only be a few minutes. I need to let Ada know what's happening, and call my office. I'm staying here at the hospital tonight."

The scowl on his face smoothed into resignation. "One of us should stay here. I tried the other night but sleeping in that hard little chair was rough on this old body. You go make your calls; I'll be upstairs wit' your mama."

I found a payphone. Ada answered on the second ring.

"I was beginning to worry when I didn't hear from you and then I got the answering machine. What's happening with your mom?"

Crouching near the floor, with my back against the wall, I tried to relax. "Pops and I just finished talking with her doctors. The prognosis is not great, but there is hope. The next couple of days will likely be the turning point, one way or the other..."

"Charlie, I'm so sorry. How are you holding up? Do you want me to come there to be with you?"

I had given little thought to how I was doing. "It would be great if you were here, but let's not make that decision now. I'm staying at the hospital tonight. I'll call you tomorrow and let you know how she's doing."

With a sigh in her voice, she acquiesced. "You're lucky to be there with your mom if these turn out to be her final days. I'll always hate that I never got the chance to say goodbye to my parents. Things can change in an instant. Treasure the moments that you have with her."

"I appreciate that. I have to make a quick call to the office and then get upstairs. Goodnight, Cera."

She laughed deeply. "Goodnight, baby."

I'd make my call to Jan as short as possible. It took five rings before she answered.

"Charlie, I was hoping you would call, but I was just leaving for a meeting. I'm late."

I was relieved to know it would be a short conversation. "Tell me quickly what's going on."

She sounded flustered, and spoke haltingly, "Uh, the budget, they're cutting budgets. Our program. It's on the chopping block. I think, well, uh, I, uh know that really, the real reason is because of our efforts, you know, to show that Koch faked his results."

She sighed after getting it all out. I should have been angry because she had pulled me into her scheme, but at that moment I felt that it didn't matter.

"Jan, there is nothing I can do from here. Things are not good with my mother. I have to go."

"Charlie, I am so sorry. I didn't even ask about your mother; how is she? I'll deal with this the best I can."

"Jan, it'll be okay. I really must go. I'll call when I can."

I hung up and suddenly felt hungry; I could not remember my last meal. Visions of ice-cold lemonade, fried chicken, potato salad, deviled eggs, and chocolate cake filled my mind. I found the cafeteria. In a far corner sat a group of doctors and nurses laughing. Nearer the door, members of an extended family were going on and on about the beautiful baby girl just born. My appetite evaporated and I left for the ICU.

I found my way to Mama's room. Through the open door, I watched as Pops sat there stroking her hand, careful not to disturb the IV tubes. Her breathing was labored, but a peaceful shadow drifted across her face. Ada was right; I should treasure the moments.

CHAPTER 9

WEDNESDAY, 9 MAY 1990/ THURSDAY, 10 MAY 1990

That night my sleep was restless, full of worry and uncertainty. The room was too cold, and the chair wasn't made for sleeping; the light blanket covering me provided little comfort. The unfamiliar sounds I heard throughout the night were unnerving. The hissing sounds came from Mama's respirator; the moans came from the patient in the next room.

The EKG and the IV system both emitted an eerie orange light that combined with the shadows to play tricks on my eyes. Through the window, sheets of lightning intermittently illuminated the sky.

Fear gradually overtook me, and I remembered the first time I faced death as a child. Images of Uncle Prince's funeral drifted through my memory. I recalled how my six-year old body trembled as his coffin was lowered into the ground while I huddled close to Mama.

My anger with Pops bubbled to the surface again. The wall of secrecy everyone was hiding behind was getting to me. I told myself that if Mama had been well, things would be different: I would have gotten the information from her. But as I thought more about it, I had to acknowledge that her side of the family was just as secretive. During several conversations I had tried to have with her and my aunts about things they experienced while growing up, I got 'Why you interested in that old stuff?' and 'I don't have time for that!' For my parents' generation, secrecy seemed to be a way of life, but I didn't understand why.

000297233365

I drifted back into sleep. Somewhere around midnight, Mama sat up and spoke to me in a hoarse voice. "Charlie-boy, don't be so worried. I'm not gonna die, at least not tonight."

I opened my eyes and realized she hadn't spoken. I dropped back into spurts of sleep, back into my tortured dreams.

During a waking moment, I stared at the ceiling, concentrating on the shadows that danced above my head. Still, my thoughts returned to Uncle Prince. To shift my focus, I tried to mentally solve an especially difficult equation I had been struggling with during the prior week. I drifted back into a semblance of sleep but heard a shuffling and saw a shadow moving across the room in the dark.

Thinking I was dreaming again, I ignored it; then she spoke. "Good morning. You must be Mrs. Dawson's son; the doctor told us you'd be here. I'm Cathy Mason, her nurse for this shift. Hope I didn't wake you."

I stood and extended my hand to the young nurse. "Yes, I'm Charlie Dawson. And you didn't wake me. This chair definitely isn't a bed."

She smiled. "You really don't have to sleep here at the hospital. We're taking good care of her and if anything should change, we'd contact the family right away." Her appearance reminded me of Ada, about 5'2" with a darker complexion.

"Everybody is doing a great job, but if she wakes with no family here, it might scare her. I can handle an uncomfortable chair."

"I understand your concerns, Mr. Dawson; it happens all the time with our patients. If you don't mind being here, we don't mind having you."

"Please call me Charlie. 'Mr. Dawson' makes me feel

old."

Smiling, she said, "Well, sure Charlie, if you call me Cathy."

"So, how's she doing?"

"I just checked her vitals. She's looking good for a woman of her age who has just had major surgery. Your mother's a strong woman. I'm about to get someone to help me turn her now. We don't want her getting bed sores. I'll be right back."

"I'm glad to help, if you show me what to do."

She nodded and started to show me how to use the air mattress to make the lifting easier. Cathy moved with the efficiency of someone who had done this often, and the speed of someone who had other patients to deal with. As we turned Mama onto her other side, I felt, for the first time since coming home that I was doing something useful. Cathy tucked in the sheet and blanket, did a quick check of the IV and ventilation tubes, and left as quietly as she had come.

"I'll see you soon, Charlie."

I returned to the chair and my restless sleep. A resounding thunderclap startled me awake; I bolted upright. The windows and everything else in the room reverberated in response to the deafening sound. The lights and monitoring equipment flickered, but returned to normal after a few seconds. Moving to Mama's bedside, I saw she hadn't moved. I leaned in close to be sure she was still breathing. Cathy Mason hurried back into the room with a determined look on her face. She reset the EKG monitor and checked Mama's pulse.

She said, tersely, "Power failure, but everything is fine. The generators kicked in so don't worry. I have other patients to check, but I'll be sure to look in on her soon."

I heard a slapping sound outside. Moving to the window, I saw large raindrops splattering the windowpane. A few pine trees acted as a buffer, causing the rain to hit the glass erratically. I pressed my face against the window, surprised by the intensity. The sky was spewing water with a vengeance. In the dim first light of morning, the dark, turbulent clouds boiled. My childhood fascination with thunder and lightning kept me there, waiting for the next flash of lightning and roar of thunder.

"What you doing, Charlie-boy, leaning up against the window like that? Everything alright?"

Pops and the Mitchells were standing in the doorway, dripping wet. Pops was in a yellow rain slick I hadn't seen in decades. Mrs. Mitchell was in knee-high rain boots and held an oversized umbrella. Mr. Mitchell wore a felt hat, a waist length rain jacket, and was the wettest of the three.

"I was just looking out at the storm, Miss Susie. Looks rough out there. Things are fine in here, though. The nurse just left. Y'all are here real early."

She said, "We left early because it was storming so bad. We wanted to have enough time to get here in all this rain."

Mr. Mitchell warned me, "You ought to know better than to stay by the window when it's storming like that. Way back when I was just a boy, I remember this man name of Willie Brown got struck by lightning standing at the window."

I couldn't resist asking, "Did it have any glass in it?"

He leered and shook his head; clearly, he didn't appreciate my attempt at humor. A flash of lightning lit the room, followed by deafening thunder. We all flinched.

"Told you so!" Mr. Mitchell was smug. "Lightning ain't nothing to play with. It's the Lord doing his work."

Pops hadn't said a word since arriving. He removed his rain gear and put it on the chair. He walked to Mama's bedside, took her hand and asked me, "How she sleep last night? I hope you didn't start..." Our eyes met and his voice trailed off to nothing.

"She slept fine. Once or twice she mumbled a few words, but otherwise slept like a baby. Better than I did. The nurse came by to check on her a few times; the doctor is supposed to be here about 7:15 or 7:30."

Pops nodded and seemed to be collecting his thoughts. He put his hand on my shoulder. "Listen son, I know you did a good job looking out for your mama. You oughta go back to the house and get some sleep. The Mitchells gonna stay here with me."

"I'll take you up on that Pops, but I want to stay until the doctor has a chance to examine her. I'm going for a cup of coffee. Do you want me to bring you anything?"

"Naw, I got up early and had breakfast over at the Mitchells' house. You go on; we'll be here."

Mr. Mitchell had found a couple of extra chairs from somewhere. He was slumped into one, busy with the remote, flipping through channels with the volume turned down.

I headed out when Mrs. Mitchell said, "Wait for me Charlie-boy; I'll go wit' you. Just give me a minute." Perched on the edge of Mama's bed, she removed her boots and put on some flats she took from her massive purse.

We waited in the corridor for the elevator. "I been knowing your mama for longer than I can remember. We went to school together; been friends since elementary school. I only had one brother, no sisters. Your mama and me are like sisters. Her two sisters been dead for a long time. So, I care about her as much as you, your brother, and your daddy do. If there's something you want to talk about, you can talk to me."

The elevator arrived and we got on. "Well, Miss Susie, I appreciate everything you've been doing."

We exited the elevator and she turned to face me. "What I'm saying is, I notice that you and your daddy don't seem to be getting along too well. It just ain't good for y'all to be like that."

I didn't want to be rude, but I was feeling tired and didn't want to get into an extended conversation with her about what was going on between me and Pops. "If you can't tell me about the shooting of my Uncle Prince in '51, or get Pops to tell me about it, I'm not sure there's much you can help with."

Her eyes widened in surprise. "So that's what the two of you is at each other's throats about. I don't know much, but I'll tell you what I can."

We got coffee and sat in a secluded corner. I told her about my efforts to find out what happened from Pops, Aunt Tillie, and Booker but didn't mention my visit to the local paper.

She leaned in close as I talked. When she spoke, it was in whispers. "I don't know what it is they don't want you to know. I think I know about as much as what everybody around here knowed about it. Your folks never told me any kind of secrets about that situation. But I wasn't here when all this happened."

"I don't understand. I thought you had been here since way back when you and Mama were in school together."

"Well, that's right Charlie-boy. But I left here for a few years to live in St. Louis. That's when I met Henry; he was from the Delta. When we decided to leave the city in '55 neither of us wanted to live in the Delta, so we came here. When Prince was shot, there was a lot of news about it in the paper."

"I'm confused because I checked with the local paper and they didn't publish anything about it."

She nodded and put her cup down. "Yeah, these folks around here never would print nothing like that. But there was a colored newspaper down in Jackson that they printed once a week. Lots of folks living away from Mississippi used to get that paper up in St. Louis. That's the only way we knowed anything about what was happening back home unless kin folks wrote to us about it. That Jackson paper had something about it for two or three weeks in a row, right on the front page."

"I saw part of the story they wrote about the shooting. That's what got me started trying to find out what happened."

Worry lines spread across her brow, as she said, "I think I see why your daddy so concerned. You been in town for a little bit more than a day, your mama sick, and already you done all this investigating and snooping around. If you know all of this, then you aware everybody knowed who shot your Uncle Prince and that man's son is the county sheriff. Maybe you do need to stop asking people about this."

My jaw dropped. "Sheriff! Is that why everybody is afraid?"

"Well, I can't say that's the reason. As a matter of fact, that Mr. Mullins one of the best sheriffs we had around here in a long time. Most of the sheriffs used to be so mean. But you ask anybody, and they'll tell you he's a man who knows how to treat folks right."

"Well why do you think everybody is so afraid? Why won't they talk about this?"

"Like I said, all I know is what I read in them newspapers. The sheriff's daddy shot Prince over some little bitty accident that didn't even happen. Next thing you know, them other peoples got shot. Maybe that's-"

I threw up both hands. "Wait a minute, Miss Susie. What other people are you talking about? Who else got shot?"

"The way I remember things, the NAACP got a bunch of folks together to go down to the courthouse and demand that they do something about your uncle getting killed. Things got out of hand and the police shot three or four peoples. One of 'em died. That's all I know. I think we need to get back upstairs now."

During the elevator ride and the walk back to the ICU, Mrs. Mitchell was silent. I wondered if she was troubled by what she had told me. Before we entered the room, I stopped her. "Thanks for the information. I won't mention our conversation."

Pops and Mr. Mitchell were standing in the corridor just outside the room. I looked inside and saw the curtain was pulled closed around Mama's bed. After about five minutes the curtain opened. Both doctors were there, along with Cathy. I could read nothing from their blank faces.

Frank Davis started talking first. Looking back and forth between me and Pops, he said, "We would like to talk with the both of you. Let's go in."

Mrs. Mitchell looked at her husband. "Henry, let's take a walk."

Frank put a hand on my shoulder. "Your mother is holding her own."

The surgeon cleared his throat and added, "A few of her vital signs are actually looking a little better. There's reason for hope. We're doing all we can. I'll be checking on her."

I asked, "She's sleeping a lot. She was awake briefly yesterday, but I don't think she's been alert since then. Is that normal?"

The surgeon replied, "That's to be expected. Her body has been through major surgery, which is an incredible shock. She should start to be more responsive in a day or so." He shook Pops' hand, then mine. "I'm sorry but I have to go; I have several other patients to check on."

Frank started out of the room also and motioned for me to follow. Once in the hall, he said, "My friend. Everything we told you and your father is true, but I want to warn you that I've seen patients at this stage who suddenly go down-hill. You need to be prepared for that possibility. But we're doing all we can. Meanwhile, prayer can't hurt. I also have to finish my rounds, but I'll check in later." He embraced me tightly. "Be strong."

I walked back into the room. Pops had little to say but did remind me of Mike's 11:30 arrival. I said I'd get cleaned up and pick Mike up from the airport. I went to the hospital parking lot. The rain had stopped, and the clouds were clearing. I decided that was a good sign.

CHAPTER 10

THURSDAY, 10 MAY 1990

I turned onto the main road and saw the storm's damage. Magnolias that had lined the roadway for decades were twisted and broken. Branches clung precariously to trunks still upright; other trunks obstructed the road. On another street, the rain had overwhelmed the drainage system and water stood in large puddles, filling all the potholes. I had to brake frequently to avoid flooding the engine or spraying sheets of water onto pedestrians.

Strong winds were sweeping away high, lingering clouds. I rolled down the car window, aware of the quiet. Even the workmen clearing storm drains and repairing broken power lines were lethargic in their movements, and not very talkative.

I turned on the radio. Even the music on WMSQ was unusually soft in contrast to their standard R&B, jazz and blues. At the end of an unfamiliar tune that sounded like a dirge, the announcer commented quietly about how fortunate we were that the storm had caused only minor injuries.

In the Northfield neighborhood, the storm damage was worse than in the more affluent, whiter, Westside. However, this part of town was busy. On almost every corner, people stood around discussing the storm's devastation. At a traffic light, I watched two men describe in billowing tones how they avoided being swept away by a wall of water flowing down the street. Half a block farther, a large woman had collected a small crowd as she wailed about the sycamore tree that had demolished half of her front porch, along with the Chevy Impala in the driveway.

I was relieved to see no signs of damage at 741. Pops probably would have mentioned any, but I took a quick walk around the house, just the same. The worst damage was to the old Live Oak tree in the back yard. When Mike and I were kids, it had been our favorite climbing spot.

I walked in the house and immediately crashed in the bedroom Mike and I used to share. The two twin beds had fresh linen. Mrs. Mitchell was probably responsible for the neatness of the room. I closed my eyes and wished for sleep. During the preceding three days, I'd had very little, and my body was feeling it.

The room was stuffy. I got up to open the window and pull the shades down, but muted sunlight still trickled in. I lay back down but was aware of all the sounds surrounding me: tree branches outside the bedroom window creaked as they resisted the wind; the house's pops and crackling noises as it settled; the steady tick of the grandfather clock three rooms away that had been there as long as I could remember. I even heard what sounded like footsteps, but knew no one else was in the house. I eventually faded into that nether world between awake and asleep.

***

I was walking in a place I had never been before, yet something seemed familiar. At the top of a low hill, I surveyed my surroundings. The area was desolate, but beautiful. The sky was filled with billowing clouds and the air was cooled by a gentle breeze. There was a lush clump of oak trees about a mile away. I followed a flock of geese flying to-

wards them. I soon discovered a small village partially hidden by the trees. Every building was identical: granite, three-stories, and cylindrically shaped. The structures were obviously old. I had no idea where I was. I knocked at the first building I reached, but there was no answer. I pushed the heavy wooden door, but it did not give. I walked to the next structure, becoming more aware of my surroundings.

Everything was eerily quiet. Night was coming, but I didn't see any lights on. The streets were cobblestone, like in that small Italian town Ada and I vacationed in three summers ago. I approached a small fountain in the village square where water trickled in short spurts. I cupped my hands to drink, and afterwards felt oddly refreshed.

I sat on the bench that encircled the fountain, then heard rustling behind me. I was surprised to see Ada standing there, head tilted back and dripping water onto her neck with a handkerchief. I watched the water flow down her blouse.

"What took you so long?" she asked casually. "I've been waiting for almost an hour."

"Cera, what are you doing here? How did you get here?"

She smiled and simply said, "Siesta time." The glint in her eyes told me we would not be napping. She took my hand. "The hotel is this way." She pointed to a building looming ahead of us. We stopped and bought two bottles of beer from a small restaurant half a block before we got there.

I started the shower as soon as we got to the room. We stripped and entered the shower, lathering each other's body with soap and exploring with our lips. Soon, the shower was over, and dripping, we dove into bed. As we traded passionate kisses, our intimacy was interrupted by loud voices outside. I went to the window and saw about twenty men waving swords, rushing the hotel. They shouted in a language I couldn't understand or recognize. Somehow, I knew they were looking for me. I turned around to warn Ada but she was already dressed and heading for the door. She tossed me jeans and a t-shirt.

"Follow me. I know a back way out of here."

Seconds later, I was dressed and sneakers magically appeared on my feet. Racing down some back stairs, ten steps behind her, I heard her say, "When you get to the street, go two blocks to the right, turn down the first alley..." I couldn't hear the rest, and I was lagging farther behind.

Sprinting down the street, turning corners recklessly, I turned onto a dead-end street. I heard my pursuers close behind me. Ahead, I saw a door ajar. I rushed in, slamming the door behind me. I saw a spiral staircase, and had no choice but to go up. As I raced up, it began to crumble ahead of me. I leapt over disintegrating sections and made it to the landing. Ahead of me was a wide window; I was probably ten stories above ground. Behind me, I saw the staircase being reconstituted ahead of the pursuing throng. I was trapped.

To my right, I caught a glimpse of a rope hanging above the opening. Grabbing it, I quickly made a loop at the end and tossed it over a large branch of a tall oak tree just outside the window. Holding *onto the rope, I swung from the window toward the ground. Seconds before impact, a white horse and a rider came galloping across the field and the arc of my swing landed me just behind the rider. The rider was topless and I saw a spider-like birthmark on her shoulder. Cera had rescued me. I initially didn't realize it was her because of the braids in her hair. As the horse began to accelerate, I held on tightly to her, cupping her breasts in my hands. I became aware of arrows and spears, piercing the air near us.*

The horse began to sprout wings, and I realized it was Jack – the horse from my recurring dream. The wings flapped rapidly, and I could vividly hear the sounds they made. Jack banked sharply to the left and started to quickly gain altitude. Through all of this, Ada had been silent. Suddenly, she screamed a gut-wrenching scream. "Oh no!" Directly ahead of us was a large jetliner, descending for a landing. Instinctively, Jack tried to get above the plane, but it was too late. I could hear the awful ripping sound as his right wing was torn from his body and pulled into the jet engine. We were in a nose-dive toward a deep canyon, with a rapidly flowing river. I was jolted awake.

***

"Oh my God! That was some dream; what did that mean?" My body was soaked with sweat. I recalled the dream with total clarity and tried to gain some understanding of the message I should receive from it. I lay still, using controlled breathing to try and relax, but it didn't help. Eventually,

I acknowledged I would not gain an understanding and I needed to head for the airport to pick up Mike.

I got out of bed and wandered aimlessly through the house; Mama's absence was even more noticeable than before. If she were home, she would already have greens or peas cooking, and starting the cornbread.

As I looked at the walls in each room, I realized for the first time, the sparse number of pictures hanging in comparison with Aunt Tillie's home. I paused to look at what was always my favorite family photograph. In a picture taken before I was born, Pops stands in his Army uniform behind Mama who is seated in an ornate wooden chair that Pops made. Mike, about three years old, stands next to her, gripping her right hand.

Another picture caught my interest – a picture I had forgotten about. It was taken during the only time Ada visited my hometown with me. My parents are seated in the backyard in wicker lawn chairs. Maya, at about age eight, stood near Mama, I stood behind Pops and Ada stood behind Mama. I looked closer at the photo and saw Ada's hair was in braids – the only time she wore her hair in that style. One of my relatives offered to do braiding for Ada. She decided afterwards she didn't like them and never wore her hair in that style again.

As I stood looking at the photo, my concentration was broken by a knock at the door. I was tempted not to answer, but after a brief hesitation, I went to the door. A teenage white boy stood there, looking uneasy.

"Good morning. Can I help you?"

He responded, "I'm looking for Dr. Charlie Dawson."

"Well, that's me. What can I do for you?"

He hesitantly withdrew a manila envelope from under his arm. "Mr. Nelson at the newspaper asked me to bring this to you."

After I took it, he turned to leave but I stopped him. I took $5.00 from my pocket. "Hold on; this is for you."

He looked surprised but accepted it before leaving.

I anxiously opened the envelope and found photocopies of numerous newspaper pages. A note was attached that simply said, 'I did what I could.' It was signed Kevin Nelson.

Included in the package was the continuation of the Jackson Informer article I had found earlier. There were several other articles from the same paper that confirmed what Mrs. Mitchell told me. The shooting of Uncle Prince had led to local "riots" that resulted in the death of one person and the injury of several others. The surprise item was a small clipping from the legal section of the local paper. Dated May 23, 1951, it said Red Mullins - the killer of my uncle – was fined $100 for the assault of a 'local Negro.'

The anger I felt was accentuated by the clock striking 11:00. It was time to leave for the airport to meet Mike.

CHAPTER 11

I didn't want to be late to meet Mike's flight, so I hurried out of the house and tossed the envelope from the newspaper office into the back seat. I decided to take the shortest, most direct route to the airport rather than the scenic route. Traveling west on Spring Avenue, I headed for the intersection with Mission Road, which helped me to avoid the downtown area and get quickly onto the west-bound highway. Street cleaning crews were finally starting to deal with the destruction in Northfield. In several places people were not waiting for the city crews. I pass three locations where neighborhood men were using chainsaws to remove fallen trees and branches.

Two blocks after turning onto Mission, I passed the old Pruitt house. I still knew all those stately old homes because Mike and I spent so much time during our teen years helping Pops to do repairs on them. As I drove by, I saw a strikingly beautiful, olive-skin sister standing on the wrap-around porch. I slowed to a crawl to get a closer look. She wore a well-fitting, floral robe and cradled a large coffee mug close to her body as she surveyed her minor property damage. *Definitely not the maid*, I decided. Not so long ago black folks were only in these places as the hired help, but that had slowly changed. For a fleeting moment, she reminded me of Maria Davidson, but she looked young enough to be her daughter.

Maria was the first girl I can remember in my life. We were childhood play mates. By fifth grade, I knew we would be married and live happily ever after. But, by our first year of high school she had become the most beautiful young woman imaginable. Every guy in town had discovered the treasure that I had always known about, and I had faded into obscurity on the sidelines. As I drove by, a vivid flash-back of the last time I saw Maria returned to haunt me.

***

It's our high school graduation night. I muster enough courage to pull her aside and blurt out 'I love you Maria.' She moves in very close to me, slowly removes her graduation mortar-board cap, smiles the most beautiful smile imaginable, and gently strokes the back of my neck. I know she's about to kiss me; instead, she simply says: 'I know Choo-Choo, I know.' She turns and walks away.

***

That moment was indelibly seared in my memory.

As I accelerated and pulled away from the Pruitt house, with my peripheral vision I saw her turning in my direction. To avoid further self-pity about what never-was, I turned on the radio. WMSQ had returned to their standard fare of up-tempo R&B. I tried to sing along with Brother JB as he belted out 'Poppa's Got a Brand-New Bag.' That was my mantra all the way to the airport.

By the time I parked the car and walked quickly to the only gate in the Silver Quadrangle Airport, it was about ten minutes after the scheduled arrival time for Mike's flight. Fortunately, the plane was about fifteen minutes late. As I got to the crowded waiting area, the PA system announced the arrival of Southern Regional Air flight 1128. Through the large windows, I saw the small plane being rocked erratically by wind gusts as it came in on final approach. A feeling of panic suddenly overtook me; I held my breath, sure that the plane was about to crash. Instead, the pilot executed an almost perfect three-point landing. Apparently, I was not the only one who sensed impending danger, because as I exhaled, I heard a sigh of relief from several people standing near me. Spontaneously, we all began to applaud.

The flight was very full; the first several passengers to get off seemed shaken by the landing; some had to be assisted by members of the ground crew. Mike was the last passenger to exit; he stood at the top of the steps for what seemed like a very long time, engaged in a friendly banter with two flight attendants. As he started down the steps, one of them, a petite, shapely redhead, touched his right shoulder. He turned toward her, and she placed a slip of paper into his hand. *Probably her phone number*, I concluded. My feeling of concern for his safety was quickly replaced by envy.

Mike had never been married, but he somehow managed to avoid the Playboy image. He'd always had it easy with women, and I've always been jealous; in fact, the only time I can remember Maria talking with me during our high school years was when she would ask about Mike. Whenever he was home from college, she showed up at our house. He often commented to me about how fine she was, but he never gave her any play in deference to me.

Mike was almost four years older than I was, but I'm about an inch taller. Nevertheless, anyone who knows us well would insist that Mike is taller. He had always had that athletic look where I had the nerdy look. He lettered in baseball and football; I lettered in chess and debate. Mike was a star athlete, and a solid B-student; I was a solid A-student.

I always felt that he could be an A-student if he wanted to, but I knew I could never be a star athlete. I had to be content with being a student of the games. I had an encyclopedic knowledge of the players, the stats and all the strategies and techniques. In high school, the coaches of the three major sports wanted me to keep their stats after they learned of my prowess with the numbers. I graciously declined; I couldn't bear being that close to the teams and not being a part of them.

Halfway down the steps, Mike paused and pulled out his aviator sunglasses. After slowly putting them on, he just stood there, carefully surveying the scenery. He took a deep breath, and I could almost hear him from inside the terminal as he exhaled. I had expected him to be wearing his flight suit; instead he wore beige slacks and a denim shirt with the sleeves partially rolled up. He carried his flight bag effortlessly; the muscles of his forearms seemed to ripple in the sunlight as he strode toward the terminal. It was obvious that he was a fighter pilot. It wasn't because of the glasses or the flight bag; it was that damn stride of his. It was a swagger. They all had it; fighter pilots have that way of walking that uniquely identifies them. Again, I had to suppress my envious thoughts.

The waiting room had almost cleared out. I stood about ten feet from the door. Mike entered, and for a moment neither of us said a word. Our eyes just locked onto each other; we smiled. He let his flight bag drop to the floor as he opened his arms in an overly dramatic gesture. "Charlie!" He repeated it in his rich baritone voice. "Charlie!"

I walked slowly toward him, feeling compelled to be the one who must move. We embraced. He was solid and muscular. I made a mental note to start working out as soon as I returned to Albuquerque.

He stepped back, gripping each shoulder as he nodded his head in approval while looking me over. "It's great to see you Charlie. You're looking good. That desert air must agree with you."

"Not as good as you, Mike. You look like a damn fighter pilot."

He chuckled, jabbed me lightly in the chest, and then his gaze turned very serious. "How's Mama? What's going on with her? Tell me everything."

"Well, she's still in intensive care, and they say the next 24 hours will be real critical. But she's doing much better than the doctors expected for someone her age."

He nodded without saying anything. I continued explaining what was happening.

"I stayed in her room last night just in case she woke up; I didn't want her to be there alone. Mama didn't wake up. She's been sleeping a lot; the doctors say that's normal after surgery of this type."

"By the way, who's her doc?"

"She has two doctors. The surgeon is Dr. Larson; he's only been in town for a short while. Frank Davis is her internist; you remember him. He speaks very highly of Larson."

Mike's eyes widen as he raised his hand for me to stop. "Wait a minute. Are you talking about your old buddy from high school, Frank Davis?"

There was a tone of skepticism in his voice, and I tried with my tone to convey my annoyance with his attitude. "Yeah it's the same Dr. Frank Davis. Don't you know he's the only doctor Mama and Pops will go to since he set up his practice seven years ago?"

Almost before I finished getting the words out, he responded with, "Well did you get a second opinion before consenting to her surgery?"

"No! There was no time for that. As a matter fact, Pops signed the consent form before I got here."

The wrinkles that quickly formed across his brow betrayed worry. As he bent to pick up his bag, he simply said, "Let's get out to the hospital."

No words passed between us as we walked outside. As I unlocked the car, Mike looked it over, and said dryly, "It's not looking too bad for 12-year-old car. How's it driving?"

"Well, I really hadn't noticed. I've had lots of other stuff on my mind. You want to drive?"

With his arms resting on the roof as he stood near the passenger side door, Mike said, "Look Charlie, I didn't mean to give you a hard time. I know you're doing everything that needs to be done to look out for her. Now let's go see about Mama."

Pulling away from the airport, I turned on the radio and moved the dial away from WMSQ, to the NPR station that broadcasts from Mississippi State. A panel discussion was in progress; they were talking about the potential for conflict in Iraq..

"Mike, we never really discussed your feelings about possibly going to war. What do you think that would be like?"

He took his sunglasses off and turned slightly to face me. "War is hell Lil' Brother, war is hell."

I flinched at the use of that nickname; but said nothing. I had wondered how long it would take for Mike to start using that again.

"We would be flying at a minimum of twenty-thousand feet, raining down death and destruction on that country. By the way, as I told you before, don't mention the war to Mama or Pops. I never told them I was in the Middle East. They think I'm in Germany."

I nodded in agreement, and added, "If something should

happen to you, it would be even more difficult to explain to them that you were in the war."

"Yeah, you're right, but the danger for us would be minimal; Iraq's air defenses are non-existent. Being a passenger on Southern Regional Air is probably more dangerous. I thought I was gonna have to get outta my seat and land the plane for that joker who flew us in here."

"I saw how hard it was to land that thing, but he pulled it off. I was concerned about you when I first saw the plane coming in. You landed in the dying winds of a large storm that came through last night. Glad you made it okay."

He jabbed me lightly on the right shoulder, and said, "Thanks Charlie." The sunglasses went back on as he stared straight ahead.

Instead of parking, I pulled up to the front entrance of the hospital. "Mike, I'm gonna find a good spot to park in the shade. You go up to ICU; I'll be right up."

He said nothing, just nodded his head. I knew that Mike probably understood my motive for not going up with him: I didn't want to see Pops making a fuss over him. Mike had always been Pop's favorite. He was proud of my good grades, but even prouder of his son the sports hero. In the real world, he understood little of what my job was all about, but being a fighter pilot was something he could fully appreciate.

When I got to the ICU ten minutes later, Mike was kneeling on the far side of the bed, holding Mama's hand and slowly stroking her brow. She seemed to be responding slightly to him. Her eyes fluttered briefly, and a weak smile came across her face. Pops stood on the other side of the bed, beaming with approval. When I approached, he whispered, "Your mama woke up when he got here. She's glad to see him."

I just smiled and nodded in agreement. Mike looked at

me and shrugged.

Mrs. Mitchell entered the room a few minutes after I did, gesturing with her usual flourish. She saw me before she saw Mike, and announced, "I left Henry down there, still eatin'; that man don't know when to stop. Where your brother at? I thought you was gonna pick him up from the airport."

Before I could respond, Mike stood up and opened his arms. She grabbed him and went through her greeting ritual. Hugging him tightly, she said, "You sure is looking good. You look like you could be one of them professional football players. I don't know when I last seen you."

Pops chimed in with, "He's a fighter pilot, not a football player."

Oblivious to Pops, Mrs. Mitchell stepped back, grabbed Mike's left hand, lifted it to eye level and said, "Boy, you looking this good and still ain't married. You need to meet my niece. She been gone away from here a long time, but she moved back; you might remember her..."

Mike interrupted, and said, "Actually, I don't know if I'm gonna have time; I really need to focus on Mama."

I felt like I had been sucker-punched by what she had just said. I was caught off guard for the same reason that Mike had interrupted Mrs. Mitchell. That was Maria I had seen a few hours earlier; Maria is Mrs. Mitchell's niece!

Turning toward Pops, Mike announced, "I'm gonna stay here at the hospital tonight."

Pops said, "That's a good idea. Charlie stayed out here last night. Y'all can take turns at nights, and I'll stay here in the daytime. Now, you oughta git on over to the house and git some sleep."

As an after-thought, he said, "You too Charlie. I reckon the storm kept you awake last night."

As soon as we were in the car, Mike said, "You looked like you had been hit by a sledgehammer. Judging from the look I saw on your face; you didn't know that Maria was back in town."

I managed to mumble, "I caught a glimpse of her this morning, but refused to believe it was really her. She looked so young; I thought my eyes were deceiving me."

"Well, it's seems that she's well preserved. By the way, I'm craving food more than sleep. Let's stop at Slick's and grab something to eat."

***

The place still had the same old tables and chairs I remembered from my high school days; the booths with cracked and faded imitation leather lined each wall. There was a Miller High Life sign in one front window and a Colt 45 sign in the other. The smell of fish grease met us at the door. Only a few customers were in the place. I spotted Chit in a corner near the entrance; he didn't look up when we came in. He was hunched over a table, deep in conversation. He nursed a can of beer that was probably paid for by the other guy at the table. I didn't recognize Chit's companion, but he acknowledged us when we entered.

Toward the right rear, a group of five young guys huddled around a TV, drinking beer and watching basketball. I decided they were watching a replay, because it was the middle of a weekday afternoon. One member of the group, the guy in the red t-shirt, was loudly proclaiming, "You wrong! The Bulls going all the way this year. They got Jordan, they can't be stopped. I'll bet everyone of y'all 50 dollars!"

Another guy responded, "You on! The Lakers gonna stop em. I'll take your money FOOL!"

Mike and I walked to the counter at the rear of the place to order. The buxom young woman behind the counter wore a tight-fitting blouse that was spotted with grease stains. She looked only at Mike, staring into his eyes as she purred her question, "Hi, I'm Larissa. Can I help YOU?"

Without asking me, Mike placed a $20 bill on the counter and said, "We'll have two catfish sandwiches and sides of coleslaw, to go."

Slick came rushing out of the kitchen, grabbed Mike's hand, while rapidly patting him on his shoulder with his free hand. He still had the processed hair that earned him his nickname; it needed a touch-up.

"I know that voice anywhere. Mike Dawson. How you doing? You sure looking good man." Turning to me, he added, "It's good to see both of y'all. Your daddy told me y'all was gonna be in town. Sorry to hear 'bout your mama. How she doing?"

I answered before Mike could, "She's doing better than expected, holding her own. We just left the hospital."

"Glad to hear that. We praying for her. It's mighty good to see y'all. The Dawson boys is back in town." He turned to Mike as he gestured around the room, "Still got you on the wall."

Plastered around the room, close to ceiling height, were faded high school and college photos of neighborhood sports stars. There were two pictures of Mike, one from baseball, the other from football.

"Slick, thanks for keeping the legend alive. I like the feel of this place. We're gonna eat here instead of getting takeout and let us have some Colt 45's with that."

"Sit anywhere you want to. The food will be at your table in a few minutes."

As soon as we were seated in a corner booth, Mike said,

"Okay, Tell me about Ada. How's my sister-in-law? And how's my favorite niece? By the way, I sent her a check for 200 bucks a few weeks ago. I remember how fast money disappeared in college."

Larissa arrived with our malt liquor and two plastic cups. After placing them on the table, she stood there in a very seductive pose, with her hands on her hips and her eyes locked on Mike.

"Is there anything else you want? Anything?"

He just smiled, and said, "No, but thanks for offering."

She shrugged, and left the table, shaking her head in frustration.

"Mike, you shouldn't do that. You're just spoiling Maya. But she's doing fine; her grades are good so far. Ada and I were going to try to get down to Atlanta for a surprise visit, but the semester is almost over. Ada is doing well, but she's working too hard at her law practice."

"Glad to know everybody is doing well, but how about you? We haven't talked in a long time. What's happening with you, Lil' Brother?"

He was doing it again. I said nothing about it; instead, I answered his question, tersely. "My health is good. Work is okay; it's fun most of the time, a few minor issues, here and there."

He nodded, and churned his hands in a motion that said, 'Come on, let's hear more.'

Larissa came back with the food, gestured for a moment, as if she was going to say something, had second thoughts, and just walked away, shaking her head. Mike reached for the hot sauce, added a liberal amount to his food and started to eat. "This stuff is still good. Dig in."

Ignoring his inquiry about the details of my life, I said, "There is something else I need your advice about. What do you remember about Uncle Prince's death?"

"Why, Charlie? That was eons ago. Why are you bringing that up?"

"I'm gonna tell you all about that, but first tell me what you remember."

After taking another generous bite of fish and a sip of malt liquor, Mike rested his chin on his interlocked hands and appeared to be thinking deeply. Slowly, and in a measured tone, he said, "A white man shot him. I'm trying to remember his name; I think..."

My hands went up, stopping him in mid-sentence. I could hardly believe it. "Wait, Mike. You knew he was shot? How did you know that?"

He shrugged, and said, "We all knew that." He gestured around the room with both hands and continued, "I remember everybody talking about it. Are you saying you don't remember the shooting?"

Unable to restrain my frustration, I blurted out, "No, I don't remember a shooting, and nobody else wants to talk about it."

I had lost my appetite. Mike had almost finished his fish; he took a large swig of his drink and said, "Maybe you don't remember because you were too young at the time. I was almost nine but I bet I can jog your memory. It was about Eight 'O May; I remember how much you-"

"Mike! Wait a minute, Mike. How can this possibly have anything to do with Ada?"

His arched eyebrows showed confusion. "Charlie what are you talking about? I was just explaining..."

"My wife! I didn't even realize you knew her middle name. Ada Mae. She doesn't like to use it, but that's her name..."

Mike doubled over from laughter. When he recovered,

he said, "That's exactly what used to happen when we were kids. People would say Eight 'O May is gonna be here soon, and you thought they were talking about a woman whose name was Ada Mae. That's the holiday we used to celebrate; the 8th of May was black folks 4th of July around here. People stop celebrating it years ago. Don't you remember?"

I closed my eyes and tried to recall. Memories slowly start to return. I vaguely remembered lots of food and baseball games.

"I'm starting to remember some of that. It's been so long. The thing I remember most is the baseball games."

"I'm surprised you don't remember the drums."

"Drums?"

He started tapping out a syncopated rhythm on the tabletop. "Yeah. The first time you went, the drums almost scared you to death. They would beat all day, non-stop. The story is that, slaves were not allowed to beat drums, because the overseers and masters were afraid that they could be used for sending coded messages. When freedom came, spontaneous drumming started all over the plantations. They kept the tradition going at the Eight O' May celebrations. There would be a drumming circle, mostly old men, with all kinds of drums. Bass drums, snare drums, congas, sometimes a hollow log. When a drummer got tired, somebody would move in to take his place. Those drums would go from sunrise to late into the night."

As Mike talked, I closed my eyes again and I could hear the drums. I was there. Images of the baseball games also started to flood into my mind's eye. "I remember the drums, but I also remember baseball."

"That's what I was starting to tell you about. We always looked forward to seeing Booker play in those games. He was a real star, but that year he took off and left here just a few days before Eight 'O May, a few days before his daddy got killed. Maybe that's why you're having so much trouble remembering, because later I overheard folks saying that he got into some trouble, but he had to leave here because of you. I don't know what that was about, but sometimes you block stuff out that you don't want to remember." Mike dropped that bombshell, and then proceeded to finish eating his food.

"What are you talking about Mike? What does this have to do with me?"

"I'm sorry Charlie that's all I know. Ask Pops about it."

"That's why I'm asking you. I've asked Pops, Aunt Tillie, Buddy, Mrs. Mitchell and even Chit. I went downtown to the newspaper office to try to find something in the old newspapers. Everybody is trying to hide something, and now you tell me that I'm somehow involved."

"Look Lil' brother, I'm not trying to hide anything. I've told you everything I know. I'll try to help you get more information, but right now you need to drive me home so I can get some sleep. I want to be rested for tonight. Don't forget that Mama is still very sick."

CHAPTER 12

THURSDAY, 10 MAY 1990

We entered the house and Mike went straight for the bedroom. Five minutes later, I could hear him snoring softly. It must be a military thing where one learns to grab some sleep whenever and wherever possible. I was feeling tired too, but also restless. Mike's statement stuck in my mind: "...Booker left here because of you." I needed to think and reflect. My first instinct was to go back to talk with Aunt Tillie. If Mike's claim was right, she had to know something about why Booker left town, something about what it had to do with me. However, I decided that trying to get any more information from her would be wasted effort. I needed to think alone.

The back porch was screened-in, shaded from the sun by several trees and much quieter than the front porch, so I went there. Mama's rocking chair looked so comfortable, and I sat in it and hoped I might soak up some of her spiritual energy. I stared at the greenery in the back yard and thought about Mama. She loved her garden so much, and I hoped she would be able to get back to it soon. Most of her plants and flowers seemed to have survived the storm because the fencing provided some protection from the winds. The grass had recently been mowed, but it would probably need to be cut again soon. As I looked around, I suddenly realized that was the setting I dreamed about when I encountered the flying horse. It was nothing like what I dreamed about, but in the dream, I knew I was in the backyard I grew up in.

My thoughts drifted to my encounter with Sara Madison as I awoke from that surreal dream during my flight. In the chaos of all that had happened, I had forgotten that she was headed to Millerton when we met. I had no desire to see her, yet I was surprised that I hadn't remembered that fact until that moment. I had also forgotten that Maria was the niece of the Mitchells. I saw a pattern. I had probably forgotten some other piece of information that was critical to all that was happening. Mike was right: I probably had repressed all memory of why Booker left town. It must have been something traumatic and horrible; I must have totally blocked it out. A wave of anxiety descended over my body. Despite the warm sunny day, the chills returned.

Many years earlier, I had practiced a form of transcendental meditation. If I could calm my body and mind with meditation, I thought might be able to put things into perspective. I began to meditate, focusing my breathing and silently, slowly repeating my mantra: "Shrim, Shrim, Shrim..." I continued for several minutes but it wasn't working. I was too aware of my surroundings. That subtle state of 'wakeful unconsciousness' eluded me. The more I tried, the more I became aware that it wasn't working.

Random images flashed into my mind, adding to the sense of chaos. Slowly, Maria's face drifted into my mind's eye and froze there. It was an image of Maria as I last saw her more than twenty years earlier, but also an image of Maria as I saw her several hours earlier. Suddenly I understood something: Maria was the surprise that Al was referring to during his traffic stop. His wife, Shirley was always Maria's best friend. If Maria were in town, the two of them certainly would be in contact. Until that moment, I had forgotten that Al had invited me to a gathering at their house that night. I wanted to go because I was certain that Maria would be there. However, I knew I shouldn't go to a party with Mama being so sick.

"Charlie, what are you doing out here? You counting blades of grass?" Mike's voice startled me as he interrupted my thoughts.

"Just sitting here trying to get my thoughts together. You sure had a short sleep."

"A power nap is all I need it. Over the years I have learned how to make maximum use of my sleep time. You have to be able to do that in the military. How about you? Aren't you sleepy?"

"Actually, I am very tired, but at the same time my mind is so restless. I know I won't be able to sleep."

As he sat in the chair next to me, he asked, "So, what's on your mind? You want to tell your big brother about it?"

"Lots of things are on my mind. I am really worried about Mama."

Mike nodded slowly, and said, "I am also."

"Another thing. I can't get my mind off that statement you made about Booker leaving because of me. I can't believe that this never came up in all these years. I have to know what that's all about."

Mike slowly rubbed his hands together, as if trying to pull thoughts together. "You know, I think you're repressing your memory about this, because I'm sure that I told you this before. I distinctly remember how you had a tantrum when I told you this when we were kids. But maybe you should just drop it. After all, it has been more than 35 years."

"Believe me, Mike. I wish I could drop it. But since I read that newspaper, things have been happening that let me know that I cannot rest until I understand what's going on."

"Such as...?"

"First of all, I had a dream during my flight to New Orleans. A dream I couldn't wake up from; it was a dream within a dream. Now, I'm sure that I've had that dream several times before."

He gestured with his hands as if to say 'tell me more.'

"In the dream I'm on Booker's horse right here in the backyard. It feels like here, only it isn't here; it somewhere else, but it's very familiar. Suddenly the horse sprouts wings and starts to fly. I know it's a dream and I try to wake up, but I can't. The horse crashes through the trees. His chest splits open; I can see the beating heart and it is so real. When I finally woke up there's..."

Mike grabbed me firmly by my shoulder. "Hold on! Hold on for a minute. There's something else wrong with that dream. Booker never had a horse; in fact, he didn't like horses. Baseball was his thing, baseball and nothing else."

I couldn't believe what I was hearing from Mike. "What are you talking about? Booker had a Quarter Horse that Uncle Prince gave him when that horse was just a colt. It was white and named Jack. I remember that well. Booker used to let me ride it with him. You have to remember that."

"You do remember the horse, but that wasn't Booker's. We had another cousin who everybody called Slim. That was his horse. Actually, it wasn't really his horse. It belonged to the man be worked for, but he took care of Jack all the time and treated it like it was his. He and Booker were about the same age and they hung out together all the time. Slim was killed when he was about nineteen."

"Mike, are you sure? I just can't believe I would confuse Booker and Slim. I don't even remember Slim. Booker was my favorite cousin. You must be mistaken."

"You were only about five or six at the time, so I can see how you might get things a little mixed up in your mind. But don't take my word for it. Ask Pops or Aunt Tillie. I'm sure they'll have nothing to hide about something as simple as that."

I shrugged, not so much in agreement as in resignation. I was more confused than ever.

Mike said," I'm about to go for a short run. You should join me. It'll help to clear your mind."

Running with Mike was the last thing I wanted to do. He was in shape. "Well, I would run with you, but I don't have the right shoes for it."

"How about this? I'll run in my flight boots. You can use my running shoes. My feet are slightly bigger than yours, but if you wear a couple pairs of thick socks, you'll be all right. Come on; it'll be good for you."

**

We started out running to the south. It was clear to me that Mike was holding back, letting me set the pace. After less than a quarter mile, I was feeling exhausted, but I tried not to let on. We reached the railroad and began running in freshly mowed grass beside the tracks. Tall trees to the west of us provided shade, softening the effects of the afternoon sun.

"You should watch out for snakes. Glad I have these high boots on."

Suddenly I was stumbling as I tried to look carefully at each spot where my feet hit the ground.

Mike started laughing and said, "Just kidding! If snakes are around here, they will be out in the sun, trying to soak up some rays. Not here in the shade. You should know that."

I lied, "Thanks Mike, But I had figured it out."

"Hey, I have an idea. Let's run over to the house where you think you saw Maria earlier. Then you can be sure if it's her or not."

Sweat dripped from my body. I was wishing I had a towel, but I was starting to get my second wind. "Thanks for your concern, but I have a better way of figuring out if Maria is still in town. Do you remember my old friend Al Jackson from high school?"

"Yeah, I remember him. What's Al got to do with this?"

"He and his wife have moved back here. He used to be a cop in Detroit; now he's a local cop. Tonight..."

Mike interrupted with a loud laugh. "Wait! Tell me you are not gonna send the cops out to look for her. You are getting desperate. You had better watch it; remember, you're a married man."

"No! It's nothing like that. However, I would like to see her, if she's in town. Al is having a little gathering tonight. His wife and Maria were always best friends. If Maria is in town, she will be at their house. I'll just call Al and ask him about her."

"Why don't you just wait until you get there? You'll see her and be surprised —sorta."

"I'm not going. Not with Mama being in the hospital."

Mike stopped abruptly. "Hold on Charlie. There is absolutely no reason for you to play a martyr. There's nothing wrong with your going over to visit with friends. I will be there with Mama tonight. Just make sure I have Al's phone number. If anything should come up, I'll call you. You can drive anywhere in this town in ten minutes or less. That's it! It's settled."

"You are probably right. But frankly, it just won't look right."

"What are you worried about? Tell you what. Just don't mention to Pops that you are going to a party." I nodded in agreement. Mike looked pleased with himself, and not a drop of sweat was visible on him. He said, "Okay, let's start back home. I want to take a shower, get something to eat and rest a little before going to the hospital."

As we started back to the house, I felt relieved by my conversation with Mike. Then he asked, "What else were you going to tell me about your dream about the horse? I interrupted you before you finish."

"I'm probably making too much of this, but it seemed significant at the time. When I woke up from my dream, this attractive young woman across the aisle from me start a conversation. She claimed that she had heard me talking in my sleep, and that she has had the same dream."

"Did she mention any details?"

"Well, I guess she didn't, but she sounded so sincere."

"It sounds like a pickup line to me, Lil' Brother. A bit unusual, but probably a very effective line," Mike said as he stifled a belly laugh. "Did you get her number?"

"She gave me her card, but she lives in San Francisco."

"That would be a very good conversation starter. I imagine that gets lots of attention."

"Maybe you are right. However, the thing that was strange is that we were flying from Albuquerque to Dallas, but her final destination was Millerton. Said she has family here. I think that's too much of a coincidence. Don't you?"

Mike started humming that little 'Twilight Zone' theme: Na, Na, Na,... Na. Then he said, "I think maybe you wasted your time in getting those three college degrees. Ever thought about giving them back to the universities?"

"Well, thanks for the vote of confidence."

"Don't take it too seriously. Since this woman is here in town, maybe you should look her up. You still have her card, right? You said she was fine; maybe I should check her out for you."

I ignored the jab and replied, "I don't have her local contact information. Her name is Sara Madison, but I'm not going to call every white person in town with the name Madison. As a matter of fact, she just ended a bad marriage; that's probably her married name."

"You forgot to mention that she's white. Not that it matters; this is the New South."

As soon as we were in the house. I headed straight for the fridge to get something cold to drink.

Mike said, "The message light is flashing. I'll check it out to see if everything is OK."

When I got back to the front of the house, Mike was smiling and shaking his head. "You are holding out on me Charlie. There were three messages. Nothing important except for the one for you. Jan wants you to call her ASAP. She says it's very important. Let's see, there's Maria, Sara Madison and now Jan. Better slow down. You are still a married man."

"There's nothing going on. She's a coworker and we have an issue at work that needs to be dealt with."

"Yeah, sure. But, remember I can read you like a book. You can tell me about it later. Jan says she's at home and you know the number."

CHAPTER 13

"Take the old Waverly Road; we have plenty of time to get to the hospital."

Mike said it nonchalantly, but I knew him well enough to sense that something was up. Waverly is a two-lane road that meanders through a new subdivision. When we were kids, that area was heavily wooded and undeveloped. The newer middle-class neighborhood was now filled with brick homes, mostly ranch-style. As we drove, Mike said nothing. He was focused on the surroundings, apparently looking for something.

In less than five minutes, we reached a familiar place where the road slopes sharply downward and flows into a tight, hairpin curve. That area was more wooded than what I remembered from childhood. When we were growing up people would say it was haunted. Downhill from the roadway, there was a place that once seemed spooky. A mist would hang low to the ground at odd times of the day. Once, Mike and I were riding our bikes when we should not have been near the place, and we both heard howling sounds coming from where the trees were especially thick.

"Do you remember how we thought this place was haunted when we were kids?"

"Yeah, I do, but that was just superstition. Do you remember when you got your first real kiss, right over there?" A big smile came across Mike's face as he jabbed his finger in the direction of a wide clearing surrounded by tall pines trees.

"Yeah, I vaguely remember, now that you remind me of it."

The memories returned vividly.

***

I was about 15, at a picnic for our church's vacation bible school. Mike shouldn't have even been there because he had already finished high school. He was interested in one of the young women who was chaperoning us, and instead of dropping me off, he stayed around. I stood near a tree, trying to impress several younger kids with how much I knew about movie special effects. I noticed a nearby group of seven or eight girls my age, whispering and giggling in a conspiratorial manner. As I was getting into an explanation of how they made movie gunshots look so real, Nancy Richards stepped away from the group and moved slowly toward me. She was an attractive girl who exuded sexuality; however, she was large for her age. Because of her size and demeanor, she seemed so much older than the rest of the sophomore girls.

When she was just inches from my face, she said, "Charlie Dawson, we were just wondering if you've ever kissed a girl."

"Uh, uh yeah, sure," I managed to mumble, unconvincingly.

"Who?" she demanded.

I knew what was coming next, but was frozen in place, or maybe I didn't want to move. In one seamless motion, she gently pushed me against the tree, grabbed my shoulders, rammed her tongue into my mouth and pressed her body against mine. In the background, I heard hoots, whistles, and cheers. I closed my eyes and imagined that she was Maria. It was not what I expected. Her tongue felt thick and coarse in my mouth. I tasted potato salad and deviled eggs and could hardly breathe. Minutes seemed to go by; then it was over. People cheered and applauded. The experience was so disturbing that when I opened my eyes, everybody's face was blurred and out of focus.

Before moving away, Nancy said softly, "Now you don't have to lie about it."

I felt sad and embarrassed but tried not to show it. Mike came over and tried to cheer me up. Somewhere in the background, I heard the chaperone that Mike had been talking with scolding Nancy. It was a long while after that before I understood what was so great about kissing.

***

The blaring horn of a car coming toward us snapped me out of my vivid flashback; I had drifted into the other lane. As we reached the bottom of the hill, I added, "Not only was that my first kiss; it was my only kiss for a long time."

"Well, I guess you're trying to make up for it now."

"What are you talking about?"

"You know what I mean – Jan! Let's hear it."

"Mike, I told you there's nothing going on."

"Okay, Lil' Brother. I believe you."

Mike got out of the car and moved quickly toward the lobby entrance. As I walked rapidly to catch up with him, I reflected on what he had just said to me, and although I hated to admit it, I knew he was right. What I didn't tell him was that before leaving for the hospital, I had returned Jan's call.

She had some encouraging news for me: she followed through on my suggestion and was able to get a senior manager to intercede for us. After talking with her, it appeared that we would get a reprieve on the cancellation of our project.

***

"I was standing up there looking outta the window when y'all pulled up and parked. Thought y'all would've been in here by now. What took you fellas so long?" Mr. Mitchell sounded as if he were talking to two little boys he had just caught with their hands in the cookie jar.

Pops and Mrs. Mitchell were standing there with him in the lobby; all three seemed irritated.

Pops said, "Thought y'all would've been here half-hour ago. We just left the room. Your mama is doing a whole lot better. She woke up two or three times, talked really good, knew who everybody was. But why are you here, Charlie? Only Mike is staying tonight, right?"

"That's right, Pops. I'm just dropping Mike off; I'm going down the road here to..."

"Now wait a minute, boy. This is the first I heard of this. I need my car to go to prayer meetin' tonight. You should've..."

Mr. Mitchell interrupted with, "Joe, that ain't no big deal. You can ride home with us, and you know I'm going to prayer meetin' too."

Pops started to open his mouth to protest, seemed to have second thoughts and just said, "Well let me have the door key. What time you gonna be back?" Before I could answer, he said, "Don't worry about it. The door will be unlocked when you get back. OK, let's go y'all."

During the elevator ride up to ICU, Mike asked, "What

did you do to Pops? He sure seems irritated with you."

"I told you. It's all because of the questions I've been asking about Uncle Prince's murder."

"Well Charlie, that's serious. We have to get to the bottom of this." The sarcasm in his voice irritated me, but I said nothing.

We arrived at the room to find Cathy Mason, the night nurse, adjusting Mama's bedding. As I entered the room, I said, "Hello Cathy. This is my brother, Mike. How's our mother doing tonight?"

Turning to face Mike, and ignoring me, she said with cheerfulness in her voice and a big smile on her face, "I'm pleased to meet you. Your mother is improving nicely. The doctor says he might move her out of the ICU tomorrow if her vitals remain as strong as they are now. And, how about you? How are you?"

Mike smiled and said, "I'm doing fine. I just got in town a few hours ago; I'll be staying here tonight."

"That's good! Tonight, I'm pulling a double shift; I'll be here until about 7:00 AM." She looked around for a moment and added, "Just let me know if you need anything."

While the two of them were getting acquainted, I went to Mama's bedside and softly stroked her hair. She moved her head slightly but didn't wake up. Her appearance seemed stronger than before, and the breathing was more relaxed. I felt encouraged. I looked at the monitor and saw that her heartbeat seemed steady at about 75. I started to look for the BP reading.

"Don't touch anything. Those are very delicate instruments."

Before I could respond, Mike said, "Don't worry. He knows what he's doing. He's well qualified."

That seemed to be adequate to satisfy Cathy. She said, "Mike, I have to check on my other patients, but I'll return soon." Smiling, she backed out of the room.

I just looked at Mike, shaking my head. "It seems that you and Mama are in good hands. I'm leaving. Here's the number at Al's house. It's about five minutes from here."

In the parking lot, I felt a gentle breeze. Looking at the western sky, I saw the remnants of a beautiful sunset – shades of red, pink and blue mixing, as if part of a watercolor painting. I even detected a whiff of honeysuckle drifting under my nose.

The trip to Al's house took all of three minutes. Seven cars were in the driveway – all expensive looking. The large brick house at the end of the cul-de-sac stood out from others in the neighborhood, and was apparently custom built. Smells of fish, barbeque and fried chicken drifted through the screen door. Gladys's voice enticed me with soulful pleads of 'If I Were Your Woman.' I heard lively conversation coming from somewhere in the house. Suddenly, I was reluctant to enter. My feeling of guilt returned. Mama was in the ICU and I was at a party.

As if on cue, Maria was standing in the doorway – the Maria of our teen years.

"Come on in, Charlie. I've been waiting for you."

My apprehensions evaporated.

CHAPTER 14

THURSDAY, 10 MAY 1990

I was enjoying it, but the experience was nothing like I had ever imagined it would be. Her lips were soft and sensuous, but her tongue didn't enter my mouth. Although I felt the urge to go further, I followed her lead. Throughout our high school years, the fantasy was always with me: the two of us together endlessly. During college, my obsession waned, but never went away. In later years, vivid thoughts of Maria would occasionally drift into my mind. At that moment, I let the reality sink in; for the first time in my life I was kissing the woman who had been the object of my unrequited desires. Standing there in the entryway of my friends' home, neither of us spoke a word. Our bodies didn't touch. Our hands were shoulder-high, pressed palm to palm, as we tacitly agreed to keep our distance. Suddenly, guilt took over. *You should not be doing this; you're a married man.* As if reading my thoughts, Maria pushed away. She looked up at me, smiled seductively, then moved closer to hug me tightly.

"It's so good to see you Choo-Choo. It's been such a long time," she whispered.

When the two of us were kids, I loved to play with trains. Choo-Choo was the name she had given me those many years ago – a name I had long ago forgotten. I was aroused by the way she said it.

"You don't know how glad I am to see you, Maria. But you must know how much I wanted you when we were teens." I surprised myself as those once-private thoughts rolled from my lips.

She took a step backward, tilted her head to one side, placed her hands on her hips and asked, as she giggled softly, "Wanted? What do you mean 'wanted'?"

Standing there looking at her, I realized she was not the Maria of twenty years ago. There were definitely a few more pounds, in all the right places. I saw hints of gray along the hairline. A few wrinkles invaded the corners of her eyes. Most of all, the whole demeanor was different: there was an aura of confidence that comes with maturity. Maria-the-woman was even more beautiful than Maria-the-girl.

"Cat got your tongue, Choo-Choo? And, please stop undressing me with your eyes; that can wait." Maria winked; I blushed. I didn't quite know how to react to the new, flirtatious Maria.

"Uh-uh, I was just, uh, looking at what a lovely woman you have become."

"It's all right to look," she chuckled," and, you're looking great yourself. In fact, I now realize how stupid I was to have pushed you away years ago."

"Okay you two cut it out. There's a party going on back here; people want to see you, Charlie Dawson."

I was temporarily released from the spell Maria had cast over me. Turning around, I saw Al's wife, Shirley standing in the doorway and smiling. I wondered how long she had been there and how much she had heard. I decided it really didn't matter because her best friend would probably tell her all the details later anyway. Shirley and Al had been a couple since long before high school. Back then they made an odd couple. Al: tall, rail-thin and high-yellow. Shirley: short, shapely, and dark chocolate. They were still the odd couple. Al: tall and high-yellow, but now solid muscle. Shirley: short, dark chocolate, and now plump. She spread her arms.

As we embraced, she said, "I heard about your mother. I'm so sorry. How's she doing?"

Standing behind me, Maria slowly stroked my arm and said, "Me too Charlie; you know that goes for me too. Let me know if there's anything I can do."

"She's starting to get better. I just left the hospital, and it looks like she may be out of ICU by tomorrow."

"That's wonderful. Praise the Lord!"

As she said that, Shirley stepped between Maria and me, looped her arms into ours and guided us into the den. "Now, let's go in here and celebrate that good news. Like I said, people are waiting for you."

For the first time since encountering Maria, I became fully aware of the music that had been playing in the background. It was the Temps, midway through telling the world about 'My Girl.' I recognized most of the people in the room, but I didn't see Al. I spotted Ray and Carolyn Thomas across the room -- also a couple since high school. Eddie Miller was there, with a woman I didn't recognize. Fred Johnson, the confirmed bachelor and fulltime player, seemed to be alone. The food was plentiful and smelling good; the mood was festive. Shirley interrupted the party before I could greet anyone.

Turning the music down, she said, "Y'all party people, listen up. Let me get serious for a minute. Charlie Dawson is here. Like I've told everybody, his mother has been real sick, but now it looks like she's gonna be alright."

Lots of 'Amen's' and 'praise-the-Lord's' rose up from the group. She continued, "Before we go on with our good times, I want to ask the Rev. Miller to lead us in a prayer of thanks."

Rev. Miller? Eddie Miller? Eddie was the biggest thug in our class when we were in school.

He must have been reading my mind or seeing the look of shock on my face because he said, "That's right brother. It's Rev. Miller now; I've seen the light." Then he shifted smoothly into that officious ministerial voice. "Join hands please. Let's bow our heads and pray."

Shirley took my right hand; Maria held my left. I noticed that Fred had moved into position to hold her other hand.

"Heavenly father, we come..."

As he prayed, Maria stroked my palm and moved closer to me. I couldn't concentrate on the prayer. She leaned in close and whispers something that I couldn't quite make out.

"...In Jesus' name we pray. Amen."

I felt guilty. The prayer for my mother was finished and I missed it. Shirley released her grip on my hand and walked over to turn the music up again. Maria turned to face me and went through the exaggerated motion of pulling her hand away from Fred. We stood there, face to face in the middle of a room full of people, holding hands.

"What did you just say to me, Maria?"

"I was just apologizing for graduation night." She stared into my eyes, as if trying to drill into the place that locked my deepest thoughts. As she turned to walk away, she added, "Other people want to see you. We can talk about it later."

People started to gather around, greeting me, and telling me how great it was that my mother was recovering. Fred took my hand, shook it furiously and then asked, "By the way, did your wife come to town with you?"

"No, she's not here. Why?"

"I don't think any of us have ever met her." He gave me that knowing kind of look and nodded in Maria's direction.

Before I could respond, Al came in from the patio. He put down a platter of ribs, talked with his wife for a moment and came over to greet me with a solid embrace. "I'm so glad you could come, man. Shirley told me your mom is getting better; that's good news. By the way, how do you like the surprise?" he said, while guiding me into a quiet corner.

"Thanks for arranging for Maria to be here. However, I'm not surprised. I figured it out, Al."

He just rolled his eyes at me.

"I happened to see her on the porch of the old Pruitt place this morning."

"Yeah man. She came into town, bought the place right away. Paid cash! I tell you there were some folks..."

We were interrupted by a large woman moving toward me with an even larger man waddling behind her. She beamed at me and loudly announced, "Charlie Dawson, you're looking great boy! You remember me? You better remember me."

I hesitated. The face was vaguely familiar; frantically, I searched my memory. "Nancy? Nancy Richards? I don't know when I last saw you. It must have been..."

"Well, you do remember me. But don't burn your brain out trying to figure out when you last saw me. I didn't graduate. Dropped out to have a baby before senior year. Give me a hug."

We embraced. I felt as if I was being crushed.

"This is my husband, Michael Gandy. I'm now Mrs. Gandy!"

Michael and I shook hands; he had a vise grip. "You're not going to believe this Nancy, but I was just thinking about you earlier today."

"I believe it. In fact, you should have thought about me a lot over the last 25 years or so!" she bellowed, attracting the attention of most people in the room.

Michael spoke up," Is this one of your old boyfriends,

honey? You never mentioned him."

I didn't like where the conversation was going; I tried to change the subject. "Well it's really nothing like that. Just an old joke from a long time ago..."

Fred butted in, with "Yeah, and that shit was funny. I was there-"

"You stay out of this Fred! It's my story, I'll tell it." Nancy said loudly, as she looked around, cleared her throat, and had the undivided attention of everyone in the room. I looked over at Maria. She smiled, shook her head and shrugged.

"It was one of those church picnics. Me and several of the girls got to talking. I know Maria was there, and I think Shirley was too. Y'all know how teenage girls get sometimes. After a while, we decided that Charlie here had never had a real kiss before. I got elected to do something about it. So, I walked over, pushed him against a tree and..."

I was unprepared for the speed with which she moved. Faster than I could respond, she did the same thing as before. She pressed my head firmly between her palms and thrust her tongue into my mouth. Again, I was the object of the joke; however, this time I reacted differently. I heard the hoots, whistles and cheers. I embraced her tightly and returned her kiss. We slowly released each other, and the first person I saw was her husband, applauding and laughing louder than anyone in the place.

Slowly, Nancy turned to him, kissed him lightly on his lips and said, "My man ain't concerned about that 'cause he knows how crazy his wife is; he knows he's got nothing to worry about."

I smiled, smacked my lips in an exaggerated manner and said," Thank you, Nancy. That was delicious. A nice hickory smoked barbecued taste. Got any more where that came from?"

Everybody laughed. She said, "Somebody please bring this boy some ribs before he tries to kiss me again, and gits both of us in trouble."

The crowd began to disperse, and Maria handed me a plate. It was piled high with ribs, fish, greens, potato salad and cornbread.

Shirley came over and said," Come on and have a seat over here. Let me get you something to drink. How about a beer?" I nodded, and she returned with a cold Bud in seconds.

The Rev. Miller joined me, followed by the woman I didn't recognize. "Charlie, I want you to meet my wife Sharon. She's not from around here; she grew up in Birmingham."

"It's a pleasure to meet you Sharon. How long have you two been married?"

"It's been about twelve years now, and we got two children—a boy and a girl. There's Eddie junior, ten and Sharon junior, eleven. In case you're wondering, I've been preaching for about seven of them years. You know what I was like when we were in school: drinking, fighting, gambling, and stealing. You name it; I did it. Me and everybody else was surprised that I graduated. Well, I got even worse after we finish school. In fact, I was surprised that I've lived to be twenty. I moved to Birmingham, started hanging with some fellows who made me realize I was just a rookie. Then I met this lady."

He pulled Sharon close, and kissed her on the cheek; she glowed with pride. He was on a roll; that preaching cadence had returned to his voice. "But guess what? Nothing had changed. I was still out there doing the same old stuff. Then, I got shot. Five times! Doctors said I should have been dead after the second bullet. You ever been shot Charlie? You know what that feels like?

"Well, no. I haven't, but I can imagine..." I wanted to get away from the conversation; I needed to find an opening to do it politely. I looked around for Al, Shirley, Maria – anyone to rescue me.

"Like I was just saying, getting shot is awful. I remember when I was around five or six, my oldest brother got shot; messed him up really bad. There was some kind of riot that broke out downtown and the white folks shot several people; he was one of them. He only got hit by one bullet; now, imagine me getting..."

"Wait! Excuse me. Hold up. What did you just say?"

Eddie, that is Rev. Miller, looked annoyed by my interruption, and showed it in the tone of his voice. "I said he got hit by one bullet. Now like I was..."

"I was asking about the other part. You said something about a riot. When was that? What else do you know about it?"

"Well, I was trying to explain about what caused me to see the light. That riot must have been around 1951 or '54. You and me would've been little fellas at the time. Why you so interested in that?"

I didn't want to go into the entire story with him. I simply said, "I think that riot started because a white man murdered my uncle and this community got upset when the police didn't do anything about it. I've been trying to find information, but it hasn't been easy. Where is your brother now? I would sure like to talk with him."

"My brother Frank lives in Dallas. He's thirteen years older than me, and like I said, it messed him up real bad. He never did get quite right from it. Truth is that his mind is starting to go."

"How about your parents? Are they still alive?"

"No! Both of my parents been gone for a long time now. But, how about your family? Why don't you ask them about it?"

"Don't think I haven't tried. But that got me nowhere. I've talked to several family members. I even went downtown to look at old newspapers. Nobody seems to want to talk about it."

He leaned in close, his voice was almost at a whisper, "Do you know why?"

"Well, no I don't, but my suspicion is that there's more to it than what it seems."

"You probably got that right. But why you think we're having this conversation?" He peered into my eyes, placed his hand on my shoulder and said, "What I'm talking about is why is it that you and me are standing here, right now talking about your uncle? A man that I never knew."

"I would have to say that it's probably because..."

"Hold on brother! Don't say the wrong thing. Think about it! Here you are, a man with all kind of degrees behind your name, a man of science. Then, there's me. I used to be a thug, now I'm a preacher. It's clear to me that the Lord put us together so I can help you out. The Lord works in mysterious ways, his wonders to perform."

Not wanting to offend, I said, "I have no doubt that you are right, but since your family members are no longer of any help, I'm not sure what..."

"When something is put in front of you, you got to be able to see it for what it is. What I did was to plant a seed with you about where to take your search. It's like that mustard seed in the Bible. Now all of us in this room is about the same age. Maybe somebody else got family that knows something. This is still a small town. Hold on. I'm gonna get folks attention so you can ask for some help. But, one more thing. This is us you talking to. It ain't always necessary to say things correctly for you to say it right. You git my drift, brother?"

He walked over, turned the music down and clapped his hands. "I want all y'all to listen up for a minute. Brother Charlie has a request of us. He's been telling me a very interesting story."

He turned to me, and I was on the spot. "I don't want to bore y'all with all the details. There was a shootin' back in '54. A white man murdered my uncle, Prince Dawson. After it happened, a riot broke out downtown, and several black folks got shot by the police. I would 'preciate it if anybody could ask around in your families and see if anybody knows anything. If so, just call me. The number is still listed in my daddy's name, Joseph Dawson. Thanks everybody. Now let's party."

Rev. Miller gave me an approving nod and seemed to be really proud of himself. Shirley and Ray stopped by to briefly mention that they each thought that what I'd talked about sounded familiar and that someone in their families might be helpful. They promised to call.

Maria returned to my side. "That's an interesting story you just told. I'd like to hear more, and I think that I may know someone who can help you."

I was aware that her parents had been dead for a long time. "I hope it's not your aunt, because I've already asked her."

"No, actually it's the county sheriff that I have in mind."

"The sheriff! I don't know if..."

"Don't worry about it. Things have changed around here. I happened to know Sheriff Red Mullins quite well. I can introduce you."

I couldn't hide the look of surprise that my facial expression betrayed.

"Charlie, I can't believe you're jealous. It's nothing like that, but I am on good terms with him."

"No! That's not what I'm concerned about, is just that, uh..."

"I tell you what Charlie. If you buy me breakfast tomorrow morning at the Gramecy coffee shop, he'll be there. All the city's movers and shakers meet for breakfast at about 8:00. I drop in occasionally when I need to talk with somebody who has influence."

"Okay, it's a date for breakfast, but let me think about whether or not I want to meet the sheriff."

"You really don't have to be concerned about him. But let's not talk about it anymore right now. It'll just ruin the rest of the evening. Dance with me. You do realize that we've never danced together? They're playing my favorite slow drag record."

I focused on the music. The Drells were pleading, 'stay darling, stay in my corner...' I pulled her close and enjoyed the moment. Later, I would explain to Maria. It's not the title 'Sheriff' that bothered me. It was the name: Red Mullins' father was my uncle's killer.

CHAPTER 15

FRIDAY, 11 MAY 1990

The waitress had been to the booth twice since I sat down. She had become a little irritated with me, probably because I hadn't ordered any food. After about ten minutes of waiting, I got up and bought a copy of The Appeal from the newspaper dispenser just outside the entrance. When I went back into the restaurant, the waitress was there, about to take my cup away. She probably thought I had left without paying for the coffee, but turned and walked away when she spotted me.

As I skimmed the paper, it was clear that most of the news was about the big storm. There were several pictures of fallen trees and damaged homes. The editorial page had a long spread about how fortunate the community was to have escaped without death or serious injury.

I sat there and looked around to take in the décor of the restaurant. My thoughts drifted to my years of growing up when the only way I could have set foot in the place was as a dishwasher or a busboy. The space was large, and probably seated more than a hundred people; it seemed about half-full. The spacious interior evoked the image of the antebellum south. A large painting on the back wall displayed an idyllic image of a plantation house, fronted by magnolia trees. The walls were paneled with mahogany, and large windows provided an excellent view of the morning activities of Main Street.

As I glanced around the room, none of the other customers seemed concerned about my presence. I was bored and started speculating about who some of them might be. Two uniformed police officers, one black, the other white, were having breakfast at a table near the window. Several young couples were eating with their kids. I quickly spotted the power table. *Looks like a few bankers. The balding guy is probably on the city council. The one in the expensive blue pinstripe is a banker.*

I was sipping my second cup of coffee when Maria arrived, and I waved to get her attention. She had to cross the entire span of the room to reach the booth. This woman had a stride that exuded the confidence of a fashion model walking the runway in Milan. For a fleeting moment, I again saw the Maria of twenty years earlier, coming to me. The sunlight streaking through the window behind her added a halo-like effect around her head. I couldn't take my eyes away because she was even more beautiful than at the party the night before. She was dressed in just the right balance of casual elegance: low heels, designer jeans that fit her perfectly, a beige linen blouse with the two top buttons undone, a silk scarf around her neck and a minimal amount of makeup. Her hair was pulled back in a bun, drawing attention to her high cheek bones.

As she approached, I rose to greet her. Looking around, I noticed that most eyes in the room were on Maria, and she knew it. We embraced, and I was enchanted by the muted scent of her jasmine perfume.

She whispered, "Too bad you didn't wait outside for me; we could've started a good rumor." I gave her a quizzical look, and she clarified. "Around here, if a man and woman show up for breakfast together, everyone assumes they spent the night together."

"We did spend the night together – in my dreams. Uh, uh, I'm sorry. I shouldn't have said that."

"Why not?" She settled into the booth, slid toward the wall and said, "Sit here Charlie, next to me." I felt awkward about it but couldn't resist her invitation. She moved very close, stroked my arm and said, "Tell me more. I want to hear about your dream."

"Let's talk about that some other time."

She giggled and said, "Why? Am I making you uncomfortable?"

"Well, actually you are."

"That's good, because I learned a long time ago that it's important not to let a man get too comfortable. When that happens, they start taking you for granted." She winked and smiled.

The waitress returned. As she poured Maria a cup of coffee, she nodded in my direction and said, "Well, good morning Mrs. Davidson. So, it's you he's been waiting for. I thought for a while he was just gonna sit here and sip coffee all day."

"Paulette, this is Dr. Charlie Dawson; he's a rocket scientist. We grew up together, but it's been ages since we laid eyes on each other."

She gave me a weak smile and said, "Pleased to meet you. Welcome back to Millerton. Y'all ready to order yet?"

"I'm ready. How about you, Charlie?"

I picked up the menu that had been on the table since I arrived twenty minutes earlier and started to scan it.

Maria said, "I'll have my usual." For my benefit, she added, "Rye toast, two eggs over easy and a slice of country ham. Their ham is great; you should have it."

"I'll have what she's having."

As soon as the waitress had left, Maria stroked my arm softly. "Sorry I kept you waiting. Hope you weren't sitting here too long."

"It's okay. I arrived a little bit early. I got up about 6:00 this morning, drove to the hospital and picked up Mike, then I..."

"Before you say anymore, give me an update on your mother. How's she doing?"

"She's doing surprisingly well. When I went in this morning, she was very alert, and recognized me, Mike and Pops. She's still very weak, but we are really feeling encouraged. I stayed and talked with her for about ten minutes before the nurse came in and made all of us leave the room. Pops is there now along with your aunt and uncle. I'm staying tonight. Mike dropped me off here and kept the car. That means you must drive me back. I hope that's not a problem."

"We'll see. I may just decide to keep you." She winked again.

"Don't I have something to say about that? And, I'm sure my wife wouldn't like that."

She frowned, leaned away from me slightly and said, "Well, since you brought her up, tell me about your wife. I'm dying to know all about her."

"What do you want to know?"

"Tell me everything. From the beginning."

"Okay, but only if you fill me in on the last twenty years of your life."

"Sure. Now tell me first how the two of you met. I especially want to know about that, because I as remember, you didn't have a girlfriend in high school. I'm really interested in hearing..."

I raised my hands in a manner that said 'stop' and whispered, "Excuse me Maria, you're right. I didn't have a girlfriend back then, but it certainly wasn't for lack of trying. As I remember it, I pursued the girl of my dreams all through high school, but she wasn't interested in me."

"Choo-Choo, you sure know how to hit a girl where it hurts. Yeah, you chased me all through high school, but frankly you just weren't the kind of guy I thought I wanted. I was a silly teenager who didn't understand much about life. I can tell you that I've learned a lot over the years." She paused; her thoughts seemed to be on something else. I waited. "My marriage fell apart about two years ago. Since then, I've done lots of thinking about what's important and the kind of man I'd like to spend the rest of my life with. You may not believe this, but even before I knew you were in town, my thoughts kept coming back to you. Of all the men I've known over the years, you're the ideal of who I would like to be with."

I shook my head, but couldn't hold back that smile that spread across my face. "Maria, I'm really flattered. But I'm happily married, and don't expect that to change. Plus, you don't really know me. We knew each other as kids and haven't even communicated in more than twenty years. A lot has happened in both our lives during all that time."

She chuckled and said, "Now don't go getting too full of yourself. I said you're my ideal; I'm interested in finding a guy like you, not necessarily you. Other men like you exist; I just have to look in the right places. You're right, we haven't been in contact in years, but I know how you were raised. I know what a great guy you were. I still know you. You're still Choo-Choo."

Paulette returned and said, "Excuse me. I hate to interrupt y'all's serious conversation, but your food is ready." She placed our plates on the table and asked, "Anything else I can bring?"

Maria responded, "We're fine. Thanks."

Paulette left the table, shaking her head.

"What's up with her? She seems disgusted with you or

me, or both."

"When things are slow in here, Paulette will sit for a while and chat with me. She has a very low opinion of men. You're a man, so she's probably not happy that I've spent more than five minutes with you. And, I'm obviously sitting too close to you." She giggled.

I picked up my fork and knife and tasted the food. "This is delicious, especially the ham. I'm glad I followed your recommendation."

"You know I wouldn't lead you astray. Now, let's get back to your story. You were about to tell me about your wife. What's her name?"

"Ada. Her name is Ada Mae. We met when I was a few months from completing graduate school in Chicago, and she was in her first year of law school."

"So, she's a lawyer?"

"Yeah. And a very good one."

"Good. Don't stop. Tell me more."

"In college and grad school I had a few girlfriends before her, but nothing very serious. When Ada and I met, we seemed to be perfectly matched. Things got serious very quickly. When I completed my doctorate, I got several job offers, but the one I liked best was in Albuquerque. It allowed me to continue the kind of research I was really interested in doing. That caused a problem. She didn't want to leave Chicago, but the job was a perfect match. I moved away and we tried to maintain a long-distance relationship, but it wasn't working out. We eventually went our separate ways."

"So, what happened? When did you two finally get back together?"

"It was almost six years later. I was in New Orleans on a business trip. While I was out for dinner with colleagues, I ran into her. She was with a guy who turned out to be just a friend. Seeing her brought back all those feelings I once had for her and, although I tried to deny it, I was jealous. Before leaving the restaurant, she asked if we could get together the next day because she had a surprise for me. We met for lunch, and I was floored to learn that..."

"The two of you had a child that you didn't know about." Maria saw the surprise on my face as she completed my sentence. "No, I'm not a mind reader. However, I've seen this movie before." She leaned in close to me, took a deep breath and said slowly, with carefully chosen words, "Charlie, I'm speaking as a friend. Please understand that. Are you sure you are the father?"

I threw up my hands in a defensive posture and blurted out, "Yes, I'm sure! Maria, you don't know anything about this. I don't understand why you think, that after all these years, you suddenly have special insight. You sound just like my brother when he found out about our daughter, and..." I immediately realized that I had unintentionally reinforced her suspicions by making that statement, but she didn't follow up on it.

"Charlie, there is really no reason to get angry about this. I'm only trying to help. It's just that over the years I've known a couple of women who were very devious about things like this. But I'm going to leave it alone."

"Thanks for dropping it. I'm not angry with you. After all this time, it serves no useful purpose to bring it up. I know that Maya is my daughter. I love her and nothing will change that."

"Tell me about Maya. What's she like?"

"She has grown up to be a very beautiful and bright young woman. She's only sixteen but is already in college at Spellman. Can't decide between law or science. My guess is that she will follow in her mother's footsteps."

"Well, what a coincidence. My son is a junior at Morehouse. Maybe the two of them will meet, fall in love and travel the road that we didn't. Now, please complete the story that I so rudely interrupted."

"There's not much to tell. We reconnected, got married about twelve years ago and she has established a very good law practice in New Mexico. She focuses on environmental issues."

"That's great. Now, tell me more about her. What's she like? Is she pretty?"

"Ada is a very beautiful woman. Not just physically, but spiritually."

Maria stroked her hair with both hands, giggled and said, "Is she prettier than me?"

I smiled without responding. "There is something else I want to talk with you about. Remember the little story I told last night at the party about my uncle's murder? Well, I learned about this 40-year-old murder because I accidentally found an old edition of the Jackson Informer. It was a front-page description of my uncle's murder."

"Wait a minute. I don't understand what you're talking about. You accidentally found this newspaper? Where did you find it? Where did it come from?"

"That's the part that's so strange. The newspaper was something that Ada had for many years. As a matter of fact, it was a paper that she happened to pick up in Jackson on the day that we met in New Orleans. She had been in Jackson for several days and had just driven to New Orleans earlier that afternoon. Ada had the newspaper because of a story completely unrelated to the article about my uncle."

"That's it Charlie? That's what you're all excited about?"

I became self-conscious about our surroundings and

paused to scan the room. I said, in a hushed tone, "Maybe it doesn't seem like much to you. But I never would have known about this murder if Ada and I hadn't gotten back together. There is something else going on because nobody wants to talk about it."

"So, what do you think is such a big secret? What are people trying to hide?"

"I don't know. I'm still searching and asking questions. I don't know why he was killed, but I do know who did it. What I didn't tell you at the party is that the man who killed him was Red Mullins. I had intended to tell you last night."

"Now I understand why you were reluctant to talk to the sheriff about this. But it can't be the same person because Sheriff Mullins is only a few years older than we are. He would have been about twelve or thirteen at the time. He is a very nice man." Her eyes lit up when she said that.

"That's because he's the son of the man who killed my uncle. By the way, you sure seem to know a lot about him. How close are you two?"

"Um, am I hearing a little bit of jealousy from you, Charlie?"

"No, I was just…"

"In case you're wondering, there's nothing going on between us. But, it's not because he hasn't tried."

I placed my hand on hers and said, "I'm sorry. I wasn't trying to get into your business."

"Forget it Charlie. The word around town is he has more than one woman over in Northfield. I'm not into spreading rumors, so I'm not naming names. He's actually a very nice man if you can overlook his skirt chasing. In fact, most people will tell you that he's the best sheriff this place has had for a long time."

"I'm sure he is, but let's get back to what we were talking

about. Fill me in on what's been going on with you for the last twenty years."

"Sure, I would be glad to tell you about it. But before I do, how about letting me introduce you to the sheriff. He's sitting right over there, just two tables away."

She nodded to my right and slightly over my shoulder. I turned slowly to look. There were five people at the table.

"Which one is he?"

"He's the good-looking guy in the blue pinstripe suit. That man always dresses well."

He was the one I had thought was a banker. He looked more affluent than anyone at the table.

"How about it? Let me introduce you to him."

"Well, I don't know. I don't think that..."

"What are you afraid of? You don't even have to bring up the shooting if you don't want to. Come on."

She nudged me and pushed me gently off the bench. Reluctantly I got up. Maria grabbed my hand and almost pulled me along as she walked briskly toward the table. When we were about four feet away the sheriff abruptly got up and turned to face us.

As soon as we were close enough, he planted a quick kiss on Maria's cheek, and said, "Well, good morning Maria. I swear you look more lovely every time I see you. And who is this lucky man you have with you?"

"Sheriff Mullins, I would like you to meet my old friend Charlie Dawson. We grew up together. He's in town for a few days and..."

He turned, looked to me squarely in my eyes, gripped my right hand firmly and placed his left hand on my shoulder. As he did so, I caught a glimpse of the TEC-9 in his shoulder holster. Immediately, I felt that this wasn't a good idea. Neither hand moved; we seemed frozen in place. "Charlie

Dawson? Are you Joe Dawson's son?"

I couldn't hide my surprise. I was speechless and could only manage to nod in response.

"So, are you the fighter pilot or are you the scientist who lives out west?"

Maria replied, "He's Dr. Dawson. The scientist."

I turned to look at her; she seemed to be as surprised as I was.

"No, I haven't been collecting intelligence on you. I know your father quite well. This is still a small town. Before he retired, he did lots of work for me. As a matter of fact, I think that you and your brother helped him out a summer or two when he worked on some of my rental places. I haven't always been the sheriff. And now, every time I run into him, he brags about his boys. He keeps me updated on everything that happens with the two of you."

He released the grip on my hand, and I thought I had recovered from my surprise. "Well sheriff, that's news to me. You can imagine how surprised I am that you know so much about me."

"But as I said, I just know what your father tells me."

Because the sheriff was so approachable, I decided on the spot to ask him about the shooting. "Actually, we came over because there's something I want to talk with you about; it has to do with..."

He raised his hand to cut me off. "Before you continue, let me introduce you to this group of distinguished gentlemen. Excuse me gentlemen. I want y'all to meet Dr. Charlie Dawson. He's one of our own, grew up here, now he's a brilliant scientist living out in New Mexico. This is our mayor, Harvey Wilson. Over here is the president of First National Bank, the man with all the money, Bob Phillips, and right here is the publisher of the newspaper, Mr. Will Carson.

And I'm sure all y'all know this lovely lady."

Each one got up and shook my hand. The mayor and the banker had firm handshakes. The publisher barely rose from his seat, offered me a limp handshake and did not make eye contact. Guiding me with a hand on my shoulder, the sheriff said softly, "I think I know what you want to talk about. Let's go back to your table." He turned to his friends and said, "Y'all excuse me for a few minutes. I'll be right back."

As we walked back to the booth, I realized, Of course he knows what I want to talk about. Will Carson told him about my visit to the newspaper offices. He's gonna politely warn me to stop asking questions. I looked over at Maria. She seemed worried, probably wondering what she had gotten us into.

We took our seats. Maria was still next to me, but this time she was sitting even closer. I thought I felt her body trembling, or maybe it was my own. The sheriff sat across from us. As he slid into the booth, I saw the gun again. Without looking, he made a hand gesture and Paulette arrived almost immediately with a fresh cup of coffee for him. She started to refresh mine, but I waved her off. Maria also declined. It seemed to me that everyone in the place was looking at us.

After taking a sip, he said, "Being the smart man that you are, I'm sure that you have figured out by now that Will Carson told me about your visit to the newspaper office a couple days ago."

I nodded in agreement. Maria turned and shot a questioning look at me.

He continued, "As you can probably tell, Will is from the old school. He's trying to change with the times, but I'm sure you understand what I mean. Will was pretty upset when he found out about your inquires. But I'll tell you the same thing I told him. I have no problem with you trying to find out what happened, and I will do whatever I can to help you." He took a sip of coffee, rested both hands on the table, smiled and waited for my reaction.

Simultaneously, Maria and I exhaled and looked at each other. "Well sir, I must say you have surprised me twice today. But I'm not sure I understand."

Maria touched my arm. "Charlie, I told you he's a very nice guy. I, uh, well, excuse me for a minute. I need to visit the washroom."

As I got up to let Maria out of the booth, Paulette arrived. She still looked irritated but said nothing and simply took our plates away.

"I know you're probably thinking that I'm not sincere. But, as I've told you, I grew up around your relatives. When I was a boy my sister and I used to play with your cousins who lived right down the road from us. Your cousin Booker and I were good friends; he was a little bit older than I was but I learned a lot from him. This shooting incident happened when I was almost fourteen; you must have been about five or six at the time."

"Yeah, that's right. I was almost six; I remember going to my uncle's funeral yet, I didn't know until a few days ago that he was shot. You piqued my interests when you mentioned Booker. What do you remember about him?"

"Booker left town a day or so before the shooting. I never saw him again, but I often wondered if the two things were related. I had only a little more information than you do. I knew almost immediately that my father had shot someone; it was two or three days before I found out it was Prince, uh, your Uncle Prince. I knew your uncle. He was a real good man. But nobody wanted to talk about why the shooting happened."

"I still don't understand why you are taking this attitude about my attempts to find out what caused your father to shoot my uncle. How did you two get along?'

"We got along about as well as any father and son in a small southern town in that era. He laid down the law, and I followed it. But my relationship has nothing to do with this."

Maria returned and I got up to let her into the booth. The three of us took sips of coffee.

"I grew up like any typical southern white boy. I went through segregated schools, and lived a very segregated life, except for with some of your family in my early teens. In college at Ole Miss, I was in ROTC. After college, I found myself as a young officer in charge of a platoon in Nam. At the time, I was eager to be there to do my patriotic duty." He paused and it looked like he might cry. "One day I almost died, but Tommy Brown, a black guy from a little rural town in Alabama saved my life. I have a big scar across my chest to help me remember."

"I'm glad you survived, and glad that you had that eye-opening experience. But, isn't there anything you can tell me about the shooting."

"Unfortunately, almost nothing. One of the first things I did when I became sheriff was to look through the old files to see what I could learn about it. There was minimal information. In those days, no one spent much time investigating white-on-black crime. Since Will Carson told me about your visit, I've been thinking about it. Most of the old-timers are dead or senile. Mike Franklin, who witnessed the shooting, is still alive, but he's 92 and his mind is gone." He paused, cupped his hand to his mouth and looked at the ceiling for what seemed like forever. I said nothing and just waited. "There may be someone who can help you – my aunt. She's my father's sister. Aunt Gladys is 78, never married and still lives at the old family home near Tomley. She has a live-in maid to help her out, but there's nothing wrong with her memory."

"Have you talked with her about this?"

"Well, there's a big problem with that. Aunt Gladys has not talked to me in years. She doesn't approve of the women I've chosen to have in my life." He paused, looked at Maria and added, "I'm sure you can update Charlie about that, Maria."

"How about your sister? You mentioned a sister. Where is she?"

"Actually, I had three sisters. I was the youngest; they are all dead now. My oldest sister died of cancer. My second sister was killed by a jealous lover. My youngest sister, Tara, and her husband died in a boating accident on the river." He pulled out one of his business cards from his shirt pocket, wrote on the back and slide it across the table. "This is my aunt's phone number."

"Do you think she'll even talk to me?"

"Yes. She'll talk to you, just don't mention my name. I suggest that you not ask straight out about the shooting. Tell her that you're doing family history research and you heard the two families were close at one time. Get her talking and you might learn some interesting things."

I got up and shook his hand. Maria stayed seated, smiled and waved to him slowly.

"One last thing, Charlie. Don't forget that old saying: 'Be careful what you ask for; you might get it'."

CHAPTER 16

I walked quietly past the bed of the large woman snoring in short, erratic bursts and tossing restlessly in her sleep. I stopped in the opening where the privacy curtain separated Mama's bed from that of her roommate. I just stood there looking at her for a short while, but it seemed like an eternity. Soft shadows from the branches of the pine tree outside the window fluttered across her face. She appeared to be sleeping comfortably, breathing deeply and slowly. It had been a little more than three days since her surgery, but it seemed like weeks. The breathing tube had been removed from her nose and the blood-gas monitor was absent from her finger. Her blood pressure and heart monitors were still operating.

Pops' Sports Illustrated, still open to a baseball article, had slipped to the floor, as he nodded in a chair in the corner. His chin rested awkwardly on his chest, and he drooled slightly from the corner of his mouth. I was tempted to wake him, but quickly decided against it. Those last few days had been very trying, and I was sure he could use the rest.

"Come on over here and let me see you. I'm not asleep."

"How long have you been awake, Mama?"

"Charlie-boy, I've been awake since you came in. I saw you trying to tiptoe in here. When you first came in, I was trying to make out who you were because your face was in the shadows. Couldn't tell who my own baby boy was. Ain't that something." She chuckled softly, grimaced slightly and then clutched her side.

"Are you okay, Mama? Do you need something?" I asked as I moved closer to her bedside.

"Don't need nothing. Just hurts a little bit to laugh but laughing is supposed to be good for you. Now come over here and give me a kiss. I know that's good for me."

As I kissed and embraced Mama, her skin seemed warm and sticky. I knew that it would take a long time before she would be back to her usual self. That was the first time she had been fully awake since I arrived in town. I was aware that she was still very sick, but slowly improving. "I'm so happy to see that you are getting better. I was really concerned about you."

"Don't be so worried. Like I've told you before, I'm not gonna die anytime soon. I don't think the Lord is ready for me yet." She saw the surprised look on my face and just smiled.

"But... uh, I thought I was dreaming the other night, and I thought you were-"

"I know you thought you were dreaming and that I was sleeping. I ain't heard nobody saying that neither one of those things was not true."

"But I don't understand what you're saying."

"All I'm saying baby, is the person don't always have to be awake to say something and you sure can hear lots of things when you're dreaming." She patted the bed next to her, and said, "You sit here for a minute." As I sat, she took my left hand, placed it on my chest and said, "You can feel your heart beating. You got it for a reason, and it's not just for pumping blood through your body. Up there in your head you got lots of knowledge, but sometimes you got to listen to this. Do you understand that?"

"I think so," I said enthusiastically, trying not to sound too tentative.

"You don't really understand, but you will. You will," she said as she tapped my chest lightly.

"I hate to interrupt, but I need to check your vital signs Mrs. Dawson. How are you doing this afternoon?"

I hadn't noticed her when she first entered the room. It was Kathy Mason, the nurse from the stormy night I spent at the hospital. She didn't look in my direction as she moved efficiently through her tasks.

"I'm doing pretty good. Just here talking to my son. You met my son? He's a scientist."

"Yes, Mrs. Dawson, I've met both of your sons." The nurse finally looked at me and smiled weakly.

Mama said, "Well, actually I do need one thing. When the doctor was in here, he told me I could get something to help me sleep. I didn't sleep too well last night."

"I don't see it on the chart, but I'll call him about that. And if he says it's alright, I'll bring you something when I come back."

After the nurse left, Mama asked," So what have you been doing when you're not here at the hospital?"

"Not much. I've visited with a few friends. I stopped by Aunt Tillie's place the first day I was in town. She asked about you."

Mama didn't hide her sarcasm when she said, "I bet she was real concerned."

"You sound a bit sarcastic there, Mama. That's not like you."

"Well, it's no secret that she was never happy about me being her sister-in-law. Always thought I was too dark for your daddy. But I'm not concerned about it. Now what friends did you see?"

"I went to Al Jackson's place last night. He had a few people over. Mostly folks we went to school with."

"Did one of those folks happened to be Maria?" Mama asked, with a sly look on her face.

"You sure know everything, don't you? I never could keep a thing from you."

"Ever since she moved back here, I've been thinking about how you used to go chasing after her. She was so fast when she was in school; you be careful you hear me?"

"Sure Mama. Nothing's going on; we just had breakfast together this..."

She just shook her head and then asked, "How you coming with the puzzle?"

I hesitated before answering.

"You heard me, Charlie. How you making out with that puzzle of mine?"

"Well, you know it's not really a puzzle or a riddle."

"I sure do know that, but you've been working on it all these years like it's a real puzzle. So, how are you coming with that?"

"Actually, it has turned out to be a very interesting science problem, and I've made progress on it. In fact, I was going to present a talk about it at a conference in New Orleans. I left early because I was really worried about you."

Mama squeezed my hand tightly and said, "I'm glad that you did come to see about me. But I hate that you had to miss your meeting. I hope you can do your talk some other time soon."

I just smiled and nodded in agreement. I was wishing that she had not brought up that subject. Ironically, it brought back painful memories for me; yet it had shaped my life in such profound ways. I know it also had to bring lots of painful memories for her, but at the same time she seemed to find so much joy in it. As much as I wanted to, I couldn't stop the flashbacks from flooding through my mind and pulling my thoughts away from the hospital room.

***

From early school years, I had a fascination with puzzles and riddles. In third and fourth grades I started out with simple riddles and devoured them. As I got older, my interest in riddles and puzzles became more sophisticated and my ability to solve them increased. Somewhere along the way, I started to discover logic. Around seventh grade, I realized mathematics was the highest form of logic, and gradually became very good at it. My math, puzzle and riddle solving abilities became legendary among my peers and family. Then, along came a riddle the changed my and Mama's life, in fact that of our whole family. I understand now that it was not truly a riddle; it was part of an insidious plot. However, in my youthful naiveté, I failed to comprehend the obvious. My memories of that April day in 1964 are as clear as if the events unfolded yesterday.

I got home early from my after-school job at Simms Market because there wasn't much to do on that day. Mama was busy in the kitchen, and no one else was home. Without stopping in the kitchen, I called out to let her know I was home, went to the room I shared with Mike, turned on the radio and caught Martha and the Vandellas in the middle of 'Heat Wave.' I flopped down on my bed to rest for a few minutes before starting my homework.

A minute or two after I landed on the bed, Mama came in, turned the radio down and said with a very serious tone, "Charlie, I have a riddle for you." She took a deep breath, let out a sigh and I saw tears welling in the corners of her eyes. Mama blurted out," How many bubbles in a bar of soap?"

"One-million, eight-hundred fifty-six thousand, two-hundred, thirty-three."

Her mouth dropped open and her voice cracked, as she asked," How did you know that?" Mama was a first-grade teacher, but over the years she had come to hold my math and puzzle solving abilities in great awe.

"I was just kidding. I don't know. How big is the bar?" I sheepishly replied.

But this was more serious than I realized. She burst into tears and rushed from the room. I stood there a long time, feeling helpless and not knowing what to do. I found her in the kitchen, still crying slightly, but trying to compose herself. The death of Grandma Lizzy, ten years earlier, was the only time I could remember seeing her cry like that.

"Mama, I'm sorry. I didn't mean any harm. What's wrong?"

"That's okay, baby. It's not your fault; I'm just a little scared," she said softly.

I stepped closer, hugged her tightly and just held her. "Tell me what's wrong."

She wiped the tears from her eyes with her sleeve, took a deep breath and said, "Okay, but promise me you won't tell your daddy."

"Uh, uh, okay. I promise. What is it?"

"Well baby, I've been going to the freedom school over at Northfield Baptist for a few weeks. Those COFO civil rights workers have been holding classes to get folks prepared to go down to register to vote. I think I'm ready. I'm going down tomorrow."

"Mama, that's great! But why don't you want Pops to know?"

"Because he'll be real mad. You know as well as I do, they don't want no Negros registering to vote. That's gonna make a lot of white folks real angry, and your dad is worried about what they might do. When we talked about registering to vote a few months ago, he said I could lose my job, or worse, and he might be right."

"You are not thinking about changing your mind, are you Mama?"

She shook her head vigorously, pursed her lips and answered, "No, I made up my mind to do this. I'm scared, but I'm still going to do it. There have been six other teachers going to the freedom school and all of us are going together. Actually, we already knew most of what we needed to know before we started going to that school. What those COFO workers did was to give us a good idea of what to expect when we get down there to the courthouse. But the most important thing is that being there helped all of us to pick up courage and strength from each other."

I smiled, hugged her again and said, "I'm real proud of you for going down there to do this. Just wait 'til I tell the kids at school. But what's all this got to do with soap bubbles?"

"I was about to get to that part. Down at the freedom school we went over everything about the U.S. Constitution and the Mississippi Constitution. I'm a constitutional expert now." She paused, chuckled softly and managed a weak smile. She continued with, "They told us that the people at the voting registration office will often ask folks to recite a section of one of the constitutions, or they will give a section to you, ask you to read it and then interpret it. I can't recite every section of the constitution, but I can tell you what every section means. The thing that bothers me is that when we were almost finished, the young man who was teaching us said he didn't want to discourage us, but when you really get down to it, they could ask us anything they want to, including how many bubbles in a bar of soap." She paused, shook her head and used a corner of her apron to wipe away a few drops of sweat starting to form on her brow. "And he said they have been known to ask some folks that question and there's nothing we can do about it."

"Nobody can answer that Mama, that's just--"

"That's the point of the whole thing, baby."

"How about this? If they ask you that question, you just turn around and ask them 'How big is the bar and what kind of soap is it?' Then you look like you are thinking for a minute or so and tell them the answer is infinity."

Mama just laughed. For the moment, that took her mind away from her anxiety about the whole thing. She shook her head, gave me a big hug, and said, "Boy, you're something else."

As I turned to leave the room, I caught a whiff of the stewed chicken simmering on the stove. "That sure smells good, and I'm real hungry." Then, after a moment's hesitation I said in the manliest voice I could muster," Mama, I'm going down there with you tomorrow when you go to register."

"No, I'll be all right. Like I've told you, a group of us will be going together, but thanks for offering. And, we're gonna eat dinner real soon. I just heard your daddy come in. Go wash up and come back to help me put the food on the table. We'll eat supper in about ten minutes. Mike should be here any time now."

As I stood at the sink washing my hands and watching the lather form, bubbles started to develop and I realized that the number was not infinite. A large bubble, surrounded by several smaller ones, grabbed and held my attention for countless seconds. I knew that there was some very complex science going on and I didn't understand it. At that moment, I promised myself that I would.

"Charlie, come on. What are you doing? It's time to eat. Mike and your daddy are already at the table."

"Okay, I'm coming."

None of us seemed happy as we ate. I knew Mama was worried about what would happen the next day. I was thinking about bubbles. Mike was complaining about the new baseball coach. Pops seemed to know that something was up.

During her attempt to register, Mama did so well on the constitutional questions that they did indeed ask her 'How many bubbles in a bar of soap?' The registrar told her he not impressed with her 'flippant answer.' She didn't get to register and did lose her job. Thus, things were difficult for our family for a long time. We somehow got by, but that meant selling things, such as the piano and Pops' favorite chair. I was glad to see the piano go be-

cause I was tired of taking lessons, but I know Pops hated losing that chair, although it was replaced about two years later with one that was even nicer.

At that time, I stubbornly refused to acknowledge to myself that the understanding of bubbles science was not the real issue. I spent the summer coming-up with a science fair project on bubbles; I won first-prize the next school year. My single-minded focus on bubbles was the spark that propelled me into a career in science.

***

"Charlie! Charlie, are you listening to me? I want you to tell me about your progress on this problem. I'm sure you can explain it in a way that will make sense to your poor mama. I still can't believe they pay you to study bubbles. Like I always said, you are something else boy."

Her words yanked me out of my flashback mode.

As I was about to answer her, the nurse returned. "I've talked with the doctor and I have a sleeping pill for you and a little bit of lemonade to help you wash it down. You're gonna sleep real good tonight. In fact, this will work really fast. You two need to finish-up your conversation soon."

As the nurse left, I answered, "They don't really pay me to study bubbles. Well, I guess they do - kind of. I study fluids for lots of practical reasons, like how to get more oil out of the ground. But I also get paid for a certain amount of time that I can use to work on just about anything I would like to. It just has to be something I can write about in a scientific journal."

"That sounds real good. Now go on and explain what you know about how many bubbles there are in a bar of soap."

"Well, it really turns out to be a very hard problem. If I know a few things about the soap, like how large it is, how heavy it is, how sticky it is-we call that viscosity, and how hot the water is, I can tell you about the bubbles. When I say I can tell you this, what I mean is that I can write down an equation that describes it. It just turns out to be hard to solve it, but I'm making progress."

"Okay, I believe you. I think I kinda understand what you're saying. It sounds like if you know how big the bar is and a few other things, you can answer the question. It looks to me like you had it right way back there twenty years ago. Them folks just weren't smart enough to understand my answer."

We both started laughing. Mama seemed genuinely happy. Then she held up her hand, waving it slightly. She flinched momentarily in pain, and then said she needed to rest.

"What's all this fuss and noise? If a man can't sleep in the hospital where can he sleep?" Pops stirred slowly from his nap, got up and kissed Mama on the cheek. He seemed to be in an unusually good mood. "How you feel honey? Everything all right?"

"Yeah, I'm fine. Charlie-boy has been cheering me up."

"I'll be right back. Just going down the hall to find Henry, then me and him can leave. I can go somewhere quiet to get some rest."

"Okay Pops, but you need to drive the car back to the house. Mike wants to use it tonight."

As he left the room, Mama beckoned me to come close and said, "Come over here Charlie-boy. Tell me one more thing. I understand you been asking lots of questions about what happened years ago to your Uncle Prince. Why you doing that?" She gave me that look that said she wanted a no-bullshit answer.

"I just found out this week about this awful thing that happened years ago. I just want to know why nobody wants to talk about it. Mama, you must know what happened. Please tell me."

"Let me tell you this one thing. What happened back then involved your daddy's people. He's gonna have to be the one to decide if you should know about it. It is not my place to decide for them. Now I need to get some sleep. I'll see you in the morning. You're just gonna have to get some-body..."

Her voice trailed off to nothing. I couldn't quite make out what she was saying. I leaned in very close. "Mama. Mama say that again. I didn't understand."

Softly, she said "...tell you about the baby."

As I turned around, Pops was standing there. He seemed angry.

CHAPTER 17

SATURDAY, 12 MAY 1990

After knocking twice, I waited for someone to come to the door. A black woman opened the door; I estimated she was forty-something. She was dressed in a dark skirt and white blouse, standard wear for domestic help in that part of the country. Obviously, she was the live-in caretaker Sheriff Mullins had mentioned. She looked like someone I had gone to high school with; I wanted to ask her but decided against it because she was trying hard to avoid eye contact.

While scrutinizing me from the neck downward, she asked, gruffly. "What can I do for you?"

"Well good afternoon. How are you?"

She grunted and asked again, "So, what can I do for you?"

I decided she probably thought I was trying to sell something. "My name is Dr. Charlie Dawson. I'm here to see Ms. Mullins, she's expecting me." I gave her my card, which she didn't bother to look at.

She flinched slightly, looked me in the eyes for a fleeting moment, followed by a raised eyebrow and a hesitation of several seconds. She said dryly, "Come on in."

I had gotten the appointment through a bit of deception and was at that moment thinking it was probably a bad idea. As Maria drove me home from breakfast earlier that day, she had suggested that I not approach Ms. Mullins in the manner proposed by the sheriff. Following Maria's suggestion, I had called with my best middle-American voice.

"Ms. Mullins, this is Dr. Dawson. I live in Albuquerque,

but I'm here in town for a few days to do research on prominent families in small southern towns. Everybody I interviewed said I should talk to you."

She giggled softly, followed by a long silence on the phone. "Well, Dr. Dawson I don't know what you think I can tell you. I'm not what you would call a historian. You would be better off talking with somebody else; I'm just an old woman."

"I really won't take up much of your time, Ms. Mullins. I just want to check a few pieces of information to make sure my facts are accurate."

"Well, I guess it's all right if you stop by for a little bit this afternoon."

The deception had worked; I had made it past the front door. I was down a short hallway that smelled ancient and looked like a scene out of the forties. A mahogany loveseat just inside the entryway was the centerpiece of the foyer. A large floral rug covered most of the matching hardwood floor; the rug seemed to be in great shape but could use some cleaning.

The caretaker slowly slid open the large pocket doors to reveal a cluttered parlor. "Have a seat. I'll go get her." As she walked away, she shook her head and I heard her chuckle softly.

I glanced around and took the first available chair. As soon as I was seated, the upholstered chair brought back vivid memories of Pops' favorite chair when I was a child. The mustard yellow color was firmly stamped in my memory. Whoever decorated the room seem to have chosen the chair to match a similar color that was heavily speckled throughout the threadbare woven rug. As I rubbed my hands across the arms of the chair, I was sure that I could feel all the bumps and ridges that ours used to have. That chair, along with the piano, sewing machine and assorted other items that I had long forgotten, was among the things we had to sell when Mama was fired from her job for daring to attempt to register to vote in 1964. Having to part with that chair only added to Pops' anger over the fact that she had taken part in the mass voter registration drive.

All I could remember was that some white folks had stopped at our yard sale and had bought the chair for almost nothing. As I sat there waiting for Ms. Mullins, I realized this could be our chair. It was possible that the upholstery had held up for this long because Mama always had it covered in plastic. To confirm my suspicion, I started searching with my right hand for my initials that I had carved into it with the new penknife I had gotten when I was eleven - an action that earned me a serious whopping. I thought I felt something there on the chair leg, and leaned over to verify, but spotted the feet of the housekeeper standing a foot or so away. I hadn't heard her enter the room.

"Is something wrong? Can I help you with something?"

"No, I thought I heard something fall." I was hoping that my voice didn't really sound as shaky as it felt to me.

She said nothing, just stood there, making me feel uneasy. I got up and started wandering slowly around the room, looking at the many pictures on the wall. Mostly family pictures, but there were black folks in several of the photos. There was a picture of a black maid in uniform, with four white children that seemed to range in age from three to ten. Another picture contained only black children: about a dozen of them sitting on the steps of a run-down dog-trot house. There were five girls and seven boys, arrayed in an apparently random order. They all looked intently into the camera, putting on their best toothy smiles. I was curious about who they were, and turned to ask the maid, but she was gone.

Immediately, I realized that was my chance to finish checking out the chair, but as I started back toward it, something grabbed my attention: a group photo of what appeared to be the Mullins family, posing outdoors. Seated in an armchair at the center of the picture was a large man with a handlebar mustache. I was sure that was him: Old man Red Mullins, the man who shot Uncle Prince. Standing behind the chair, with her hand on his shoulder, was a woman of about 50 who was probably Mrs. Mullins. Near the right arm of the chair stood two young boys; one was surely the younger Red Mullins I had met earlier that day.

The three girls in the picture seemed to range in age from preteen to late teens or early twenties. Judging from the clothing styles, the picture was probably taken in the early fifties. The family members looked like they could be straight out of an old movie. The girl standing near the boy was strikingly beautiful. As I looked closer, the face looked vaguely familiar. And I noticed something else: the face had been cut out and pasted back in place. As I studied her, it came back to me: she bore a strong resemblance to...

"Well, Dr. Dawson. What a wonderful surprise you found me; I'm impressed."

...Sara Madison, from the plane. I was speechless. As I turned to face her, I managed to recover sufficiently to ask, "What are you doing here Sara? Are you part of this family?"

"Well, yes I am. But, aren't you glad to see me?"

"It's great to see you again. It's just that I'm still in shock, seeing you here. How do you fit into this family?"

"That's my mother's picture you were just looking at. Her name is Tara." She paused, looked back at the door, and added, "In case you were wondering, she and my grandfather had a falling out years ago. He cut her out of the family-

figuratively and literally. Just disowned her. What he didn't know was that one of my aunts saved her face from that picture. Years later, after he was dead and buried, Aunt Maggie put her back into the photo."

"That's an interesting story. Do you have any idea what caused the riff between the two of them?"

"All I know is that he was unhappy about some man in her life. Isn't that what usually causes problems between fathers and daughters?"

At that moment Ms. Mullins entered the room with a flourish; dressed as if going to a party. She held my business card in her hand, using it as a makeshift fan. The maid entered, a few steps behind her, stopped, then just hovered there, waiting to see what would happen next.

Halfway across the room, Ms. Mullins stopped dead in her tracks. She looked around the room for a moment, seemed confused, but recovered nicely. "So, you must be Dr. Dawson. Nobody told me you was colored." She turned around halfway to look at the maid, who just shrugged and glanced at Sara for a split second.

"Aunt Gladys, you're not being very nice."

"I didn't say I have nothing against coloreds, just said somebody should've told me." Turning to me, she added, "I don't think I can help you with anything you want to know."

"Like I said on the phone, Ms. Mullins, I will not take much of your time."

We were all still standing. I glanced toward the sofa, but she didn't offer me a seat. Sara intervened with, "Have a seat Dr. Dawson. I'm sure she's willing to spend a few minutes talking to you. Isn't that right Aunt Gladys?" Before Ms. Mullins could respond, Sara added, "Thelma, please bring us some cold iced tea." She gestured toward the sofa, "Please sit."

I took a seat at the end of the overstuffed sofa. Ms. Mullins looked confused but sat in the yellow chair. Sara sat at the other end of the sofa. Thelma shook her head and slowly left the room, looking back as if she might miss something. Ms. Mullins fidgeted with my card for a few seconds and then said, "Well Dr. Dawson, just exactly what did you say you wanted to... Wait a minute! You Joe Dawson's boy, ain't you?"

"That's right, Joseph Dawson is my father."

"I should've knowed. Two people have called me today to tell me about you and my nephew having a long talk downtown yesterday. I'm an old lady and I might be a little bit slow, but I ain't senile yet. You didn't come here to talk about no history; you here to ask about the shooting."

Sara almost leapt off the sofa as she heard this and looked back and forth between me and her aunt. Apparently, this was her first knowledge of the shooting.

"I sure would like to know about the shooting, but if you don't want to talk about it, I won't push the issue. However, I do understand that your family and my uncle's family were very close at that time."

Thelma reentered the room hurriedly, apparently having heard mention of the shooting and just stood there waiting for more.

"Thelma, you can put the tray here on the table. Thank you for getting the tea," Sara said, as she smiled and nodded toward the coffee table. Thelma put the tray down but made no effort to leave.

"Let me just tell you that I know nothing about that shooting. I was just a young woman at the time. The only thing I know is that it was because of some kind of accident. That's all I know. I can't tell you what caused Red to shoot Prince, 'cause them two was friends at one time. That situation made me sick to my stomach when I heard about it."

"You just said the two of them were friends. My Uncle Prince and your brother? Do you really mean that?"

"Of course I do. White and colored could be friends back then. Just didn't have to do all of this mingling and mixing."

"Did your brother ever talk about any of this around the house?"

"No, he never did, at least not around me. By the way, why you asking me all these questions? Why in the world you bringing this up after all this time? And, why ain't you at home asking your folks about this?"

"It's been years since I lived here, and I just found out about the shooting a few days ago. I did talk with my father, but I wanted to get the other side of the story." I've decided to play a hunch. "One more thing? Who was the black, uh colored, fella that your niece was involved with back in those days? What does this have to do with what happened? That's why your father cut her out of the picture, isn't it?"

Ms. Mullins shot an accusing looked at Sara, who responded with a questioning look. Thelma's mouth dropped open. Mrs. Mullins' answer confirmed my suspicion. She shot back, "You know very well who. You know that it was your cousin Booker. I have absolutely nothing else to say to you."

"Please, just one more thing. This is the last thing." She pursed her lips but said nothing. I continued, "When did your brother find out? When did Booker leave here?"

She looked at the ceiling, as if trying to decide if she would answer. Finally, she said, "I think it was a few days before the shooting. Yeah, that's right; it was about two days before the shooting. I remember my niece thinking that Red must've done something to him. Nobody I know of ever saw him again. Maybe my brother did do something to him."

"Thank you. I promised not to ask anything else and I won't."

However, she wasn't finished. She added, talking to no one in particular, "Yeah, one of them colored children started talking about it, and somehow word got back to Red. He sure was mad, he..." She threw her hands up. "That's all I got to say."

Her statement had the effect of someone kicking me in the stomach. I felt nauseous and could hardly breathe. Ms. Mullins also seemed drained by all of this. She gestured for Thelma, who came over to the chair to assist her. She said nothing else, just left the room with Thelma supporting most of her weight.

Sara got up quickly, grabbed a scrap of paper and a pen from a desk in the corner. She scribbled something and gave it to me.

"This has been quite a visit, but I need to go upstairs and make sure she's OK. We need to talk. Meet me here tonight."

"I think I can do that. I'll see you later."

I looked at the note. It said Saturday, 8:00 PM, Big Daddy's Place, Lee Hwy.

CHAPTER 18

SATURDAY, 12 MAY 1990

I knew what it was going to be like, and I thought I had prepared myself. I gave lots of attention to the image I wanted to present when meeting Sara. I showered, but used no cologne. I left a hint of a 5 o'clock shadow on my face, but used no after-shave. I carefully selected my clothes to convey the sense that this was no big deal – just the right degree of casual while appearing not to be a working stiff. The khaki slacks and the denim shirt seemed to provide the effect I was looking for.

Finally, I decided it was time to put on my most important piece of armor: a call to Ada. As expected, she was still in the office. She was in the middle of reviewing her notes for the next phase of her big water rights case.

"Hi Cera. I was just thinking about you, and how much I miss you. I will be home next week, let's get away and spend a few days at that bed and breakfast we like so much up near Santa Fe. Remember the last time we were there? Remember how hard it was for us to get out of bed? Remember how much fun it was? Let's do it again."

"Honey, that sounds great, but let's talk about it when you get here." In a whispered tone, she added, "You're making me blush. I'm not alone; we're still working."

"We? Do you mean you and Fernando?"

"Yes, that's right. We'll be here late. I have to go. But, are you okay? Is everything all right?"

"I'm fine, just missing you. I love you baby."

***

During the drive to Big Daddy's Bar and Grill, I tried to focus only on Ada. But my apprehension about this entire thing pushed through to intrude on my thoughts. I was very nervous about meeting a woman like Sara in a place like that. After all, it was still the Deep South. My old friends repeatedly told me that things had really changed- that it was the New South. Still, I was not totally comfortable. However, the real source of my apprehension was what I thought she had in mind. I knew that she wanted me – probably just for the night; it seemed to be some kind of game with her.

The dialogue going on in my head reflected my apprehension: *During the nine years of my marriage, I haven't cheated on Ada. I've maintained my integrity by not letting myself get into situations like this. Now, here I am knowingly walking into a problem. Sara Madison is a fine woman, but this is different. She has information that is very important to me, not just because of what happened to Uncle Prince. It was deeper than that somehow.*

I had never been to Big Daddy's, but I knew exactly where it was. It was an institution in this little town. I had passed nearby many times before. Years earlier, several of my friends had worked there as bus boys or dishwashers, but in those days, no black person dared try to enter as a customer.

I arrived about twenty minutes early. The parking lot was almost empty, but I took time to look around for the right spot. The lot was large, and I decided I wanted to be close to the door, but not too close; near the light, but not too much light. As I went through that routine, I asked myself what all the caution was about, and decided I wasn't sure. Finally, I took a space very near the door; the light was poor.

Pausing for a moment and looking off toward the west, I was reminded of the beauty of the place where I grew up. I was on a bluff that gave me an excellent view of the river and of the sprawling farmlands beyond. Out there was Tomley – the place where Pops, Uncle Prince and all of the Dawson family had grown up – the place where all of this started.

As I went through the door, I paused to try to get a sense of what the place was like. Something about the look and feel of the place said: 'things happen here.' It was a Saturday night, with a larger crowd than the cars outside would suggest. Lots of pictures on the walls of people who seemed to be somebody – a few of them black people – something I viewed as an encouraging sign.

The lighting was moderately low, mixing with the last few rays of the setting sun coming in from the large windows on the west side of the building. I was vaguely familiar with the lyrics of the soft country rock tune playing in the background, something about a 'cheating woman' and a 'broken hearted man.' I became aware of smells; the aromas from the kitchen were vying with the music for my sensory attention. Those smells were wonderful; I recognized the Bermuda onion mixed with the subtle hint of... *Is that rabbit?*

"Hello sir, you must be here to meet Miss Madison." Those words dripped like honey from the lips of the young woman who greeted me. I could feel my facial muscles involuntarily revealing my surprise. Before I could respond, she followed up with, "She told me to keep an eye out for this beautiful man who was looking for her."

Instantly, a quip came to mind, but I thought better of it and simply responded with a nod.

"She's right in here, please follow me sir."

"Thank you; with pleasure"

I had planned to arrive before Sara; this threw me off

my plan. I had intended to have time to scope the place out, and to find a table at just the right spot. Ce la vie, I thought.

"Thank you, Sara darling, for finding him for me," Sara said. She was seated at the bar, and the guy next to her seemed to be really into her. She simply told him, "Nice talking with you, my friend is here." and turned to face me.

I made a mental note of the way she was dressed: a calf length, lavender dress, unbuttoned so as to reveal just the right amount of thigh. I remembered reading somewhere that lavender was the color that was found to be most appealing to engineers and scientists.

"Have a seat. Please buy me a drink, sir," she said as she tapped the empty barstool to her right.

"Is everybody here named Sara?" I asked as I sat down, partially facing her.

"I'm drinking Jack and branch water; how about you?" she said, hesitated for a moment and then added, "She's my little cousin, named for me. My uncle bought this place when Big Daddy died about fifteen years ago. She works here from time to time. Pretty little thing, isn't she?"

"In that case, I'll have what you're having," I responded as I nodded toward her and signaled the bartender.

"Marvin, this is my new friend, Charlie Dawson. Dr. Charlie Dawson. He grew up here, lives in New Mexico now. We met on the flight to Dallas; he's here for a few days.

Marvin was a large guy with a cherub-like face and blond hair pulled back in a ponytail. He leaned on the bar in a manner that conveyed too much familiarity.

"Pleased to meet you, Dr. Dawson."

"Thanks. Please call me Charlie"

"Sure Charlie, and just let me know if there's anything I can do for you. What y'all drinking?"

Before I could get the words out, Sara tapped the glass in

front of her. "Two."

"Well, I see she's got you drinking her drank already," Marvin said and gave a knowing look in my direction.

I turned to Sara, smiled and said, "This sure is a different town from the one I grew up in. You know, I was very uneasy about meeting you in public in a place like this. At one time, a black man around here could get lynched for a lot less. And speaking of that, you know this will get back to your uncle. Aren't you concerned about how he will react when he hears?"

"Well Charlie, Uncle Phil knows that I'm a big girl now. Besides, if he could deal with my husband being black, he can deal with this. I was married for seven years to my college sweetheart. He was the finest man on campus, and one of the best basketball players to every play at Ole Miss, 2nd round draft pick. Golden State. Just got traded to Detroit. When he got ready to make that move, I knew I couldn't go. I was tired of having to wade through the crowd of groupies that were always hanging around. They can have him. I'm through. Furthermore, the fact that Uncle Phil has a black mistress is an open secret; that hasn't kept him from getting re-elected twice as sheriff."

I just nodded slowly.

"Relax Charlie, lighten-up, it really is okay," Sara said as she took a sip of her drink and smiled a big, wide smile.

I hadn't even noticed our drinks had arrived. I picked up the bourbon and water, tapped my glass to Sara's, took a sip and tried to relax. The music! I was suddenly aware that it had changed to a soulful ballad by Bettye Swann. I recognized the lyrics immediately: 'Make me yours, I just wanna be yours...' *She probably had them play this, probably provided a play list. I imagine the entire evening is scripted.*

As if on cue, she picked up her glass, softly touched my

hand and said, "Let's go to our table; I had Sara save the best one in the house for us."

I found it difficult not to notice her figure as she walked away. *Very nice*, I thought. The dress fit loosely but clung to her in just the right way to emphasize her hips. *Lovely figure, from here I might think she's a sister*. The dress was plain, not showy, but obviously not cheap. I noticed she wore flats, not heels. She walked those few feet to the table, subtlety moving her hips in a way that made it obvious that she thoroughly understood the power her body could have over a man.

She sat before I got to the table, on the side nearest the bar. This gave me an opportunity to sit across from her and still have a view of most of the room. *Not a bad table*, I thought. *Probably, the one I would have picked.*

The number of people in the restaurant seemed to have doubled since I first arrived. I noted, with some relief, that no one seemed to be paying any attention to us. I even thought I may have seen another interracial couple, but I didn't want to stare. Still, I quickly estimated that the emergency exit was only about twenty yards away, with only two occupied tables between us and the door. *I could be at the door in about five or six seconds if I needed to*, I thought to myself, then tried to relax.

I took a small sip from my glass, but was determined to drink very little that night. I sat there and looked at the woman across the table from me – really looked at her. *She really is a very good-looking woman*, I thought. *But, there's something about her that I can't quite figure out.*

I observed her more closely and made mental notes. She wore a minimal amount of jewelry; jade earrings and a small jade and gold pendant. Understated, but I knew jewelry well enough to know that they were expensive. I couldn't avoid noticing the beauty of her dark eyes, but I thought I saw a sad edge. The small amount of makeup she wore seemed to be perfectly applied. I tried to avoid them, but my eyes were drawn to her ample breasts, with just the right amount of cleavage showing. She wasn't wearing a bra. I was beginning to imagine what it might be like to spend a night with her. *Obviously been somewhere in the sun recently to get a tan like that.*

"Well, how do you like me so far?" Her words pulled me out of my daydreaming. I didn't answer. "Charlie, now it's your turn. Tell me about your wife. What's she like?"

"A beautiful and brilliant woman. She's an attorney."

"Oh, I must be careful. I could find myself in court." Smiling a wicked smile, she continued with, "How did you two meet? Any children? Tell me all of it." She spoke with very animated gestures of her hands and a gleeful smile.

"We met in Chicago; I was in grad school she was in law school. We have one daughter; she's in her first year of college," I replied, as tersely as possible and leaving out the details. "There's something else I would really like to talk with you about."

"What's the rush Charlie? Relax. We have lots of time. Let's order first, afterwards we'll see where it goes."

"What do you recommend?"

"Well, everything is good, but you really must try the house special as an appetizer. They make this thing with sautéed rabbit, onions and various hot peppers, it's great, has a real zip to it. It's right here on the menu. You're going to love the name – Hot Peter. We should share it," she said with a little hint of naughtiness in her tone.

"Excuse me. Are you ready?"

Because I was so focused on Sara, I didn't notice the other woman's arrival until she cleared her throat. I looked up to see a pretty, young waitress ready to take our order. The smooth, dark tone of her skin and the broad shape of her nose reminded me of someone. *Probably the daughter of someone I went to high school with.*

"I took her advice. We'll share the Hot Peter to start," I indicated to the waitress, as I nodded toward Sara.

The waitress, who was about the age of my daughter, was not shy about showing her irritation. "Are you sure that's what you want, sir?" She nodded in Sara's direction. To ensure her meaning was not lost on me, she continued with, "I would recommend the dish called the Black Bottom – strips of marinated rump steak, served blackened; it's real good."

Sara, visibly annoyed, interrupted with, "We both know what we want. Also, bring another round of drinks for us; the bartender knows what we're drinking."

"And, who are you?"

"You must be new here, honey."

I tried to defuse things by saying, "Sara's family owns this place."

"Oh, I see. It's like that. Thank you, sir," she said before leaving.

"Charlie, you were so concerned about somebody in here messing with you, but that child was ready to kick my ass for sitting here with you. She doesn't know a damn thing about either of us, but she takes it as a personal affront that we're together. I could have her fired, but I won't even bother. I'm used to it; I saw it all the time, even in San Francisco."

I decided I wouldn't try to explain the actions of the waitress to Sara. I felt no responsibility to do so. "Just because nobody hasn't decided to jump up and teach me my place doesn't mean some people in here don't harbor those views. I imagine you'll still get some flak about this."

"Charlie, you really are hung up on race; let's just try to

be two people who like each other's company."

"Maybe you're right; however, I have something I would like you to read," I said, as I carefully removed the folded paper from my shirt pocket. I gave her a photocopy of the newspaper article. Sara took what seemed to be an eternity to read it, pausing several times to stare away blankly. I was anxious to see her reaction, but there was none I could detect.

"Where's the rest of the story?"

"That's why I'm here! To get the other facts from you."

Again, I looked for a reaction. I saw none.

After what seemed like an endless delay, she said, "Charlie, I would love to help you; I really would, but I know nothing of this. I wasn't even born when this happened, and I can't recall a single mention of anything like this when I was growing up."

"There must have been something. I'm certain this is connected to the riff between your mother and your grandfather."

"What you don't know is that I didn't grow up here. I lived with my mother and father in a little town north of here: Jonesville. We didn't get down here to visit that often. I only started to come here on a regular basis when I was a student at Ole Miss. In fact, that's how my husband Art and I met."

"Sara, I really don't...," I said as I raised my hand to stop her. She ignored me.

"Ole Miss played a big basketball game at State, a game that's always a big rivalry. I drove down to the game with three of my friends. I had arranged for all of us to stay with my aunt and uncle at the old home place where my aunt still lives; they have lots of room. The four of us had the guest house to ourselves. There was an after-game party at somebody's place in Millerton; we all went. Several members of our basketball team came – actually, all the white guys on the team, and Art. Everybody there was surprised to see him, but nobody was freaked out by it. Art had had a great game that night; he was almost like a god when he walked in. All the women in the room wanted to make a move on him, but they were all concerned about what people would say. He looked so good, and I wanted him so bad. On impulse, I decided 'to hell with it,' walked right over and asked him to dance. We ended up back at my family's guest house; my friends found other places to stay that night. The rest is history."

"Well, that's a great story, but why are you telling me all of this? Are you trying to divert my attention from what we're here for?"

"No, Charlie. I guess I was just reminiscing. In some ways you remind me of Art; not in appearance, but in demeanor – you have that air of confidence that I liked so much in him." I wasn't feeling very confident at that moment, but she continued with, "Like I said. I do want to help you, but I'm afraid I know little, or nothing of this." She twisted the ends of her hair through her fingers and smiled seductively.

"You can start by telling me about your mother. Tell me about her face being cut out of the picture. In fact, that's why I'm here. You implied that you could tell me about that picture."

"Here's what I know about it. When my mother was about 20, or 21, she and my grandfather had a big falling out. She left home, got married, moved to Jonesville, got pregnant and here we are."

"It's not as simple as you describe it, Sara. Where is your mother now?"

"My mother died about ten years ago. My parents were

out on the lake on a Sunday afternoon. The other guy was drunk when he crashed his speedboat into them; he got away with just a few scratches; they never saw him coming. It devastated me; I'm still trying to get over it. I have a very good therapist."

"I'm sorry Sara; I had no idea."

"No need to apologize. My therapist encourages me to talk about it. So, what else would you like to know?"

"What about your...?"

"My dad is going to be of no use to you. He survived the accident with some major broken bones and a ruptured spleen. But he's been in a nursing home for about four years now. Advanced case of Alzheimer's."

Our next round of drinks arrived. The waitress asked about our entrée orders – again. I hadn't really looked at the menu or given any real thought to dinner. Hurriedly, I decided on pan-fried trout, something I hadn't had in a long time. Sara selected a casserole with another name that was obviously made up: Shoo-Fly Pie. Several menu items seemed to be a play on words; somebody obviously thought it was cute. The waitress was pleasant this time; she had either gotten the message or had decided it wasn't worth the trouble.

I continued the conversation, but decided I wasn't ready to play my trump card yet. I thought a slow start was the best approach. "Tell me what you know about how your mother grew up; she must have talked about what things were like when she was a girl."

"I really don't understand why you are so obsessed with this. What little of her youth I'm aware of can't possibly be of any significance to what you want to find."

"One thing I have been able to learn is that the lives of our families were interlinked over a long period of time.

Little tidbits can eventually add-up to a more complete picture."

Then, she asked the obvious question, "Why aren't you asking these things of your family, instead of me? Are you sure that's why you are here?"

I dodged the second part of her question. "I've talked with several relatives. But memories are getting pretty dim for the few who were old enough at that time to know what was going on. I still have a couple of others I need to talk with. But, just like the blind man touching parts of the elephant, I need the bits and pieces to try to understand the whole. You may be able to fill-in some parts of the puzzle. You can start by telling me why your mother's face was once cut out of that picture, and the conditions under which it was put back."

"Again, I know little, or nothing about that part of her life. From as far back as I can remember there was no contact between her and her father. But my grandmother – Grandma Sylvia – stayed in contact, although I'm pretty sure he didn't know about it. She would come up to Jonesville to visit us. Uncle Phil or Aunt Millie would drive her, and they would sometime bring along a black woman who worked for them. They never stayed more than about an hour. After I was old enough to drive, I started coming down on my own to visit with my grandparents; my parents encouraged me to get to know them. I still have vivid memories of the first time I went there to visit. It was late spring, I was seventeen. My grandfather was outside under the shade tree, sipping something cool. He was alone. No, I remember the black woman who took care of him was there, sitting, occasionally fanning him. He looked so frail."

I took another sip from my drink and sat for a moment mentally reviewing what she said. "That must have been some experience. How did he react when he saw you?"

"He looked as if he had just seen a ghost; he dropped his glass. The woman who was caring for him immediately patted him on his hand and said 'It's okay Mr. Red, that's your granddaughter, Mr. Bob Logan up in Jonesville is her daddy.' Gradually, he calmed down and beckoned me to come over to him. He was glad to see me. I told him all about myself – at least three times. He was obviously becoming senile. He never mentioned my mother. The one time I brought her up, he looked at me with the coldest eyes I've ever seen, never said a word, then he just dropped his head. I went back to visit many times; I saw both him and my grandmother on those visits. However, all my visits with him were just like that first one, except I never mentioned my mother again."

Something she said about the woman who was taking care of him grabbed my attention. "Sara, what do you know about his nurse, who was she? Why do you think she found it necessary to tell him who your father was?"

"Unfortunately, I don't know much about her. Everybody used her first name. Hattie, I think. That's all I know. She lived around there somewhere. I remember she did tell me later that day how much I looked just like my mother, the way she looked when she left there. Said she didn't want him to get confused. Hattie told me she had worked there since 1942; said she was like a member of the family, but I don't know her last name. I never thought about that."

"Please do me a big favor, ask your aunt about Hattie, just try to get her name and find out where she is now. But right now, I would really like to know about your promise that got me to come here tonight." That really grabbed her attention; I continued, "The picture from which your mother's face was removed is very significant, I believe. You implied that you could tell me more about the story behind that. I'm convinced it has something to do with my uncle's story."

Before she could respond, dinner arrived. The waitress was still very professional, almost overdoing it. After easing the plates onto the table, she asked, "Anything else I can do for y'all?" Then she was gone, as quietly as she had come.

Both plates looked great; the chef was very good with presentation. The aroma was even more alluring, but I wasn't hungry. It must have been written all over my face because Sara said, "I'm not hungry either; let's dance," as she got up from the table, reached for my hand and started toward the dance floor. I really didn't want to, but decided because she was halfway to the dance floor, it wasn't a good idea for me to refuse.

The DJ was just finishing a fast, upbeat tune, but as we got to the dance floor the mood suddenly changed. Almost on cue, the music was now a slow drag. I was surprised to see how crowded the dance floor had become during our conversation. As we started to dance, I recognized the tune: 'Choose Me.' Sara used subtle movements to encourage my body to melt into hers. I told myself that I didn't want to, but I was starting to enjoy the experience. Sometimes a deer can see the headlights coming, have time to get out of the way, and yet make no movement. At that moment, I was the deer.

I had always understood that I was often a mystery to others, but at that moment I realized I was also a mystery to myself. I was totally wrapped up in enjoying that moment, all the while telling myself that I didn't want to enjoy it. She was gently pulling me in even closer, while Teddy P. reiterated 'You're my choice tonight.' The scent of jasmine that was emanating from Sara was calling up sensations I hadn't experienced in a long while. She whispered, "I know I'm gonna love this."

I was only able to meekly respond with, "Me too."

The elbow that collided with a spot a few inches to the left of my right shoulder blade jolted me out of my altered state of consciousness. The sharp pain raced down my back and into my legs. It took every ounce of my strength to keep my knees from buckling, and Sara helped me remain on my feet.

I turned to see that the elbow belonged to the son of Capt'n Bubba, the idiot with whom I had a traffic altercation on my first day in town. From the look of venom in his eyes, I knew immediately it was no accident. He didn't say a word, but the woman he had been dancing with smiled weakly and said, "We're sorry," as she tugged at his sleeve. "Come on Billy. Let's dance," she pleaded with him.

The look of surprise on Sara's face let me know she understood as well as I did what was happening.

"Sara, it's time to leave."

She nodded in agreement and led me toward the emergency exit.

"Why don't we just head for the front? Your people can help."

"It's too crowded. Let's go this way."

I decided she was right. We were trapped in a corner. Only a few people dancing very near us were even aware that anything was out of the ordinary.

As we got outside, I realized it was raining. I reached into my pocket for car keys, and Sara said, "Let's take your car."

"Where's your car Sara? I'll take you there and then leave."

"We don't have time for that," she said with some sense of urgency as she pointed toward the exit we had just come out of.

Without another word we both walked hurriedly toward my car. I unlocked the passenger door for Sara. That was a mistake, because as I started heading to the driver's side of the car, I heard a woman shouting, "Billy Joe, just forget about it! Stop it! Do you hear me, stop it!"

I didn't even look in that direction as I rushed to unlock my door, but I could tell from the sound of feet pounding on the asphalt, that I didn't have enough time. I turned to face Billy Joe and he was within seconds of pounding me into the pavement. I knew my only hope of salvation was to drive my foot, as hard as possible, into his balls. Instinctively, I shifted my weight onto my left foot and began the forward snap of my right leg. I could see the whole thing unfolding in slow motion.

As he began to fall and scream in pain, exhilaration rushed through my body, but the feeling quickly faded as I realized that I didn't touch him. The rain had brought oil up from the asphalt, making it slippery. He had slid feet-first, ending up halfway under the pickup that was parked near me. That was good enough. I quickly got into my car, started the engine and drove away.

"Damn Charlie. That was something. You're good!"

"No, I just got lucky."

"That's wasn't luck. But I think you're gonna get lucky, Charlie."

CHAPTER 19

SATURDAY, 12 MAY 1990

As I drove toward the exit of the parking lot, I checked my rearview mirror and saw a large pickup truck pulling out; I knew it was him. I floored the gas pedal and Sara was thrown back against the seat. I was surprised that the Impala was able to move that quickly.

"What the hell are you doing, Charlie?"

"Sorry, but we have company," I said, as I nodded to our rear.

In the wet, loose gravel at the exit, the car fishtailed to the right. It felt just like skidding on ice and snow, which I was accustomed to dealing with in the mountains of New Mexico. After lifting my foot slightly off the gas pedal and steering into the skid, I had the car under control.

"Damn Charlie. You're a good driver too. I'm impressed."

On the wet pavement of the two-lane highway, I accelerate a bit slower, but quickly got up to about 70. As I entered the gentle curve at the bottom of One-Mile Hill, I caught a glimpse of the truck in the rearview mirror and saw it spin out of control at the spot where I had problems. We didn't have to worry about him following us.

"Okay Sara, how do I get to the place where you're staying?"

"Just continue in this direction until you get into town. On Main Street, when we get to the post office, I'll direct you from there."

In the excitement of almost getting beaten to a pulp, I had forgotten where things were headed between Sara and me. Away from the passion of the moment, I was having second thoughts. I said nothing, but my body language apparently revealed my distress to Sara.

She leaned over and began stroking my ear lobe. "Relax. Everything is gonna be fine," she whispered. Her hands moved to the base of my neck with her left, while stroking the inside of my thigh with her right. I was relaxed and helpless. So relaxed that I almost didn't see two kids chasing a dog across the street. I hit the brakes and swerved sharply, which pulled me out of my almost-trance.

Sara directed me to the next two turns and said, "It's the large white house on the left; turn at the corner and park in the side driveway. I had the garage door opener, but I left it in my car. Too bad."

I recognized the house and asked, "Whose house is this, Sara?"

"My good friend Judy and her husband live here. They're in Natchez for a few days. I often stay here when I'm in town. They have a wonderful little apartment above the garage; I have it all to myself."

"Did you know that used to be the maid's quarters?"

The cynicism was unmistakable in her voice as she asked, "And how do you know that?"

I lied by saying, "My aunt was the live-in maid. She did a great job taking care of the Wallace family who used to live here, but never had time for a family life of her own."

That wiped the cynical sneer from her face. In truth, I knew that house because I helped Pops with the remodeling job – the summer of '64. I will never forget that hot, awful summer. There had been intense civil rights activity in Mississippi, climaxed by the infamous murder of three activists: Chaney, Goodman and Schwerner. I wanted so badly to be involved in The Movement; instead, I was stuck working on the homes of wealthy white people. But I didn't feel up to talking with Sara about it. My lie had the intended effect: it conferred a momentary morally superior status upon me.

I rolled the car slowly into the driveway, eased it into park, but left the engine running. To my soft declaration of, "Goodnight Sara," she responded with the most sensuous smile I had ever seen. As she shifted her body to face me, she caressed my face between her palms and planted a very wet kiss upon my lips, lingering for a few seconds.

Abruptly, she reached for the key, turned the ignition off, quickly exited the car and simply said, "Let's go!"

Without the keys I was going nowhere. I called out, "Sara, come on. Let me have the keys. I need to go."

She stopped halfway up the staircase, and just stood there, dangling them above her head. As she turned and walked away, I slowly followed her up the stairs. I knew where this was going but couldn't think of an alternative. As she walked, she lifted her skirt slightly to avoid tripping. I had a wonderful view of her shapely legs and apple bottom.

She opened the screen door, pushed the main door open, reached inside and flicked the light on. The room was bathed in a soft, blue haze. "Isn't it wonderful that people here still don't feel the need to lock their doors? I'm always amazed by that whenever I come back to visit. Come on in. I won't bite."

The door opened into a small entryway floored with Mexican tile; I remembered helping Pops to install it. The combination living room-dining area was small, cozy and attractively furnished with a circular table, adequate for four people, a sectional sofa and an easy chair. Because of the limited lighting, I couldn't see colors very well. From somewhere down the short hallway, I heard keys clinking on marble as she said, "Your keys are here; now you can't say I kidnapped you."

I couldn't see Sara, but I heard the distinctive sound of a stereo being powered on, and I recognized Houston Person's horn as it began to wail, followed by Etta Jones softly imploring, 'Don't Go to Strangers.' I heard a match strike, saw a brief burst of flame and detected the smell of jasmine wafting through the air. I could have grabbed my keys and left at that moment; instead, I stood there in the middle of the room, taking it all in.

"There's a wet bar in the corner. Help yourself and fix me a drink; you know what I like. I'm going to freshen up, be right back. There's a small bathroom to your left."

As the bedroom door clicked shut, I entered the bathroom. With the excitement of an almost-fight subsiding, I realized that I needed to relieve myself. After washing up, I took a quick look through the bathroom. The toilet bowl and sink were extra clean and fresh hand towels were on the rack. There was a new bar of soap on the sink. Under the sink, I found a can of Comet and a damp sponge. In a wall cabinet, I found a box of lubricated Trojans; it had been opened and two or three were missing. Clearly, Sara had a plan.

At the bar, I fixed the Jack and branch water for Sara and tonic water with a wedge of lime for me. I decided that I didn't need the additional confusion of alcohol raging through my mind.

I sat in the easy chair at the far end of the sectional sofa and placed the drinks on the straw coasters on the marble top coffee table, with her drink positioned toward the center of the table. I told myself that as soon as she returned, I would have a quick sip of my drink and leave.

From where I sat, I had a perfect view of the door as she walked out. The light level was still low, but back lighting from the bedroom provided an exhilarating view. She wore a sheer, flowing negligee. Her hair was pulled back to reveal cheek bones higher than I had noticed before. Sara stood there for a moment and turned her body at just the right angle for me to see her erect nipples pressed against the translucent fabric. She remained in the doorway long enough for me to take in the full effect. She started moving slowly toward me with the exaggerated stride of a large cat stalking its prey. From the look in her eyes, I knew I was trapped.

Raising her drink toward her, without getting up, I managed to say, "A toast."

She paused, took a sip, and said, "To the two of us, to the start of something wonderful."

As I took a sip from my glass, in one seamless movement, she put her glass down, took my glass away, lifted her garment to just above her knees, spread her legs and straddled my body. I knew I shouldn't be there. I was telling myself it was happening too fast for me to do anything about it. Slowly, I mentally extracted myself from the situation. I wasn't there; I was outside watching the events unfold before my eyes. I told myself I shouldn't even be watching, but a part of me wanted to know how it all would end. I saw my hands begin to grasp her and pull her closer. The first contact of her lips upon mine pulled me back into the moment.

As our bodies became more entangled, a part of me wanted to stop, but another part of me felt helpless. I managed to say, "Sara, this isn't why I'm here. We need to talk." Her eyes locked on mine, and I saw in them a promise of intense PLEASURE that I couldn't seem to resist. I told myself, *"Charlie, you are weak."* I got an immediate reply, *"At this moment, I don't want to be strong."*

I felt her slow, rhythmic breathing that sent waves of cinnamon over my face. She whispered, "Charlie, don't fight it. There's nothing wrong with what we are doing." At that moment, I believed her. She alternated between planting soft kisses upon my face and nipping playfully at my lips. I responded with nips of my own. Our bodies eased into a slow, hypnotic grind, in time with the music. I was aware that the music had changed, but I had no desire to know who the musicians were. Yet, I was still saying to myself, *"Man, it is not too late to stop."*

My hands were everywhere on her body. Slowly, very slowly my fingers paused at all the right places to explore the finely sculptured details of her body. Her nipples were erect and sweaty, the breasts felt more perfect than I had imagined. Her ass, in my hands, had just the right amount of firmness. There was soft fuzz covering her body that felt like the skin of a ripe peach.

I became aware that I was no longer wearing my shirt and my pant were somewhere down near my ankles. Her fingers explored my body in all kinds of places that sent ripples of ecstasy through my body. She whispered, "I have condoms."

Again, I mentally exited the scene; my point-of-view changed. From somewhere above, I could see our bodies joined: in the chair, moving to the sofa, on the thick rug on the floor, and, inexplicably, we were rolling on wet grass. Our bodies were entangled like two snakes, shedding their skins. Slowly the image changed; both faces turned toward me and began to morph into the faces of someone else. I recognized her from the picture, and I'd never forgotten his face from so many years ago.

She whispered, "Charlie, what are you waiting for? Enter me now. Don't make me wait."

Instead, I stopped and pushed her away. I had a moment of clarity. I blurted out, "Your mother and my cousin Booker conceived a child together 35 years ago. I believe that was you. We need to talk."

She rolled over onto the sofa, "Charlie, I'm 31 years old!"

All the passion had died for both of us.

CHAPTER 20

The encounter with Sara left me shaken. I was totally confused about what I was doing and needed to clear my head. It was obvious to me where I needed to be: near the river. I started in that direction, but just before turning onto River Road, I saw a phone booth at the corner of Main and River. I quickly found the number in the small notebook that I always carried. As I dialed, I had second thoughts about why I was calling, and I paused after each digit. Still I continued. She answered on the second ring.

"Hello."

"Hi, this is-"

"You don't have to tell me, Charlie. I recognize your voice. Actually, I was hoping it was you."

"Please tell me this isn't too late for me to call."

"No worries. I'm snuggled into my favorite easy chair, listening to some music, reading a good book and sipping some cognac. You're welcome to join me."

I was silent for countless seconds. "Uh, uh... I don't know if..."

"Then, why did you call? You know we're both grown folks."

"I guess you're right. I'm less than ten minutes away. See you soon."

I stood there, shaking my head and questioning myself as I hung up the phone. Charlie, what the hell are you doing? I offered a reassuring thought, Calm down. You can handle this. The internal debate continued as I drove. My mother's warning surfaced in my mind.

After parking, I sat for several minutes trying to regain my composure. I walked slowly to the door and lightly rapped the tiger-shaped brass knocker on the ornate solid oak door. A gong-like sound rang out, startling me. As I waited for the door to open, I took a deep breath, and the creaking sound of the opening door pulled me out of my reflective flashback.

Maria stood there in silk, lavender, lounging pajamas. She took my hand and pulled me into the foyer. Tiptoeing and raising her face toward mine, she kissed me softy on my lips. We embraced; my eyes locked onto her momentarily. Then, I let my arms drop and pulled away.

"Welcome to my home, Charlie." She gestured toward glasses of cognac on a small table near the door and whispered, "Please join me."

As we entered the spacious living room, we tapped glasses together in a toast. I said, "To the two of us."

We each took a sip and she responded, "Okay, but don't tease me."

"I'm not here to seduce you."

"Are you sure?" she asked as a sly smile spread across her face.

"I need someone to talk with. I know it's late, but I need a friendly ear."

She motioned me to a seat on the large gray sectional sofa. I placed my glass on the coffee table and sat at one end of the sofa; Maria sat at the opposite end. "Okay my friend, what's on your mind?"

"I want to tell you a short story. It's about coincidences."

She folded her legs onto the sofa in a lotus posture, took a sip of cognac and nodded for me to start.

"A few hours before leaving Albuquerque for a conference

in New Orleans, I accidentally found the reprint of a news article about the shooting of my uncle. The date that paper was reprinted was the same day I reconnected with Ada, after more than ten years. That's the first coincidence." I paused to get her reaction.

She smiled and simply motioned for me to continue.

"During my flight to New Orleans, I sat across from a young white woman who happened to be traveling here to Millerton. That's number two."

Maria took another sip and said, "Interesting. Go ahead."

"The moment I checked in at my hotel I got the message that my mother was critically ill. Coincidence number three."

She shrugged.

I amplified that statement by explaining, "If I hadn't been in New Orleans, I wouldn't have gotten here so quickly."

"Where is this going? You seem to be trying to make something weird out of all of this."

"I'm about to get to the good part."

"Please do," she said with a giggle.

"Shortly after I got to town, I found you..."

"Okay, that's the good part. Is that why you are here?"

"...and you lead me to the sheriff, who happens to be the son of the man who killed my uncle."

"I know this part. Remember?"

"He sent me to his aunt – the sister of my uncle's killer."

"So far, what I'm hearing just tells me that you are doing a good job of following the trail of information."

"Here's the punchline. I made an appointment with the aunt, got there and guess who I encountered."

She appeared to have a hard time restraining her belly laugh as she said, "I have no idea, but please enlighten me with this startling revelation."

I blurted out, "The woman I told you about from the plane!"

For the first time during our conversation, I saw real surprise on her face, as her mouth dropped open. Recovering from her surprise, she said, "You know, coincidence is God's way of remaining anonymous."

I laughed at that comment and said, "Now, you are quoting Albert Einstein to me. I had forgotten he said that. So, you think all of this is God's work? Also, I learned that her mother had an affair with my cousin, Booker. The two of them had a baby. It was Booker's father who was killed. I know Booker left town just before the shooting."

"What makes you so sure that your cousin left town? Maybe they dumped him in the river somewhere and shot your uncle afterward. But either way, it looks to me like you've solved the mystery."

"All my family members say that Booker left town. I can see why they might kill his father if they couldn't find him. I still want to know what happened to the baby."

"Maybe you were talking with her."

"No, that can't be the answer; she's too young."

"So just how well did you get to know this young woman?"

I hesitated before responding and thought about how much I wanted to reveal.

She must have detected something in my facial expression or body language because she said, "Come on. What are you holding back from me?"

Slowly, I told her, "We met tonight at the restaurant her uncle owns. Because of an altercation there, we ended up at her place. And, uh, I almost slept with her."

She threw up her hands and said, "Now I understand

why you are here. Well, I can't be the one to tell you that what you did is okay. You need to have that conversation with your wife."

Slowly, she rose from the sofa, gestured toward the door and said, "Good night, Charlie."

It was 1:30 AM when I got back to 741. I creeped quietly into the house. When I passed Pops' room, he said, "Boy, do you know what time it is?"

CHAPTER 21

I was awakened by a loud knock, knock, knock on the bedroom door. Pops was shouting, "Get up Charlie, we got some talking to do before you fool around and git us all killed. I got some coffee on the stove; come on out here."

Those words from Pops were even more surprising than his loud knock on the bedroom door. *What the hell is he talking about?* In all my years, Pops had never shown much interest in initiating a conversation about anything other than baseball or the bible. Suddenly, he wanted to talk.

I wasn't totally awake, but couldn't sleep after that. The sunlight coming through the small opening at the bottom of the window shade provided added incentive for me to get up. As I tried to shake off that haze between asleep and awake, I mentally reconstructed the events of the previous night. A quick check of my body reassured me that I wasn't injured, but I was having trouble remembering details. I knew I had only one drink the night before but was feeling hung-over.

Pops knocked again. "You coming out here boy?"

"Okay just give me a couple minutes," I replied as I hurriedly pulled on sweatpants, wiggled my head into a t-shirt, and starting down the hall to the bathroom.

After quick attention to body functions, a splash of cold water in my face helped to remove some of the fogginess from my mind. I almost slipped on the newly installed linoleum floor as I walked into the kitchen. The feel of the slick surface against my bare feet reminded me of the slippery asphalt in the parking lot the night before. The events in the restaurant and the brief "chase" were coming more clearly into focus. I remembered going to the old Pruitt house, remembered being almost seduced, and memories of ending the evening with Maria brought a smile to my face.

The strong aroma of Pops' freshly brewed coffee completed the job of shaking me out of my mental fog. He used the old percolator coffee pot instead of the Mr. Coffee unit I had sent to Mama three years earlier.

Pops was seated at the kitchen table; shaking his head and holding his coffee mug tightly against his chest with both hands. "Come on in, sit down and let me explain a few things to you Charlie-boy. In case you have forgotten, let me remind you that this is Mississippi. It's been a long time since you really lived here; things have changed, but not that much. It's still not a good idea to be hanging out with a white woman. Did you know her uncle is the sheriff here?"

My first thought was, *How the hell does he know all this detail about last night?* I feigned disinterest and replied, "I know that Pops. I also know her granddaddy shot Uncle Prince. You must know that too."

"Boy, I told you not to waste your time with that stuff that happened way back then. It's all over and done with." He put his mug down and slapped his palm against the table. "So that's your excuse for running around wit that woman. You don't have to go to a café late at night; you could talk to her during the daytime if you really wanna get some information from her. You sure don't have to be going out dancing wit' her. But, that ain't my business; that's between you and your wife."

That statement stung me, but I was determined to not let the impact show. But, as I started to respond, I detected a waver in my voice. I took a moment to get a mug, poured my coffee and took a seat facing him. "Pops, nothing happened." I tried to shift the focus of the conversation. "How did you manage to keep track of all my business anyway?"

The smirk on Pops' face said he didn't believe that nothing happened. "Sure was a lot of nothing going on. Lula Wood's granddaughter works out there at that place where y'all was at last night. Lula came by here first thing this morning, told me about the whole thing. Way I heard it, you was lucky to get away from that big fellow. Where did you go after that,' cause you shore didn't git back here 'til well past midnight?"

I decided everybody in the neighborhood had the whole story – the wrong story. I also knew it was too late to do anything about it. My mind was replaying the events of last night. I clearly saw Sara's face as she reacted to my speculation about a baby.

"Well boy, you gonna just sit there and ignore me? I asked you a question."

I took a few sips of coffee, picked up the morning paper, still folded on the table, looked through the first few pages and said, "I'm just checking to see if it's in the paper yet."

Pops leaned in close, looked me squarely in the eyes and said, "Ain't a damn thing funny about this. You better treat it like it's serious."

Smiling and shaking my head, I replied, "We just went somewhere to talk. By the way, did you know that Booker and Red Mullins' daughter had a baby back in '54?"

I expected to see surprise on his face; instead, I saw anger. "That woman must've told you that. You just keep on poking and digging. What you trying to do? Why do any of this stuff matter to you? What's done is done."

"All of this happened for a reason. Like you always told me, years ago when I was a young boy, 'There's a reason for everything; the Lord puts stuff in front of us and then it's up to us to pick it up and do something with it.' You remember telling me that?"

From the glazed look in Pops' eyes, I sensed that my quoting of what he used to say was having an impact upon him. I was even starting to believe the wisdom of his words.

My finger jabbed into the empty space between us, as I continued, "I told you about finding that newspaper that got me started on this, but I didn't tell you the rest of it. I found that paper on May 8th of this year. Uncle Prince was shot on May 9th, 1951. It was in a box of old papers that Ada had. She got that paper in Jackson, the 8th of May, 1981. That also happens to be Ada's birthday and the day that we saw each other for the first time in almost seven years. She got the paper in Jackson that morning, put it away, drove to New Orleans and just happened to run into me. That's when I found out about our daughter, your granddaughter Maya. I've never been superstitious, always believed in logic – in science. But there is something going on here that I just can't ignore. Don't you see, I have to keep on digging?"

When I finished, I felt totally drained emotionally. Pops looked as drained as I felt. I could barely hear him as he said, "That was her birthday too. Eight O' May. That day used to mean something around here."

"Who? Whose birthday?"

"The baby. I don't think they gave her a name. I just know it was a girl."

A stream of questions began spewing from my mouth, questions I was not consciously formulating: "What else do you know about this Pops? How did you find out? What happened to the baby? What else do you know about all of this? Why did it take all this time for you to tell me about this stuff?"

The look of disgust on Pops' face said he didn't like all of my questioning. I could see his mouth starting to form the word 'why,' but it never came. He stopped, pushed his chair back from the table, got up, poured himself another cup of coffee, turned and asked, "You want some mo'?"

"Sure Pops, you know I never turn down your good coffee."

He stood there, leaning against the stove, as he slowly said, "You know boy, if I thought it would do any good I would just tell you to shut up, but you jest gonna keep on picking at this thing, just like you use to do when you got a cut on your arm. You would just keep on picking at it, wouldn't let it heal. Drink your coffee, then put some decent clothes on, I'm gonna take you to somebody who can answer your questions."

I felt my heart pounding against my chest; I was about to achieve what I had been seeking so fervently. I started to ask who, but had second thoughts. I wouldn't push it, just wait and see what developed.

"Okay, how far we gotta go?"

"I reckon about twenty miles."

"Alright, it'll take me about ten minutes to get ready."

While getting dressed, I heard the squeaky front door. Whoever was arriving didn't even knock, just walked right in.

A woman's voice called out, "Joe, Joe, where y'all at?" I recognized the voice; it was our distant cousin, Mattie. I had never known her age, but it seemed that as far back as I could remember Mattie was always the same age: Old. Old, but somehow ageless.

"Back here in the kitchen, Mattie. Come on in."

I changed into cotton slacks and a fresh shirt, and returned to the kitchen. She was pouring herself a cup of coffee. Pops was fumbling with some paper bags in the corner;

he was probably getting his morning shot of bourbon.

When Mattie saw me, she said what she always said, "Charlie-boy, come here and give your old cousin a big hug. Every time I see you, you look more like your mama." After we released from our embrace, she added, "I heard you was in town. I figured you wouldn't find time to come see me, so I walked down here to see you, and I had to find out how your mama was doing. How is your family? You didn't bring that wife of yours wit' you? I think she been here wit' you just one time. And, how about that little girl of yours?"

"Ada is doing well; she has a very busy law practice, and our little girl is in college. She's almost nineteen."

I was thinking, *This is too early to be dropping in to see anyone unannounced.* It was almost 7:30 AM. The day was already shaping up to be a hot one. Mattie had always been something of a mystery to me. In all the years I had known her, I could only remember being in her house once. When I was about fourteen or fifteen, Pops took me along to help repair a leak in Mattie's roof. When we were finished, she invited us in for a slice of cake. I still recalled the tangy, sweet flavor of the concoction she called simply Mattie's Special.

I also had vivid memories of her house: small, cluttered, but somehow orderly. Most of all, I remembered the smell of stale roses and darkness. No shades were in the windows, but there were so many things hanging from and around them: plants, banners, small knitted rugs, cloves of garlic, clusters of dried peppers, and the strangest of all – locks of hair. As kids, we used to think Mattie was a witch, and at that moment I started to wonder about her. She had always lived alone; no husband, no children. I could never remember her working.

Mattie wasn't just any cousin; she was the oldest person I knew of in the family, and keeper of the collective family oral history. Yet, I had no idea how she was related to us. It occurred to me that I should ask Mattie about the mystery I was trying to unravel. Then, I had another thought: Maybe this is who Pops had in mind for me to talk with. Maybe all this talk of going somewhere is just a ruse... I started to ask her, "Mattie, what do you know about-"

Pops interrupted, "We 'bout to drive out to Cal'donia. We in a hurry."

"Well, I ain't got nothing to do, be nice to ride out there wit' y'all. I can't remember when I've been out that way, and I ain't seen Buddy since he buried his wife 'bout three years ago. What y'all going to see Buddy for? He ain't sick, is he?"

The scowl of his face let me know that Pops was getting more frustrated with the whole thing. He just shook his head, and said, "I didn't say we was going to see Buddy. But he's doing fine; ain't been sick a day in his life. We just going out there to visit with him. Ok, come on let's go."

Buddy! I just saw him a few days ago. If he has answers to this, it would explain why he was so nervous when we talked.

When we got to the driveway, Mattie announced, "I gotta set in the front seat, can't ride in no back seat. I gets real sick settin' back there."

Pops said, "Well, maybe you oughta just stay here. We can drop you off at your house..."

I interrupted, "Pops, this car really does have a comfortable back seat. I used to ride in the back seat a lot when I was growing up. We don't have that far to go. How about this? You drive and I'll ride back there."

He said nothing, just got in the backseat and slammed the door.

After she and I were in the car, I said, "Mattie, you have to fasten your seatbelt."

"Boy, I don't mess wit' all these belts and thangs. If you have a wreck, I can't git outta the car."

"I'm sorry, but you have to fasten it. You don't want me to get a ticket, do you? Here, let me help you with it."

"Alright, go on and fix it. Hurry up so we can git going." Then she added, in a mumble, "Chillun grow up and forgets who the grown folks is."

As I backed out of the driveway, Pops said, "Let's stop by Slick's Place and get some quick breakfast. He's got real good food. Go up there to the stop sign, turn on..."

"I know how to get there. Been eating at Slick's all my life. And, remember you had me stop by there on the first day I got to town."

I pulled up in front of the building. A hand-written sign in the window said, 'WE IS NOT OPEN ON SUNDAY NO MORE.'

Pops asks, "When did this happen? Slick ain't open on Sundays?!"

Mattie replied with a sneer, "Oh yeah. I shoulda remembered. Folks been talkin' bout how Slick done got religion. Don't work on Sundays no more."

"I know a place that's open. We can go to the Magnolia Café in the Millerton Hotel downtown."

Pops shouted, "Naw, we ain't going there! Let's just go on out to Buddy's house. I ain't hungry no more."

CHAPTER 22

SUNDAY, 13 MAY 1990

As I drove through the downtown area, the town was just starting to wake up. The car windows were up, the air conditioner was on and low-volume gospel music flowed from the radio. Mattie was trying to have a conversation with Pops, who was replying with an occasional grunt to what she was saying. I glanced at him in the back seat and saw that he was reading his bible and ignoring her. We continued west across the bridge before turning north onto Dixie Highway.

After about a mile, the landscape started to open up into gently rolling hills. My thoughts wandered to my encounters with both Sara and Maria the night before. I suddenly realized I hadn't thought for a moment about Ada during either experience; I promised myself, *I will call her as soon as we return from the visit.*

I chuckled softly as I thought about how my confrontation with Bubba had ended. Mattie blurted out, "It ain't funny, Charlie-boy. I seen it with my own eyes, back in '51. And turn that radio down, old woman like me can't stand all that noise."

Until that moment, I had been oblivious to what Mattie was saying. "I wasn't laughing at you Mattie; my mind was on something else. Say that again."

"Like I was telling your daddy; I saw a hoss flying, right over yonder. Colored man was riding his hoss real fast, coming 'round the bend in the old road over there. At first, I thought he was riding fast for the fun of it. Then, I seen about five or six white mens chasing him. All of 'em had guns. There was a old crick used to come through here. It's all dried-up these days." I pulled over to the side of the road because Mattie's story had piqued my interest. I remembered my dreams of the flying horse; a chill ran down my spine.

"What you stopping for?" Pop asked, with a tone of impatience. He closed his bible and looked up to see what was happening.

"I'm just taking a minute to understand what Mattie is talking about."

She continued talking, "It'd been raining a lot; the crick was full of water. That hoss didn't slow down one bit. Jumped up in the air, trying to get over that crick. They didn't look like they was gonna make it. Just then, that hoss sprouted wings, right out of his neck. Started flapping them wings, hoss started rising up in the air, jest like a airplane. They was just kinda hanging there in the air for a little bit, then they took off, landed way over yonder by that stand of trees right there."

She pointed, with a shaking hand, at a small cluster of trees, the largest of which stood out from the others because it was so crooked. "These trees was a lot smaller back then. Them white fellas was scared to death. They turned white as sheets, didn't know what to do. They hosses was jumping around, making all kinda noise. One of the mens spoke up said 'Let's get outta here'. He turned around and started riding fast as he could back where he came from. Them other fellas took out after him."

Pops said, "Mattie, I don't think it happened quite like that. And I don't think it happened around here. Now, can we get on where we going?"

I must have heard this story before. That has to be the reason for those dreams I've been having. "Pops, I wanna hear the rest of her story." I turned to Mattie and asked, "What did this colored man look like, who was he?" I waited for a moment, and added, "Was it Booker? Did this have something to do with him?"

She shook her head vigorously, and said, "I don't know who he was. Tall fella, real good looking. Ain't never seen him before. Ain't seen him since."

"Well, what about the white men? Did you recognize any of 'em? Did they see you?"

"Sure, I knowed 'em. One of them was Mr. Red Mullins oldest boy. Thank they called him Jimmy; boy got kilt in that Viet Nam war 'round about '63 or '64. I remember when his folks got the word; I was there. Working."

"Mattie, I didn't know you ever worked for the Mullin family. Were you working there when old man Mullins had that stroke?"

"I sure was there. Took care of that man 'til the day he died. I was also working there when..."

Pops said, "Let her finish with one thing before you jump to something else. Go on and finish telling us about the flying hoss, so we can go." The sarcasm was hard to miss.

I realized, *When Sara said her grandfather's caretaker was Hattie, she was almost right: it was Mattie.* My mind was racing, trying to make sense of the whole thing.

Mattie continued, "One of the other fellas was Mr. Cliff Jurden's boy. Him and that Mullins boy was best friends. You couldn't separate 'em. The other fellas worked on the Mullins' place. I didn't know they names, but I always seen 'em around. When it happened, I don't think they seen me. Cause, the next day I seen all of 'em down at the lil' ole store what Mr. Jurden used to have. They was setting outside there talking real quiet. When I come by, they seen me, but didn't none of 'em bat a eye."

I wanted to know many things from her, but at that moment I could only pull myself together enough to ask, "What were you doing out here by yourself Mattie? Did you tell anybody what you had seen?"

"I never said I was by myself. There was five of us seen it. Me, my baby sister Kattie, you know she had that stroke four years ago, died 'bout a year after that. God rest her soul."

Although I wasn't aware of her sister's death, I nodded in agreement. She just sat there with a faraway look in her eyes, and I waited for her to continue.

"Susie Johnson who lived down near us, she's the one that married one of the Walker boys and moved to Dallas back around '56 or '57, ain't seen or heard from 'em since. She was there wit' that Walker boy, the two of 'em had been courting for a long time."

"You said there were five. Who else was with you?"

"Jace, Jace King." She smiled a broad smile, sighed and continued, "Jace King, Lord knows he was something. Prettiest man I ever laid eyes on. He knowed it too. Jace King, um huh!" Again, she seemed to let her mind drift to some faraway place.

Pops grumbled, "Come on, let's go where we started to. It's getting hot out here and we gotta make it over to Buddy's place."

As I pulled the car back onto the road and started for Buddy's house, Mattie said, "Turn that air off, it's cold in here."

I complied with her request; Pops didn't object. In less than a minute, the car was hot and muggy, causing me to feel as if I were in an oven. I turned the air conditioner to low; she didn't seem to notice. "Mattie, tell me about the horse. What was he like?"

"I don't know if that horse was a he or a she, but it was

white. Whitest horse I ever seen."

As hot as it was in the car, that answer sent a freezing chill down my spine. *Just like in my dreams.* I was starting to feel emotionally overwhelmed by the conversation about the horse and wanted to end it. Within seconds after we stopped talking, images of that horse invaded my senses. I saw the white horse a few yards in front of the car, slowly prancing along. Although I knew the images weren't real, I couldn't take my eyes away. Slowly, the horse began to spout wings. In seconds, I was no longer driving the car; I was astride the horse and we were in flight, rising above the trees.

"Charlie-boy, you need to be looking for two crooked trees on the right side of the road, not to far up the way from here," Mattie said, casually.

Her words shook me out of my trance-like state. We had entered a section of the road where thick sycamore trees formed a canopy, shielding us from the sun that was just starting to break through cloud cover. After less than a minute more of driving, I descended a low hill; at the bottom, Mattie was proven right: the crooked trees were there like she said.

From some deep forgotten memory, I began to recall climbing those trees. They were easy to climb because the branches were so large and many of them extended almost horizontally from the trunks. I vividly remembered being up in those trees with Mike and our cousins, feeling as if we were on top of the world, feeling so free.

Slowly other images started to come through: images of something strange, something sinister, something painful. In memory flashes that seemed to be illuminated by strobe lights, I saw a limp body hanging from the tallest tree. *What is this about, and who was that?*

"Watch where you going boy; you 'bout to run us in the

ditch!" Pops shouted out. "You missed your turn too."

"Sorry," I said, as I braked and began to slowly back up. "My mind was on something else. Pops. Mattie. What do you know about somebody getting hung from one of these trees out here, long time ago?"

There was dead silence in the car. The windows were completely up to keep out the road dust. As I turned onto the small gravel road, I heard only the hum of the air conditioner and the muted sound of the tires on the rutted lane. I waited.

After what seemed like minutes, Pops finally said, "Who you been talking to now? You just keep on dragging up stuff."

"I haven't been talking with anybody about this. Seeing those trees made me remember. I was here; I saw it. I don't remember much detail, but I know that I saw it."

"Stop the car," barked Pops. I did. "Back up, keep going, back to the black top road." I did that too. They were commands, not requests. "Stop here."

Then I heard Mattie. One soft grunting sound, then a second one that was much louder. Next, she started to moan – soft and plaintive. I turned to look at her. Her eyes were open, ever so slightly. No tears. She was slowly rocking back and forth, her hands clasped in her lap, gripping a handkerchief.

"Mattie, are you okay? What's wrong?"

"Come on," Pops said, as he got out of the car and softly closed the door.

By the time I got out too, Pops was walking slightly ahead of me, with his head down. For the first time since arriving in town, I became keenly aware that Pops was starting to age. The limp was more pronounced, the gait not nearly as brisk as it once was. I always had an image of Pops as age-less. *Nothing lasts forever.*

Pops stopped abruptly. He just stood there at the edge of the road, looking down at the ground, at nothing in particular.

"Was that Booker who was hanging from that tree?"

Pops jerked his head up with surprise in his eyes. Shaking his head vigorously, he said, "No, no way. That wasn't Booker. It was her oldest sister's boy. That was a long time ago. You wasn't quite six years old." As Pops gestured toward the car with a nod of his head, he continued, "We called him Slim; his name was William Edward Bankhead. Tall, good-looking boy, musta been no more than about twenty. She was about seven or eight years older than he was, practically raised him. She was crazy about that boy, just like they was sister and brother."

"What does this have to do with what happened to Booker? Is this why you brought me out here?"

"This ain't where we're headed. This has got nothing to do with Booker. Them two boys was friends, but this is different."

"But, what happened here?" I asked, almost pleading.

"See that lil' crick over yonder?" Pops pointed to a small creek flowing from the north and branching into two smaller streams near the two large trees – trees that now seemed very sinister to me. The smaller branches, as they swayed in the breeze, seemed to reach out, trying to grab us with razor sharp fingernails. The chill down my spine returned. I shivered. "Mr. Deeberry used to live down the road there, had lots of horses, had one real fine horse, used to take him everywhere to race him. Slim used to take care of that horse; he was real good with horses."

Without warning, the strobe-lit images returned. I tried to bring the scene into focus as it replayed in my mind's eye. The image was fuzzy, but for the first time I thought I recognized Slim. *Did I ever know him?*

For a millisecond, it was all in focus, and then it was gone. I knew I had to remember. I closed my eyes and tried to concentrate. I started breathing deeply, slower, slower, slower... Gradually, the image started to come into focus. I was five years old again.

The large bloody spot surrounding the stake driven into the chest, the limp body, the eyeballs almost exploding from his face. In my mind, I gradually turned up the volume, then slowed the replay speed down to a crawl. Suddenly, I heard the crying, saw the reddened eyes, both men and women. I smelled the awful stench. Someone got sick and started to throw up.

That awful smell of the vomit rising from the warm ground; it seemed to set off a chain reaction. Then came the laughter. Turning around, I saw a group of about a dozen white men with large guns – rifles and shotguns. White men, smoking and laughing and passing the bottle of whiskey, men finding so much humor in the pain and misery playing out in front of them. A pair of hands covered my eyes.

"...and she said that you didn't see much of it. They wouldn't let nobody cut him down from that tree 'til the sun went down. They wanted people to see him hanging there; said it would teach colored folks a lesson."

"Pops, Pops," I interrupted. "I'm sorry. I missed lots of what you just said. It all just came back to me; I just remembered everything, but I still don't know why they did it."

"He was out here riding that horse, like he was supposed

to do. Horse tried to jump that lil' stream, but he didn't make it. Landed right there in the crick bed, landed on a big tree limb that was sticking up out of the mud. That limb tore that horse's chest wide open. He didn't die right away, they had to put 'im down. I didn't see it, but folks said you could see his heart beating in his chest."

The effect was like that of someone pouring a large tub of ice-cold water on me. The chills and shaking were uncontrollable. I remembered all of that from my dream during the flight.

Pops, unaware of the effects of his words upon me, was still talking "...they did all that to him because of that horse. It was a accident with a horse. They just treated him like he was a hog, or something." Suddenly, he stopped. "Charlie, what's wrong with you? You look like you just seen a haunt."

"Pops, I dreamed about that horse a few days ago, just like you told it. I had forgotten about it, but I must have seen the whole thing. It's all come back to me." I tried, but could not hold back the tears that started to trickle down my cheeks.

"Son, I'm so sorry. I didn't know you saw any of that. All this time, we didn't know. Your Aunt Tillie came out here to see one of her friends. She brought you with her; said she didn't know what was happening, but she stopped to see what the crowd of people was looking at. Said she covered your eyes and took you away as soon as she knowed what was happening."

I slowly nodded my head in agreement, as Pops said, "Stuff like that can sure eat at you. It's good that you finally letting it out."

"Mattie and the other four was the ones that found Slim hanging here. Only thing is, she made up a story, in her mind about a flying horse. There was no water in that crick, dry as a bone. That's her way of dealing with it."

I was totally unprepared for what Pops did next: he turned toward me, took a couple of steps forward, reached out and embraced his son. I couldn't remember the last time he and I had embraced. For one moment, we both cried silently. We looked each other in the eyes, and were lost for words.

"You fellas come on, let's go on down to Buddy's house!" was the shout that came from Mattie. She was standing about halfway between us and the car, with her hands on her hips. "Y'all come on before I get in there and drive this car myself."

For the next few minutes of the drive, we all made small talk. No one was emotionally ready to revisit the subject that consumed all our energy just a few moments earlier.

"It sure is gonna be a hot summer."

"This ole road's as bumpy as a washboard."

"Looks like somebody's gonna have a real nice crop of corn this year..."

"Here it is," said Mattie. "This is it alright; there he is on the porch. Booker looks just like his daddy. That boy is looking more and more like Prince."

Confused, I turned to look back at Pops. His head was down; he looked up at me, but said nothing.

CHAPTER 23

SUNDAY, 13 MAY 1990

As we turned from the main road onto the narrow one-lane path leading to Buddy's property, I noticed fascinating things about the way things were set up. I was a child when I was last at Buddy's place and was much less observant than I was on that day. The place we were about to enter was the home of a man who lived in fear of someone. The house was a modest frame structure with a wrap-around porch, perched on the only hill in the area, sited about 60 or 70 yards from the roadway. It was small, but appeared to be well maintained. A row of pine trees stood along the roadway spaced about two yards apart, such that the branches interlocked in many places. They formed a barrier that made it difficult for anyone on the road to have a clear view of the house. Behind the nest of trees, I saw a heavy chain link fence with three strands of outward facing barbed wire across the top. Two rows of tightly spaced rose bushes had been planted just behind the fence. Assorted vegetables were planted in about a dozen rows behind the roses. I also noticed flood lamps attached to several large trees in strategic locations around the property.

I stopped the car at the gate and Pops got out to open it, but it was secured with a heavy chain and padlock. Buddy was walking briskly toward the gate to let us in; I noticed a double-barreled shotgun leaning against the wall near the chair he had just left. As he headed toward us, three Doberman dogs appeared suddenly from under the porch; I saw two other dogs that didn't move. He gave a barely perceptible signal with his right hand, and they all heeled behind him. He opened the gate, and Pops motioned to me that he was going to walk back with Buddy. As the two of them closed the gate behind the car, I saw in the rearview mirror that they were having a spirited conversation.

Speaking barely above a whisper, Mattie asked, "Do you remember Booker? You was just a lil' fella when he left here, but I remember how you would always follow him around everywhere he went. You sure was crazy 'bout Booker. Charlie-boy, do you remember him?"

I simply nodded and said, "Yes, Mattie. I sure do."

The trauma of revisiting that lynching scene is messing with her memory. Buddy and Booker are cousins, but now she's confusing the two in her mind. As I parked the car, I asked, "Mattie, exactly how is Buddy related to us?"

"That's what I been trying to tell you-"

Tap, tap, tap.

Buddy was tapping on the window, and I hadn't even noticed when he approached the car. Mattie stopped talking, gripped my right hand tightly and smiled at me. As I exited the car, Buddy greeted me with a firm handshake, then pulled me in and warmly embraced me. He stepped back, gripped my shoulders with both hands and said, "I'm not gonna say you look like your daddy, 'cause you look just like yourself – a grown-up Charlie." After hesitating for a moment, he added, in a somber tone, "Charlie my man, it's great to have you here. I've been expecting you; we have lots to talk about."

His deep voice revealed only a tinge of Mississippi. His thick beard was sprinkled with bits of white. I estimated him to be about 6'2" or 6'3" and, weighting about 250 to 260; he appeared to be mid-fifties. He gripped my right shoulder firmly and slowly nodded his head.

I looked up at him, made eye contact and studied his face; I saw a man I knew nothing about. I couldn't bring myself to say a single word. I didn't really know Buddy at all. I could remember being at his house with my parents a few times. I had vague memories of playing with his kids, but I couldn't recall their faces or names. In my high school and college year, I had almost no contact with Buddy or his family. Questions rattled through my mind: *Why did we come here? What does Buddy have to do with all of this?*

We stood looking at each other for what seemed like an eternity. Booker appeared to be waiting patiently for me to say something. I was vaguely aware of Pops and Mattie whispering on the other side of the car. Finally, I managed to say, "Buddy, it's good to see you again. When we saw each other a few days ago we didn't really get a chance to talk. As we were pulling into your place here, I was trying to figure out exactly how we are related. Now, I realize that I have never known."

He looked silently into my eyes, and turned momentarily to look at Pops and Mattie, who by this time had come around to the driver's side of the car. His eyes again fixed firmly onto mine as a smile slowly crept across his face and the words seem to ooze out, one syllable at a time: "We-are-first-cous-ins-Char-lie. I'm-your-cous-in-Booker."

It took a few seconds for the significance of his words to register; I was speechless. I was shocked and surprised by those words, but neither of those terms captured the essence of any of the complex emotions and sensations darting through my mind and body at that moment. *What the hell! This can't be happening!*

When I was a child, Booker was my hero. That strong, smart, and gregarious eighteen or nineteen-year-old who took an interest in a scrawny five-year-old made a lasting impression on me. With an intensity far exceeding the attention span of the average preteen, I clung to childhood memories of him long after he disappear. With time, the vivid memories faded, to be replaced by fantasies that were viewed through the distorted lens of childhood imagination. My recent discovery of the newspaper article generated a renewed interest in someone who had become a mythical figure in my mind.

Through the years, I'd built so many images of him. In my early teens, I knew he was somewhere playing major league baseball. In the early sixties I was certain he was a civil rights activist, probably a member of SNCC, and was going to show up at any moment back in his hometown to free us. Around 1965 I knew he had been drafted and was probably kicking ass and taking names in the Nam. As my attitudes about that conflict changed, I knew he was in the leadership of 'Vets Against the War'. By the early seventies, he certainly had to be a trusted confidant of Huey, Bobby Seale and all rest of the Panthers. When Geronimo Pratt was arrested, I thought: That's about how Booker would look now. But that wasn't him. In the late seventies and early eighties, I was confident that Booker had gone through college and law school, and was surely an activist lawyer, either litigating on environmental issues or advocating on behalf of political prisoners. But of the all the things I knew that Booker might be, it never occurred to me he could be a small farmer back in Mississippi and he definitely couldn't be Buddy.

I had never really known Buddy; I never even knew his real name. He was an infrequent presence in my life, a friendly cousin who occasionally passed through selling vegetables. Now I was being told that he was the person I idolized all through my childhood and teen years. As I stood there, motionless and speechless, with my mouth hanging open, I must have appeared to the three of them to be in shock. Perhaps I was.

Mattie said, "Well, say something." Everyone laughed nervously.

I managed to say, "I don't understand. How can that be?" Looking briefly into each of their faces, I added, "If this really is you Booker, why am I just finding out? If you've been here all these years, why didn't I know?"

The clouds had started to clear, and we were standing in the sun. Booker pulled a handkerchief from his back pocket and wiped the sweat that was beading on his brow. He straightened his back, which made him seem almost a foot taller. In a slow, deep voice he said, "Well, first of all, it ain't been all these years. I left here for a while because some white folks wanted to kill me; they probably still do. I went to Chicago and changed my name. Back in them days you didn't need no papers to prove you was who you said you was. I made a life for myself; a pretty good life. But I finally got to the point where I couldn't take the city life no more. That's when I moved back down here, just before my mama died. I kept the name I took in Chicago. George Baker is the name on all my papers, but for some reason the folks started calling me Buddy."

He shifted his weight from one foot to the other, wiped his brow again and smiled broadly. "Any ways, I looked a little bit different, but just about all of our kin folks and other people in the community knowed it was me. They went along with my new identity, and white folks didn't know the difference. Back then, you were too young to trust with that kinda information. It just didn't come up later on. A few days ago, I heard from your daddy how you been asking around recently about stuff that happened way back in the

'50s. After thinking about it, I figured this was a good time to tell you. Actually, I thought you might have figured it out by yourself before now."

"I don't think I would have ever guessed that you are really Booker. Maybe I didn't want to know. But now I have to know everything, I especially need to know why some folks seem to think that you left here because of me."

"Charlie, I'll be happy to explain. But before I do, y'all come up on the porch, out of the sun. I just finished eating my breakfast, but I got some ham, biscuits and coffee left. Come on and have some."

Pops said, "We didn't eat before we left the house, so I appreciate anything you got to offer. How about you Mattie? Charlie-boy?"

Mattie's mind seemed to be focused somewhere else at the moment; she stared at a grove of trees in the distance and did not respond.

"After the shock of what I've just heard, I don't have an appetite, but I could use some coffee."

Booker, Pops and I walked toward the porch and left Mattie standing there.

"Y'all have a seat at the table 'round on the west porch, while I get the stuff together. It's real pleasant out there this time of day."

As Pops and I started for the table, Mattie was still there, just taking in the view. I was starting to get a little bit concerned about her, but she turned and started toward us. As soon as she was at the table, she shouted in the direction of the door, "Hey Buddy, bring me some biscuits and ham too and some coffee with lots of cream!" Turning to me and Pops, she said, "We used to come down this way all the time when I was a girl. That was long before Booker moved anywhere near here; they was living at Tomley like the rest of us. My oldest sister Sarah and her husband Willie was living out here. It was they middle boy William - we called him Slim- what them white mens hung in the tree back up the road where we passed. All because of that hoss. Some of these white folks sure can be mean."

This time, I saw or heard no sorrow, only anger. Pops and I nodded along in agreement with her. I didn't want to say anything to cause her to slip back into mental confusion and I was pretty sure Pops felt the same way.

Booker returned with a tray containing a coffee pot, four cups, a plate of steaming hot biscuits, another plate with thick slices of country ham, and jars of pear and fig jam.

Mattie asked, "Who fixed all of this stuff? I know you didn't do it."

"Well Mattie, you're wrong. I cooked the biscuits from scratch and fried the ham too. In fact, I cured the ham from hogs I slaughtered last fall. The figs and the pears came from my trees. I did have Mrs. Coleman up the road here make the jam, but I coulda done it myself if I wanted to."

"Well, hush your mouth Booker. Looks like you don't need no woman 'round here for nothing."

Booker chuckled a bit, and said, "I don't think I would agree with that."

Pops and I nodded, as Mattie focused her attention on the food. Booker distributed the cups, reached for the pot and poured coffee for everyone. Pops held out his cup, and asked, "Hey Booker. What you got to go in this?"

"Go in the kitchen and look on the top shelf of the pantry. You'll find some scotch, bourbon and gin. Help yourself."

I took a few sips of coffee but had lost interest in it. "Booker, I'm dying to know what this is all about; don't keep me in suspense."

"Let's go for a walk. I wanna show you around my place.

It's been a long time since you've been here; I bet you don't remember most of it," Booker said as he pushed his chair back and rose slowly from the table.

Mattie seemed to be concentrating on the jam and biscuits. Booker tapped the table in front of her and said, "Mattie, if you see anybody coming to the house, just ring that big bell hanging up there. Charlie and me are going for a little walk."

She just nodded and continued eating. We left the porch, and two of the dogs followed about three or four yards behind us; the others remained near the porch carefully watching Pops and Mattie. Booker turned, gave another hand signal and they all slowly retreated under the porch. As we walked, it was clear that Booker was right; I didn't remember this place. The trees and rows of vegetables that I had seen from the roadway completely encircled the house, except for a broad path that led to the north, directly behind the house. I couldn't see how far the patch and vegetables extended, but it was apparently a much larger spread than I remembered.

"It took me a long time to get this place the way I wanted it to be. I started out with three acres; that was more than 30 years ago. At one time, I built it up to almost 100 acres by slowly buying land next to mine." He paused and I noticed a few tears welling in his eyes; he wiped them away with his sleeve and continued, "In the last few years I've sold off about twenty acres. I love this place; I'm just sorry that Sarah isn't here to share it with me. I put down $300 on those first acres and paid the rest over the years. It's all paid off; it's mine now."

"How did you manage to get a mortgage on this place when you came back here with a new name? You had to have history, some documentation to get a mortgage."

"I did have papers, but it wouldn't have mattered much anyway. I bought this without a mortgage - well without having to go to the bank for a mortgage. The man who used to own this place hired me to work for him right after I got back here. It was about a year after I started that he decided to sell those first three acres. He carried the papers on it; after he died his family continued to carry the papers 'til I paid it off. Those were some of the best people I ever knew - white folks."

"There's so much I want to know about this whole thing; please tell me all about how this got started. I especially want to know all about you and Sylvia Mullins."

Booker stopped walking, slowly reached down and picked up a rock. As he stood, a smile came onto his face. For a moment, the look in his eyes told me he was going to hit me with it. Then he took it in his left hand and flung it. I turned to watch the arc of the throw and saw it land in a small pond that was at least 100 yards away, far enough that I only saw the splash but heard no sound.

"I used to play center field; I was good... real good. I could hit, run, catch and throw. When I was a young man, that throw you just saw would've been a short fling for me. If times had been different, I might have made it to the majors. When I was a youngster playing ball around here, the Dodgers had already called Jackie up. I always thought I could do it, but my whole life changed when I got mixed up with that girl – Sylvia. I know you wanna hear about that. Come on, let's go over here in the shade by my little fishing hole. In fact, we may as well do a little bit of fishing; I bet you ain't been fishing in a long time."

He was right; I couldn't remember when I had last been fishing. However, I had been right about one of my fantasies about him: we both had dreamed of his going into the majors. As he talked about that, I notice a smile on his face fading, and the look in his eyes transitioned into sadness.

We strolled over to the pond without exchanging a word. As we walked, I noticed thin, high clouds slowly forming. The smell in the air was a scent that I always associated with spring thunderstorms during my youth. In the distance, I heard a flock of birds. They were either blue jays or mockingbirds; there was a time when I would've been sure of which.

"Pick the rod and reel you want and get one of those small shovels; we're gonna dig for bait."

He pulled a key from his pocket, unlocked a metal box near the pond, and took out four rods and reels that all seemed to be the same. I went through the motions of choosing, before selecting one. Within about a yard of the edge of the pond, we dug for worms, and in a few minutes had about a dozen that were suitable for fishing. I followed Booker to a well-worn spot in the shade, sat and followed his lead in baiting my hook. I had forgotten how disgusting that part of fishing could be. Booker cast his line into the water; I did the same.

"By the way, what are we trying to catch?"

"Don't really matter much, does it? I got a few perch in there, some bream, a few catfish too; let's just see what's biting." Booker tapped me on my left leg with a tight fist. He looked at me and his tone turned serious. "Okay, Charlie Dawson. Here's the story you been wanting to hear."

CHAPTER 24

I saw weariness in Booker's eyes as he took a slow deep breath and started talking. "I was born down at Tomley, spent all my boyhood there; I didn't know about nothing but Tomley. You grew up in town, but I was out there in the country. It wasn't easy. When you and Mike would visit, you thought it was fun to be there, but that was just for a short time. We were around white folks all the time, but we knew our place. When I think back on it, things were not too different from slavery - them giving the orders and us obeying."

He stopped talking for a moment and just stared at me. "When I was growing up out there, before I was in my teens, I used to play with Sylvia and some of the other Mullins children. It was no big deal for us to be playing with white kids. I wasn't thinking about no girls at that time, and she was about two or three years older than me. But when I got old enough to get interested in girls, I didn't play with white kids no more. Us young boys sure understood we didn't mess around with no white girls. We heard about colored boys getting lynched for looking in the wrong way at them; I was old enough to understand what it meant. And my folks made sure that we understood. When I was growing up, I was around the Mullins place a lot, did little odd jobs over there. My mama worked over there; so did Mattie. They had several folks from the community working for them, but Mama was their favorite."

Apparently, Booker saw the look of amazement on my

face because he stopped, smiled at me and said, "Yeah, that's right. They both worked in the Mullins place. Mama's job was to take care of the children, all four of them. When she first started working there, my daddy was sharecropping for them. But he was saving his money, and all five of us boys working whenever we could and adding to the savings. He managed to buy a few acres and stop sharecropping. First colored man around here to do that."

Booker stopped again and just nodded his head. I saw a look of pride on his face. He turned to look at the surface of the water, reeled in his line, checked the bait on his hook and cast his line again, this time about a yard beyond his original fishing spot. I thought that perhaps I should also move my fishing line, but I did nothing other than swat a fly away from my face.

He continued his story, "When I was a child, Sylvia was a scrawny little thing, but when I saw her in 1950, she sure wasn't a little girl anymore."

"Booker are you gonna get around to telling me what happened?"

"Just be patient, Charlie; I'm getting to that part." He chuckled with a sly grin on his face. "I know you want to hear the good stuff."

He gestured toward the water, without saying a word. As I reeled in my line, he got up, picked up a small bucket, filled it with water from the pond and placed it next to me. A small fish dangled from my line.

"Throw it back," he said before continuing his story. "In '50 I had a regular job with the county. I was helping to pave the new highway that was coming into the county. It was hard work. When they put that hot asphalt down, I had to come behind the truck with this big broom and smooth it out. It didn't pay much, but it was about the best a colored boy could expect to get back in them days. I also helped my daddy out with his farm work whenever I could, and I even did some odd jobs on the Mullins place now and then. Early in May, they asked me if I could do some painting in the guest house - a nice little two-bedroom place out back of the main house. Sylvia was off a college; Ms. Mullins said she would be coming home soon for the summer and wanted to stay in the guest house. She said they wanted to fix it up some, asked me to paint the kitchen and the bathroom."

As Booker continued his story, I reeled in my line and casted it closer to his line.

"I started on the kitchen, got it finished pretty fast; but I got a lil' bit behind on finishing the bathroom. I was almost done, but I still had some trim work to finish, stuff like the baseboard and some edging up around the ceiling."

Booker seemed to be stalling. I sighed, not very loudly, but audible. He rolled his eyes at me but continued talking. "They'd told me Sylvia would be home from college on Saturday, so I got up real early on that Friday to go over and finish that touch-up work. I figured it would take no more than about an hour. The foreman on the road work job let me come in a little bit late. He wouldn't have done that for most of the fellows, but I was his best worker, and he really did like me. So, I'm there in the bathroom, under the sink with my shirt off, painting the baseboard. I was right on track to finish. Now, the bathroom had two doors, one from the hallway and the other one from the bedroom."

Booker gestures to with both hands to make sure I was clear on the layout and preceded with the story. "I didn't even think about anybody being there. Suddenly, the door from the bedroom opens and almost scares me to death." He grabbed his chest to illustrate.

"I looked up, and she's standing there smiling and

wearing almost nothing. She's got these little pink panties on with lace stuff all over them. Her little robe comes down to just below her waist. Her nipples are sticking up in the air, just as perky as can be. Man, I didn't know what to do. I wanted to get a good look, but I knew I shouldn't. She says, 'I remember you, you're Booker. You sure have filled out. How do you like the way I've filled out?' She turns around and shakes her butt a little bit. I'm still down there on the floor, with my eyes about to come out of my head. I can't get out a single word."

Booker shook his head vigorously to make his point. "And she says, all giggly like, 'Well, get outta here for a minute. Let me pee.' Man, I jumped up as fast as I could, and rushed out in the hallway. I was scared, my heart was beating fast, and I was breaking out in a sweat. I sure knew what could happen if a colored fellow got caught in a situation like that. My mind told me to leave; I might have done that but then I realized my shirt and all my painting stuff was in there. I knowed I couldn't be seen outside with no shirt on. I was real scared. Then I heard the toilet flush, the water running, and then the door to the bathroom opens, and she sticks her head out, tells me she's finished, and I can come back in. I waited until I heard the door to the bedroom open and close. After a minute, I walked over, looked in the bathroom and she was gone."

As Booker talked, I sat there transfixed by the whole thing. I had forgotten about fishing, until something tugged at my line. This one was larger, and as I reeled it in, Booker gestured toward the bucket.

He said, "I went into the bathroom, locked the door to the bedroom, put my shirt back on, and started collecting all of my painting materials. I was about to leave when I heard this awful scream come from the bedroom. It was a scream like I never heard; it came from deep down in her belly like her life depended on getting that scream out. Then she shouted out real loud, 'Booker, come here! I need you right now!' Without taking a minute to think, I unlocked the door and rushed in. There she was in bed, not a stitch on. Laying there looking like a pretty woman from one of them magazines. Her hair was all fluffed up, spread all over the pillow. A little bit of sun was coming through the window next to the beds, sparking through her hair making her look like some kind of angel. But she was no angel; a wild woman is what she was. She was flat on her back, her knees up, her thighs together, using a couple of fingers to play with herself between her legs. With her other hand she was pretending to pull me to her. She was talking like a baby, 'Booker, please help me. I need your help so bad.' Charlie, I had never seen nothing like that before."

As Booker talked, I visualized my encounter with her daughter, Sara, from the night before. I said, "Booker, I can see where this is going."

"Man, I knew for about two seconds that I needed to be running. But my Johnson just took over from my brain. Up to that point in my life, I just knew that I was some stud with the women. You know, before that time I had been with a few girls, but never in a bed. It was always a thing of sneaking a little bit behind the barn, up in the hay loft or out in the woods somewhere. This was different. This woman—this white woman—is laying there looking real good, and she's ready for me. Before I knew what was happening, I was peeling my clothes off. I hopped in that bed, but she let me know of right away that she was in charge. She told me to slow down, not to rush it. I thought I knew how to handle a woman, but she taught me some things that morning. Had me rubbing and feeling and kissing in all the right places.

She put it in when she was ready. It seemed to last forever, but when I think back on it, we probably wasn't there very long." Booker hesitated, looked up at the sky and chuckled, "But it sure was good."

I thought for a moment about not asking what I wanted to know, but I had to. I cleared my throat, took a deep breath and asked, "Booker, is that when she got pregnant?" Before he answered, I realized my mistake: *Of course not, the dates didn't fit.*

Booker's face filled with confusion, from the startled look in his eyes to the gaping mouth. His confusion was quickly replaced by what seemed to be fear, the most intense fear I've ever seen in a man's eyes. That was slowly replaced by anger.

"What the hell do you mean? Who said anything about a baby?"

I didn't respond; I let him rant.

"Where did you get such foolishness from? Who made up a story like that?"

He was now talking to himself, and a light seem to come on somewhere deep inside him. "Sounds like something Mattie would say." I was still silent; he continued to talk to himself. "First I ever heard of a baby. If I had a white child around here, somebody would've told me. No, it can't be."

"I didn't realize that you didn't know. Just about everybody else knows. I can't believe that in all this time nobody said anything. This didn't come from Mattie. I first heard it from my mama, when she was delirious in the hospital. They confirmed it when I went to the Mullins' house. That's why they kicked her out of the house. That's why old man Mullins was so angry. That's why he..."

I stopped. I didn't need to say it. The reality started to sink in for Booker; I saw a few tears pooling in the corner of his eyes. Neither of us wanted to say it. I did the math quickly. "Your baby was born in early May. That means you impregnated her sometime in August. You must have been aware that she was pregnant."

"Charlie, why are you making all these assumptions?"

"Well, it is logical that-"

"Let me tell you that your logic happens to be wrong. In the first place, I wasn't around the place that much after that."

He hesitated, looked around wistfully then said, "But, I sure saw a lot more of her. After the first time, we must've met up every week for the next few months. Sometimes it was two or three times a week. I was careful - most of the time. I didn't work around the place a whole lot anymore, just a little job now and then. After the second time we got together, we had a little system she used to send me a little note, right out in the open." Booker's eyes lit up as he said, "You'll never guess how we did it. You wanna know?"

With a tinge of sarcasm, I said, "Yeah tell me how you did it."

"Well it was like this. My mama still worked over there. Almost every day she would bring home a little paper sack of some kinda food. Sylvia would just write on it. If she wrote something like F8, it meant we were gonna hook-up on Friday at 8:00. Always the same place. She set the schedule." He paused and nodded his head rapidly, for emphasis. "In her car; it was a nice new Ford," he chuckled. "Man, we wore that back seat out. It was too dangerous to me to be going out on the Mullins place, could have been seen too easily. I would wait in the bushes down by the old artesian well. She would drive up and open the back door. I would run over and jump in the backseat real fast and lay down on the floor."

As Booker talked, it occurred to me we had been there longer than I had intended. I was sure Pops was ready to leave. Still, I really wanted to hear the rest of the story; I tried to speed it up. "Booker, how did all this end? What finally happened?"

He turned slowly to look at me. "Well, youngblood, we got caught; somebody told!" Booker paused, as if waiting for my reaction. I knew from his intense stare where this was going.

CHAPTER 25

SUNDAY – 13 MAY 1990

Booker continued his story, waving his hands in the air as he talked, "We had three or four different little clearings where we used to park the car. We could hide well off the main road. Most of the time, we stayed in the backseat, but now and then we would get up the nerve to spread a blanket out on the ground. This one hot night we was out there on the grass, all our clothes off, going at it real slow and easy. The mosquitoes were biting a little bit, but we didn't care. Both of us was wrapped up in what we was doing. Me on top of her, feeling real good."

He paused and smiled slightly with this sad looking curl of his lip. "They came upon us from the direction I was facing, so she didn't see 'em when I did. I looked up; first thing I saw was a dog right in my face, an old coon dog. Next, I saw somebody's boots, then a shotgun in my face. I knowed I was dead. Don't mind telling you that I was scared to death. Sylvia stopped moving; she was dead still. She couldn't see 'em at first, but she knowed something was wrong, knowed somebody was there.

"It was five or six colored fellows out hunting. I didn't know 'em, but I was relieved 'cause at first, I thought it was a bunch of white mens. Then the talks started.

'Boy, look what we got here.'

'Woo wee, I want some of dat.'

'Naw man, I'm first; I found 'em.'

'Looks like that little fella knowed what he was talking 'bout.'

'Alright, git up boy; let's see who you wit.'

Them rough looking fellows was gonna take what they wanted."

Booker clenched both hands into fists, pounded them against his thighs and just shook his head before continuing with his story. "I didn't move until I felt that cold shotgun barrel up against my butt. Before I could do anything, Sylvia says, 'You men better get outta here. You don't know what kinda trouble you're asking for; y'all must not know who I am.' There was dead silence for what seemed like minutes. I could feel her heart beating, and mine too. All I could think of was that the two of us was gonna die on the same heart-beat. Then somebody says, 'Oh damn, she's white!' One of the other fellas said, Naw, that's that high-yellow Phillips girl what lives down there by the river.'"

He paused and looked at the sky. "Sylvia nudges me out of the way, sets up, brushes her hair back and smiles. No-body said a word; they didn't have to, just started moving away from us. When they got about twenty yards away, one of them says, 'Boy, you is one foolish Negro. Looking to get yourself killed. You better git' as far from her as you can.'

"He was right. I knew it; so did Sylvia. We barely said a word to each other for the rest of the night. Riding back to where she was gonna drop me off, laying there on the floor of her car, I kept thinking to myself, Fool, what in the world is wrong with you, what are you doing this for? But most of all, I was mad at her, because she was the one who saved us. It was her whiteness that did it. Until that happened, I knowed I had no power to protect myself against white mens, but I always thought I had some power against other colored mens. I couldn't do a thing against all of them guns, but all it took was her white skin."

I heard the venom in Bookers voice as he spewed out the words 'white skin.' I felt his pain, but I couldn't resist any longer. I interrupted him. "Booker, I have to know something. What did those men mean when they mention 'That little fellow knowing what he was talking about?"

He pulled his handkerchief from the bib of his coveralls, wiped his brow slowly, turned to face me and fixed his eyes on my mine. In a voice that was barely above a whisper he said, "I think you know the answer to that already."

It suddenly seemed much warmer than when we first sat down to fish. I was keenly aware of each beat of my heart; it seemed so loud that I'm sure Booker could hear it. I wanted to say something, but the overwhelming dryness in my throat choked off my voice. Slowly I managed to get the words out, "It was me, wasn't it? That's why people say that you left here because of me."

He just nodded. His upper body rocked in rhythm with his nodding. He took a slow, deep breath and his chest expanded so much that it seemed in danger of bursting like a balloon. Then, he exhaled a long, slow stream of air. When he spoke, a weight seemed to fall from his shoulders. "Charlie, I thought about this for a long time. It was my fault and my responsibility. I never should have told a five-year-old my business, especially when it was so dangerous. It's not right for anybody to try to put this on you." He reached out and hugged me tightly. "It's over."

I said nothing. He continued, "For the first couple of days after this happened, it looked like nobody was gonna say anything about it. Then, slowly the guys started saying little things like: 'Heard about you boy, you better be careful.'

'Tell me the truth, is it really all that good?'

'Is it worth it, man?'

'Boy, if her daddy ever finds out, he's gonna have somebody whacked your Johnson off.'

"When they talked at me like that, I never would answer, just smiled and kept moving. But I was getting awfully scared; didn't know what to do. A few days after we got caught, I got another one of them little notes from her; I just ignored it. I tried as hard as I could to keep my mind off what happened, but I knew that eventually somebody was gonna talk too much, and it was gonna get back to her daddy. Pretty soon, they would find me one morning, hanging from some tree."

He stopped to bait his hook and said, "The next Sunday, we had a baseball game against some fellows from down near Columbus. We had a good team, but they did too. Game was tied all day; it was down to the last inning. We was leading by one run. They had a man on second base, had they best batter up. He was a lefty; I traded places with the fella who was in right field."

I wanted to ask Booker what any of this baseball talk had to do with what we have been talking about, but I resisted the urge to interrupt.

Gesturing as if shading his eyes, as he peered into the distance, Booker said, "Then I saw 'em; them white folks was real hard to miss. Sylvia comes driving up with some of her friends. It was two fellows and another girl. It was a pretty rare thing for young white folks to be showing up at our games. I concentrated on the batter, trying to take my mind off the fact that Sylvia was there. The batter swings hard on the first pitch, a curve ball, and misses by a mile. That made me focus even more on him 'cause I knowed he was hungry for a good hit. The second one was a great pitch: an inside curve that broke toward the batter. Somehow, that left-handed hitter managed to get a piece of that ball and pulled it toward left field. As soon as I heard that ball against that bat, I could tell it was gonna be a homer unless I did something. That ball was headed for a place about 50 yards behind the left fielder. When he figured out that he needed to be running in that direction, it was too late. The center fielder was just standing there too, looking at that ball. But I was already running toward where I knowed it was gonna land. I manage to get there just in time to throw my body straight out in the air for a diving catch. The ball landed right in my glove while I was in the air; I managed to hang on to it. I hit the ground hard, right on my stomach and chest. But I was able to keep the ball, roll over real quick, jump up and throw the ball as hard as I could. It reached home plate just in time for the catcher to tag the other runner. The crowd went wild."

From the glassy look in Booker's eyes, it was as if he was seeing a playback of all those things right in front of his eyes. While he was telling his story, it seemed that he was not even aware that I was there. Slowly, I could see his mood shifting from joy to sorrow.

He said, "With all of this happening, I forgot she was even there. We had won the game, and I was all excited. I ran in from the outfield, everybody crowded around me, patting me on the back and congratulating me. There was a big crowd around me. Then, the crowd started opening up." He paused and chuckled to himself, "It was just like Moses parting the Red Sea."

I heard his voice cracking just a bit. He went back into his trance-like mode and said, "I can see her now, just as clear as I did that day. Standing there in this flowing white dress, looking prettier than I've ever seen her. For a long time, she was frozen there looking at me with just a little smile on her face. Then she starts jumping up and down, and squealing like a child, 'You did so good; that was great.'

"Then, she runs toward me, throws her arms around

my neck and hugs me tightly. She whispers, 'I gotta see you Booker.' She suddenly turns me loose, steps back and looks at her dress. She was covered with half of the dirt that was on me. She smiles this weak little smile and starts brushing the dirt off. At first, she's doing it slowly, still smiling. Then she starts brushing harder and harder, beating her body as she brushes. All of that happened so fast that it takes a little while for her friends to react to what's going on. Suddenly, this white fella comes rushing up and steps between me and Sylvia. I can smell corn liquor on his breath as he stands toe-to-toe with me, staring into my face with the most hateful look I ever seen. Then he turns to her, grabs her arm and says, 'Let's go, you making a fool of yourself. You are a white woman, have you forgotten that?'

"She left without a word, walking backward just star-ing at me. And everybody else was looking at me. When she was almost at the car, she waved with this weak, pitiful little motion. That was the last time I ever saw her, and I ..." As his voice trailed off to nothing, Booker covered his eyes and lowered his head.

"You really cared about her, didn't you?"

"Yeah, I did, and I think she really cared about me. When this thing first started, it used to be about just screwing. But later, it was a lot more to it. Sometimes we would just set out there in the woods, looking at the stars and talking. Sometimes we talked about the good old days when we used to play together as kids; other times we talked about what we wish the world could be like. We talked about how we would..." He stopped, I could see him steeling himself, fight-ing back the tears that were starting to well-up in his eyes.

Without stopping to think, I said, "You know, she was probably pregnant at that time."

He nodded in agreement.

Bang! Bang!

Startled, I looked around for the source of the shots. Booker had already reacted. In one seamless move, he threw down his fishing rod, leapt to his feet, bounded to the box from which he had taken the fishing gear earlier, and pulled out a double-barreled shotgun. He ran with long strides toward the house, with the gun clutched in his right hand. I took off after him, not sure what was happening, or what I would do when I got to the house. As he ran, I saw him as a teen, chasing down a fly ball in the outfield. This man of more than 60 years moved like someone fifteen or twenty years younger; he left me in his wake.

As he neared the house, he started toward the east side, still in full stride. Apparently having second thoughts, he slowed slightly, bounded up the steps to the wrap-around porch, and then moved slowly toward the west side. He rounded the corner with both hands gripping his weapon in a ready position. In a semi-crouched posture, he moved silently, but quickly around the corner. I stood there transfixed as I watched him.

Unexpectedly, he halted and lowered the gun; fear raced all through my body. I expected to see his hands go up at any moment or to see him brought down by a shot. What could I do? Try to hide? Tried to run and get help? Suddenly, he started laughing a deep, roaring laugh. I heard relief from all the tension that must have been pent up in him as he rushed in to face the unknown. Still laughing, he motioned for me to move forward.

I reached the front porch and it was clear what had just happened. Mattie stood there with a pistol in her right hand. Splayed on the floor of the porch, near a large chair was a rattler, the apparent victim of her gun. Pops was standing on the lawn about three yards from the snake, slowly shaking his head. As soon as he saw me, he started explaining. More precisely he started complaining. "I'm sitting here have a nice little nap. Next thing I know, bam! bam! bam! bam!"

"Naw, I only shot twice."

"You wrong woman. I heard three shots, or four."

"I don't care what you heard, I shot that snake two times, not three."

I interrupted the conversation." Pops, it's not important how many shots it was. Mattie probably saved you from getting a pretty bad snakebite. You ought to be thanking her."

"I beg your pardon, Charlie-boy. It is important on many shots it was. I took two shots to kill that snake; it didn't take three. I hit him the first time a few inches behind his head, but he was still moving. Hit him the second time right in his head."

Booker lifted the snake with the barrel of his gun, examine it closely and he offered his conclusion. "You right, Mattie. A bullet went through his body about three or four inches from the head. That's some awfully good shooting. What you doing with a gun anyway? Where did you learn to shoot like that?"

Waving the revolver in the air, she said, "I'd been shooting since I was a little girl. My daddy learned me to shoot. I been carrying a gun since way back when they hung my sister's boy, Slim. I promised myself that if they wanted to mess with me, they had better be ready for some of this."

"Thanks, Mattie. I'm sure glad you know how to shoot that thing." With that statement, Pops put an end to the discussion. He looked at his watch and said," We've been here for a long time; we needs to be leaving."

I nodded in agreement and turned to Booker. "I had a lot of surprises today, but I would like a couple of quick answers before we go. When did you finally decide to run away from here?"

"I remember that day like it was yesterday, the 8th of May. Mama came home from work 'bout an hour later than usual. That was a big celebration day for us, and I had planned to be out having fun with my friends and family. But they made me work that day on my job with the road crew. I went home first to take a quick bath and put some fresh clothes on. My daddy was still out somewhere. I didn't hear Mama when she first came in, but she walked right up behind me and called my name. When I turned around, she was crying, she just grabbed me and started hugging me real tight. She turned me loose, looked in my face and said, 'You gotta go, if you don't Mr. Mullins is gonna kill you. You gotta get out of here now; you don't have no time to waste. Go in there and get a few things together while I put a little bit of food together for you. Hurry!'

"I asked, 'Mama, what's this about? What's going on?' She just answered, 'Boy, you know what this is about. We got no time to talk about it. Now, you hurry up!' I got a few things together, put 'em in a croaker sack and then it was time to go. When I came out of the back room, everybody was there: Papa, Mama and my little sisters and brothers. Papa gave me one of his pistols, showed me it was loaded but didn't say a word. My sisters and brothers didn't understand what was happening, but they knew something was wrong. They just started crying; made me feel real bad. Mama held her tears back while she hugged me, but she couldn't seem to bring herself to say anything. I just said,' Mama I'm sorry all this happened; I love you. I'll be back.'

"I hugged everybody and took off running into the woods with my little sack and pistol. That was the last time I saw Papa. I made it through the woods to the railroad tracks about four miles away. I hopped a freight train and eventually I made it to Memphis. I didn't contact anybody around here for a long time, and I didn't find out about Papa getting shot until almost four months later, when I finally let my folks know where I was."

I asked the obvious, "Did they shoot him because they couldn't find you?"

"I reckon so, that's what everybody said. When I finally got up the nerve to move back here, I was sure they was still after me. That's why I still keep things locked-down around here."

Mattie had been silent for several minutes, but she grabbed Booker by his right arm and said, "I'm an old lady. Ain't got much time left in this world. I'm probably the only living person who knows what I'm about to tell y'all. Guess there ain't no reason why I should take it to my grave. I'm gonna explain the real reason why old man Mullins shot your daddy."

A hot wind was blowing. All the clouds had cleared away. Mattie closed her eyes, raised her head toward the sky and began to mumble. Slowly, the mumbling became audible, "...Forgive us our trespasses as we forgive those..."

CHAPTER 26

SUNDAY – 13 MAY 1990

Mattie finished her prayer but didn't raise her head nor utter a word. Her silence engulfed us and the quietness frightened me. *Have I suddenly gone deaf?* Wringing her hands, she slowly shifted her weight from left foot to right, but still didn't open her mouth. The longer she delayed, the greater my anxiety. I was sweating more heavily than before.

I glanced at Booker and saw a blank stare. Looking toward Pops; his face was shrouded with confusion. I tried to imagine what he was thinking. For the last several days, he had put lots of energy into keeping me from knowing what he knew about the shooting of Uncle Prince. Yet, we stood there waiting for Mattie to reveal information she claimed no one else - not even Pops – was aware of.

As she slowly raised her head, we all focused our attention on her. Those piercing gray eyes locked onto mine; I saw only sadness. I could almost hear her saying: you forced me to do this. Tiny waves of nausea started to cascade through me, and I was wishing that I were someplace else. From nowhere, the words of Sheriff Mullins invaded my thoughts, 'Be careful of what you seek, you may find it.' I told myself he couldn't possibly know whatever Mattie knew.

Impatiently, Pops broke the silence with, "Well?"

Mattie shot him an under-eyed look as she cleared her throat. When she spoke, her voice was surprisingly weak. Turning first to Booker, she said, "Way back in the twenties, all of us used to live down in the Delta. I'm talkin' about all us: yo' daddy's peoples, yo' mama's peoples. Me and yo' mama was sister's childrens, so we growed-up real close. Course I was younger than yo' mama."

A hot breeze blew over us; it felt hotter than air should feel, and I remembered the scorching heat of my Mississippi youth. Mattie stopped talking, shielded her eyes with one hand and looked off into the distance, as if trying to find something. She started talking again and had found the vigor I was accustomed to hearing in her voice. "The Mullins family use to live down there too. In the Delta we knowed the whole Mullins family. Knowed 'em better back then than we did after all of us got up here in this part of the state."

I heard rustling in the brush about ten yards from where we stood; no one else seemed to hear it. I looked up to see two brown foxes. All of the dogs fixed their eyes on them but didn't bark or move. The foxes stopped and stared me down, as if taunting me. When I was a child, the old folks used to say, if a fox looks at you like that, he's telling you that trouble is approaching. As suddenly as they had appeared, they lost interest and went away.

Mattie was gathering steam; she rubbed her hands together and a smile crept onto her face. "Them peoples wasn't living much better than the colored peoples was, just some po' white trash. In fact, people used to say you can't tell 'em from colored if they wasn't wearing that white skin."

She chuckled at her own quip, then turned to talk directly to me. I chuckled along with her, uncomfortably. Pointing her bony index finger at me, she said, "Back then me and yo' daddy was teenagers."

Turning toward Booker, she said, "Yo' daddy was already a young man, and married to yo' mama."

I didn't dare turn my eyes from her, but in my peripheral vision, I saw Pops nodding in agreement; Booker seemed transfixed.

"Twenty-seven is when it happened. It started raining like I've never seen, and that ole Mississippi was already full; soon it started flooding. The peoples what built that levee said that it wasn't gonna hold unless mens git up there and build it up. It was in the spring, right at planting time. White folks started calling they workers out of the fields and having them get up there and start filling up sandbags and puttin' 'em up there to build up the levee. They was working hard as they could, but the mo' they worked, the mo' it rained. Them that was doing the work could see it wasn't doing no good and they started leaving, but white mens wit' guns started showin' up and wouldn't let 'em. By this time, it wasn't just colored working up there; they made the po' white folks stay up there too. Some folks got away, but when that levee broke lots of folks got drowned. We lost some kin folks, but most of us got away."

Mattie stopped talking, tears started welling-up in her eyes and began trickling down her cheeks. She shook her head and wiped her face with the back of her hand and the crook of her arm. I looked away from her and saw a flock of blackbirds flying swiftly toward us; when they were about twenty yards away, they veered off to the south without making a sound. Mattie glanced up at them and shook her head again, as she said, "That's a bad sign. Real bad."

She resumed her story. "Booker, your daddy saved several peoples out there at that levee—including Tom Mullins. A group of mens was working at a place on that levee where the water started coming through and they started sliding down into the river. Prince grabbed a rope, tied it to a big stake that somebody had put in ground and started pulling peoples up. Tom Mullins was one of the ones that he pulled out. He owed your daddy for that. Of course, most people what didn't get killed had nothing left, lost everything, water washed it all away. That's when we left the Delta, both families. We didn't know where we was going, but we loaded up our wagons and ended up in this part of the state. That's how we come to be here in this place." Pointing to Booker and then to me, she said, "That's how you two mens come to be born here."

Booker and I looked at each other and smiled. Pops managed a weak chuckle, but I heard sadness in his voice.

"Soon after we moved here, we found out that Tom Mullins had made it up here too. Down in the Delta, he was po', but when he got here, he fixed hisself up and managed to find a rich woman whose daddy had land and money. He married into that Mitchell family. As time went on, he started doing better and better. Our family started doing better too, but compared to him we didn't do that good. Any way, he did give us some work now and then, 'cause of what your daddy done for him."

She stopped again, straightened her back and her eyes glistened, and she said in a rapid-fire cadence, "Booker, that's why I was there when your baby girl was born. Me and your mama delivered that baby."

She paused to let the impact of that statement settle in; Booker's mouth dropped open, his eyes got big, but he said nothing.

Continuing at a slower pace she said, "That Mullins family didn't kno' that girl was pregnant until 'bout a week befo'e she dropped that baby. They didn't kno' she was coming home, but she showed up from college on a Friday night and everybody could see she was pregnant. She told her folk that the daddy was some white boy at college." Mattie stopped talking again and slowly turned away from the three of us. She wiped her face again and turned back toward us.

"Me, yo' mama, and Miz Mullins was in that room when

241

that baby was born. I could tell soon as I seen that baby that it was a colored baby. Yo' mama and Miz Mullins could see it too. Miz Mullins asked the girl who the daddy of that baby was. At first, she didn't say nothing, but her mama grabbed that girl by her throat and shouted, 'Girl, tell me what nigger you been laying down wit!' She started crying and then whispered, 'Booker.' Lawd, it felt like somebody cut my heart out when she said that. Yo' mama started crying. Miz Mullins left that room and came back in a few minutes with her husband. He said to your mama, 'Git outta my house and don't ever come back.' I thought he was gonna send me away too, but Miz Mullins told me to take care of that girl and that baby until she got somebody else to come over there. That when yo' mama went home and told you what happened."

Booker broke his silence for the first time in a long while; he said, "She told me I needed to run away, but didn't say nothing about a baby. I found out about that a few minutes ago from Charlie."

Mattie looked surprised, but didn't respond to what Booker said. She forged ahead with the story. "I stayed there until 'bout 7:00. Around 4:00 it had started raining real hard. The rain that night reminded me of that rain that started the flood down in the Delta. 'Bout a hour after yo' mama left, I heard Tom Mullins telling his wife that he had thought about it and he was gonna get rid of that child as soon as it stopped raining long enough for him to make it down to the river. I didn't kno' what to do, but soon as I could, I made my way through all that rain and mud to y'alls house and told yo' mama and daddy."

Mattie pointed at Booker and says, "You had already ran away by then."

Pops stepped closer to Booker, puts his arm around his shoulders for a moment, but said nothing.

Mattie continued, "Prince said he knowed what to do. Took off right away, sneaked in that house 'cause he knowed the door was always unlocked. He managed to get that baby out of there. He almost got away, but old Tom Mullins heard 'em leaving, came out on the porch with a shotgun and stopped him. He would've kilt your daddy right then and there if it hadn't been for Miz Mullins. She stopped 'em from shootin' yo' daddy. Latter Prince told us he turned 'round, looked that man in the eyes and said, 'Do you remember the Delta?' Then he just walked away 'cause he known them peoples wasn't gonna tell the sheriff about him takin' a colored baby." Mattie just stopped, slapped her palms together and folded her arms as if the story was complete.

Pops was nodding as if he knew all of this. He picked up the story, "Booker, I know that my mama and your mama got on a bus and took that baby up to Memphis to a place where people wanted to adopt colored childrens."

"Well, does either one of you know what happened to my baby girl after that?"

Pops just shrugged; Booker turned to Mattie waiting for an answer. "That's what's no living soul but me kno's. I done seen that girl after she got to be a woman. When that baby was born, she had a birthmark on her shoulder that was like nothing I've ever seen befo'. I seen it one mo' time, on her 30th birthday. She said it was the first time she ever been to this town."

Mattie paused and turned to look straight into my eyes. I glanced at Pops and Booker, they looked confused. She blurted out, "It was Eight O' May, 1987. That's the only other time I ever seen that birth mark that looked like a little red spider."

My knees buckled. Booker managed to grab me before I hit the ground.

EPILOGUE

I stand here at the front door to my home, reluctant to put the key into the lock. It's an unusually cloudy New Mexico afternoon. The smell of rain is in the air; we might get a short thunderstorm. Ada is expecting my return, but I have no idea how I will tell her what I know. Six days have passed since I found the answer to the mystery I've been chasing. Now, I'm wishing I hadn't caught it.

When Mattie made that fateful announcement, Pops had stood scratching his head, clearly unsure of the significance of what had just been said. Within seconds, Booker understood what was going on. Still holding onto my right shoulder after having rescued me from almost falling to the ground, he grabbed me by the other shoulder, spun me toward him and shouted, "Charlie, this ain't right. That's my daughter!"

"I know..."

"I know! That's all you got to say?"

"I learned the truth at the same time you did. I'm still trying to process all of this."

"Ain't nothing to process. Y'all can't stay together!"

I slowly removed both of his hands from my shoulders, stood as erect as possible, and said, "Booker, I mean no disrespect to you, but this ain't your decision. Ada and I are grown, we've been together for more than fifteen years, we love each other and we have a daughter."

He backed-up a few steps, wiped his brow with the handkerchief from his coveralls, shook his head and murmured,

"You right. But, what would your mama have to say about all of this?"

Indeed, what would she have to say about the situation? There wasn't much else Booker and I could talk about. Before we drove away, he pulled me aside and said, "Look, I don't know what you intend to do, but I want to see my daughter. I never been on an airplane, but I'll give you a week after you get home, then I'm flying out to where y'all live."

I nodded in understanding, but told him, "That won't be necessary. I'm going to bring her down here. She needs to get acquainted with all of her family."

During the trip back into town, not much was said by either of us. Shortly before I turned onto the main highway, Mattie placed her hand gently on my right shoulder and said, "Charlie-boy, I'm sorry about all of this, but I felt it needed to be told."

From the back seat, Pops offered his opinion, "It didn't need to be told. You shoulda just kept it to yourself." Mattie didn't respond; I remained silent.

Later that day, I told Mike what I had learned. A grimace came across his face; that was quickly replaced by a smile. He said, "Lil' Brother. You certainly do live an interesting life, but I'm sure you'll figure something out." After explaining that I was going to bring Ada back with me in a few days, he volunteered to extend his leave from his Air Force unit until I returned. He added that would give him more time to get better acquainted with Cathy Mason, the nurse who was caring for Mama.

The doctors decided to release Mama from the hospital on Monday. Mike and I took care of establishing a good support system for her during her first day at home. Initially, she slept a lot, but by Wednesday, she called me to sit and talk with her. She took my hand and said, "I know that something is bothering you. What is it? I hope you ain't worried about me; I'm gonna be fine soon."

Reluctantly, I told her the abbreviated version of what I had learned about Ada. She didn't seem surprised, but she did surprise me when she said, "Don't worry about it; there's already lots of that in the family."

Before leaving town, I had two loose ends to deal with: Maria and Sara. I called the Mullins' home and left a message for Sara with the maid. I didn't really expect to hear from her, but she called back within about two hours. Our conversation was brief. After letting her know that my mother was getting better and that I was returning home, I added: "I'm truly sorry about the way things developed between us."

With a chuckle, she responded, "I think you mean – didn't develop. It's not that critical, but if you're ever in San Francisco, you have my number. Goodbye." I didn't tell her that my wife is her sister—maybe later.

I wanted to speak with Maria face-to-face. I called and arranged to visit at her home yesterday afternoon. As we sat on her front porch, sipping lemonade, I told her the story of learning that Ada was my cousin. As we talked, her eyes got bigger and bigger. Finally, she touched my forearm and asked, "Well, what happens next?"

"I don't know where this is going. Ada doesn't know yet. I'm going home tomorrow and will tell her then. But I want you to know that I really treasure what happened between us. I just have no idea what the future holds."

"Listen, I didn't ask that question in a self-serving way. I expected nothing more than what we had that night. It would be wonderful if you were available, but I'm a big girl. Life goes on."

We parted with a light kiss on the lips and a gentle hug. This morning, I said my temporary good-byes to the family and reminded them that I would return soon with Ada. My itinerary required that I make a change of planes in New Orleans. Something still weighed heavily on my mind and I knew the answer would be found in New Orleans. I had time between flights for a quick phone call. I found a pay phone and dialed Harold's number. It was his request for old college pictures that lead me to find that critical bit of information in that old newspaper. But I never knew why he wanted it so badly. He answered on the second ring. I updated him about Mama's condition but wasn't ready to tell him the news about Ada.

"I only have a few minutes left before I have to board my flight. Please tell me why those old pictures were so important to you."

"I was going to tell you this when we went to dinner, but after you told me about your mother's condition, I knew it could wait. I hate to drop this on you in this way, but I don't know any easy way to do it. I'm dying. I have, at most, another month to live. For several weeks, I've been planning my own funeral. I want pictures of things that are important to me to display there. And, by the way, I want you to give the eulogy. Sorry to hit you like this, but I'm running out of time."

That conversation happened a few hours ago, but I can't remember what was said after I heard that. I've been emotionally numb since I hung up the phone. Now, I've run out of time. I hear Ada's shoes as she approaches the door to greet me. I must tell her, but the right words are not forming in my brain.

TO BE CONTINUED IN BOOK TWO...
COMING EARLY 2022

ABOUT THE AUTHOR

William T. Brown grew up in Columbus, Mississippi. He received a B. S. degree in mathematics and physics from Dillard University in New Orleans. He also earned M. S. and Ph. D. degrees in physics, from the University of New Mexico and performed physics research in New Mexico for more than two decades and for two additional decades in Northern Virginia. He is now retired and lives in the Washington, DC metropolitan area. This is his first book.

CPSIA information can be obtained
at www.ICGtesting.com
Printed in the USA
BVHW031936110221
599932BV00008B/164